FINAL
CROSSING

Also by Carter Wilson

Revelation

The Comfort of Black

The Boy in the Woods

FINAL CROSSING

A NOVEL OF SUSPENSE

CARTER WILSON

Oceanview Publishing
Longboat Key, Florida

ISBN 978-1-60809-234-5
Published in the United States of America by Oceanview Publishing
Longboat Key, Florida
www.oceanviewpub.com

10 9 8 7 6 5 4 3 2
PRINTED IN THE UNITED STATES OF AMERICA

For Dad

"The sun will be darkened, the moon will not give its light, the stars will fall from the sky, and the powers of heaven will be shaken loose."

— Matthew 24:29

FINAL
CROSSING

PART I

CHAPTER ONE

SUBURBAN PHILADELPHIA
MARCH 31

RUDIGER WATCHES THE man who watches him. Dark eyes. Flecks of amber. Eye contact is difficult. His gaze wants to pull toward the ground, but Rudiger forces it to stay level. The man smiles. Rudiger tries.

The man's not too big. Good, Rudiger thinks. About five-ten, maybe a hundred and seventy pounds. Two hundred or more would've been a problem. He knows he's strong, but there's a limit. Hard work ahead.

"You're quiet," the man says. His upper lip twitches. Nervous. He wears a pressed blue Oxford; the monogram on the breast pocket reads MLC.

"My first time," Rudiger says. Appalachian accent coats the words in a glaze.

"Mine too," the man says.

Liar.

A cell phone rings in the corner of the bar and a woman answers. She's drunk, she tells the caller. A Neil Diamond song dribbles from an aging jukebox. The chrome sides of the machine are tarnished. Glass case covered in dried spit.

"So," the man continues. "What made you respond to my ad? Was ... was it the photo?"

The photo showed an erect cock that Rudiger doubts belongs to the man sitting across the booth from him. Who knows? Doesn't much matter. Preacherman would've had a mouthful to say about *homasechuals*, but Rudiger doesn't care. He didn't choose this man because of who he fucks. He chose him based on his words.

"Liked your wording, I suppose."

"That so?" Eyebrows raised in confusion.

"Yeah."

Internet personal ads. All the words, the arrangements. They seem random, but they're not. Random doesn't happen. Random is only for those without the ability to see all the patterns.

Rudiger sees the patterns.

The man sitting in front of Rudiger had written an ad on a local website, looking for a discreet encounter. Rudiger had found it. He didn't give a toad's left nut about what kind of deviant had written the message; the ad he needed to find could have been in any of the categories on the site. Rudiger hadn't been trolling the Internet to seek pleasure. He'd been there because the website was a wealth of words, and Rudiger appreciated nothing more than words. They were his playthings. He could do things with words no other person could, at least no one he had ever met.

He looks closely at the man to see if there's something special about him. Some kind of sign. *Man doesn't even know what he wrote*, Rudiger thinks. But he wrote it all the same, so that's just about the sum of that.

Rudiger sees the black letters of the computer ad float before him, as though he was still staring at the smudged screen of the library computer.

HOT **LONELY **BORED ****m4m

He looks at them in his mind once again, one by one, re-arranging, reinterpreting. The letters dance in his mind, switching places, twisting and tumbling, falling into new words and phrases.

Holy Blood Enter.

"Nothing special about the wording," the man says. He drinks Scotch, holding the glass with a delicate hand that quivers just a little. Manicured nails. His name is Michael, he says. Not Mike. Michael. "My God, I hardly knew what to write."

"Caught my eye," Rudiger says.

"What's your name?"

"Gabriel." Rudiger orders a Coke. "Not Gabe," he adds. "Gabriel." He scans the tabletop and focuses on a half-filled ketchup bottle, its insides streaked from use.

"Where are you from?"

He glances around the bar, sees more people than he wants but fewer than he expected. "Not here," he says.

Michael smiles, then reaches across the table to brush fingertips. Rudiger retracts his, a spider in retreat.

"Shy?"

"Jes want to make sure you're the one," Rudiger mumbles.

The man leans forward, his salt and pepper hair coiffed just so. "I know I'm a little older but I'm in great shape and I'm totally disease-free."

Michael is funny, but Rudiger doesn't think he knows it. "Everyone has a disease, Michael. Some jes have it more than others."

"What does that mean?"

"Nothin'."

Michael studies him. "My God, you have great arms. You must work out all the time."

"Body is a temple."

Michael looks ready to worship.

"What happened to your ear? I mean, if I can ask."

He's not surprised by the question. The scar is obvious and he makes no effort to hide it. His blond hair is no more than a sprinkling of dust on his head. "Childhood accident."

"I'm sorry."

"Why? You didn't do it."

Michael takes a sip from his drink and looks downward. "Maybe ... maybe this isn't right after all. You don't seem into this whole thing."

"No," Rudiger says. His powder blue eyes blaze against his alabaster face. "You jes don't know me. Trust me, I am very happy we met tonight."

"So ... so what next?"

Rudiger pulls out a small roll of bills and drops a twenty on the table. "Figured on goin' to my car."

Outside, cold night air stings Rudiger's face, making him even more alert. Michael follows behind him. Well-trained dog. He pictures Michael as a boss of many during the day, a powerful man. By night, his weakness builds by the hour, straining for release. Dog needs to shed his collar.

Rudiger leads him to a white van, front windows dirty and back windows non-existent. Michael hesitates. Rudiger smiles and nods. It'll be okay, the smile says. It's all good. *Get in*. Michael smiles back after a bit then climbs in the passenger seat, his movements delicate, a cat walking around puddles. Inside Michael fidgets. Doesn't know what to do next.

"Buckle up," Rudiger says. He presses a button and both doors lock. Michael slowly pulls the strap across his chest and clicks the belt into place.

"Where are we going?"

"'Bout twenty miles from here."

Hesitation. "Is that where you live?"

"No." Rudiger leans down and picks up the bottle of ether on the floorboard. He unscrews the cap and dabs the top of the bottle against a black piece of cloth until it's saturated. The smell is strong, so he cracks just his window a few inches. Screws the cap back on. Bottle falls to the floor. "Not close to anything, that's the whole point there, Mike. Only thing waitin' out there is a big cross I built. That's where we're goin'."

It takes a few seconds, which is about five minutes longer than logic says it should have taken. The fear hits Michael. Rudiger glances sideways at him and sees in one second a lifetime worth of second-guessing on his face. All those times before. All those strangers. Never had a problem, though it was always a chance, wasn't it? Always a risk. But the reward was worth it, each and every time. Probably swore to never do it again. But couldn't. Just couldn't stop. Now he'll never do it again, but not by his own choosing.

Michael's frantic fingers scramble for the release button on his seat belt. Rudiger begins to hum. Scraps of something he heard on the radio, little bit of country.

Michael can't find the button because there isn't one. Seatbelt locked tight, strap holding him down like he's on a roller coaster.

Rudiger lunges, his speed preternatural, a monster attacking in a child's night terror. His hand with the rag covers Michael's mouth and nose while his other hand squeezes his throat. Just enough pressure. Michael shouts but his voice is muffled and weak. He thrashes but it doesn't mean anything. Not a thing. Rudiger stops humming.

"You're not dyin,'" he says, for no real reason. Not to placate. He doesn't care about what Michael thinks or about his feelings. "Need to stay alive a little longer. Can't be dead when we start. Doesn't work that way."

Michael's body begins to go limp. Rudiger barely feels warm from the struggle, but he knows the real work is just ahead of him. It'll take all his strength to drag Michael far from the road and lift the cross with the man's body nailed to it. He's never done it with a real person before, though he practiced three days earlier with a two-hundred pound dummy.

Took him nearly an hour.

And the dummy hadn't been screaming.

CHAPTER TWO

WASHINGTON D.C.
APRIL 3

Why don't you feel anything?

Her words came back to him with the unpleasant certitude of an alarm clock reveille. Jonas downshifted, much to his Audi's protests, and deftly maneuvered around the minivan in front of him. The speedometer told him he was going almost eighty, but Jonas had a bad habit of ignoring things that tried to slow him down. Besides, it was the Beltway. It would slow down soon enough.

True to his thoughts, a sea of red lights illuminated before him, causing him to brake hard. Again his Audi protested. Jonas and his decade-old car had a love-hate relationship. He loved to drive it hard. The Audi hated him for it. He swerved behind a Fiat *(who the hell drives a Fiat?)* and hoped for a faster current in the swirling river of D.C. traffic.

Jonas cursed under his breath. There were directions for his anger to fly. Juliette, for one. She was beautiful, intelligent, and had the sexiest accent he'd ever heard. For almost six months, she had also been his.

Until this morning.

The Fiat slowed. Jonas cursed. The lane to his right was packed. The shoulder was to his left, and he had just enough respect for the law not to drive on it. Nowhere to go. Goddamn Juliette. Bad enough she dumped him, but why the hell did she have to live so far away? Now Jonas was going to be late to work. The traffic growled around him. He was trapped.

Trapped.

Trapped? Juliette had asked this morning. *How the hell do you feel trapped? You have all the freedoms of the world. I don't ask you for hardly anything. What the hell do you mean trapped?*

Bored was more like it. But how could he be bored with such a beautiful and intelligent woman? How is that even possible?

Jonas gritted his teeth, wanting to gnash out around him. But all he could do was seethe and let the frustration of another failed relationship wash over him. Why couldn't he ever feel satisfied?

He checked his rearview. What was it women saw in those eyes that convinced them Jonas was *the one*? Were they trusting eyes? Eyes that bespoke long-term commitment and a deep desire to procreate? Or were they just pretty blue eyes that God shoved inside the skull of a heartless bastard?

He rammed the shift hard against the gearbox and made the Audi growl. It wouldn't get him where he was going any faster, but it made him feel good.

Then he saw the problem. Stalled Jeep, two vehicles up from him. No emergency vehicles on the scene yet.

Traffic wasn't moving. Horns started. Everyone trying to maneuver around the stall, pressing on.

The Jeep's driver – older man, maybe sixty – had gotten out of his car and was rummaging under the hood.

Not smart, thought Jonas. Too many impatient drivers out here. Wandering around on foot's going to get you killed.

The Fiat managed to get around the Jeep and Jonas crawled behind the stall. He turned on his hazards and studied the man for a few seconds. After that time, Jonas made his assessment. The guy had no clue what he was doing.

Jonas ignored the honking behind him and climbed out of the Audi.

The frosty morning air smelled like exhaust. Jonas paused, thinking he should put on his coat. Decided against it.

"I'm fine," the man said, waving Jonas off without a hello. "Tow truck's on the way."

"Then why are you still looking under the hood?"

"Thought maybe I'd find the problem."

"And?"

The man stared at him. "Not finding anything."

"Not safe out here, sir. I can help you push it to the shoulder. Let's clear this lane, then you should sit in your vehicle and wait for help."

Jonas saw the man's reaction to his advice. He was going to obey, Jonas knew. Civilians always did. They could see the military infused in Jonas's posture and his attitude, and, though he no longer wore a uniform, people always did what he said.

Almost always.

Chrissakes, Juliette, just stay so we can talk, will you?

"All right," the man said.

The Jeep inched forward after an initial effort. Jonas heaved against the back of the car, and then immediately realized how much dirt transferred from the vehicle to his suit. *Goddamnit.*

The man shook Jonas's hand and thanked him for his help, though he didn't seem thankful in the least. Then he got in the driver's seat, turned on the hazards, and waited.

Jonas looked at his watch.

Shit.

He was supposed to meet with the Senator in twenty minutes. He'd never make it. He wondered if this day was supposed to be shitty or if it just decided to turn that way, suddenly and on a whim.

He didn't wonder for more than a flashing moment. The next three seconds lasted just long enough for him to assess the situation and see he was fucked.

He reacted calmly and objectively to the sight of the Ford F150 smashing into the back of his parked Audi. His mind even wandered enough to consider it was probably a good thing – the Audi was released of its misery and would no longer be subjected to his daily torture. He considered the distance between his legs and the front of his car. Years of military and physical training even allowed him the reaction time to jump high enough to clear the top of the hood as the Audi careened beneath him.

He offered his shoulder to the windshield rather than his head or back. Absorbed the impact perfectly, just as his body had been trained to do.

As the impact propelled him into the next lane of traffic, Jonas then knew his luck had run out. Yes, he would try to do something about it. Maybe he could roll out of the way before a car crushed him. But, statistically speaking, he would most likely die. He accepted it. It did not anger him. It was just math.

He fell hard onto the concrete. He had a moment to look up.

Jonas saw the odds had caught up to him.

Then he saw nothing.

CHAPTER THREE

Red dust caked Jonas's lips.

He was face down, his body armor pressing painfully against his torso. He lifted his head, aware his helmet was long gone. He squinted and tried to focus, succeeding after a few seconds. Pain rifled through his core, the kind that came not from the clean wound of a bullet but from the crushing blow of a three-story fall. He remembered it all – the little girl, that fucking Army grunt Sonman, the grenade ... The concussive force of the blast had blown him out the window, and he remembered thinking it would have been more desirable to die from the grenade rather than from the impact of a spine-shattering fall. But the corrugated tin awning had softened the blow. By the time he rolled off and onto the empty Mogadishu street, he still had a chance of survival.

He tried to push himself up but couldn't. Searing pain. If the sniper was still anywhere in the area, he could place as many rounds into Jonas's back as he wanted.

Silence.

Jonas turned his head to the left and saw the dead U.N. soldiers twenty feet away. Looking forward he saw what he hoped for – a platoon of U.S. soldiers double-timing it toward his position. He had seen them out the window of the building, just before falling to the ground.

Jonas felt a sudden and inescapable desire to close his eyes as he waited the final seconds to be either rescued by his brothers or shot by the sniper. He turned his head once more and placed his left cheek down on the warm dust of the street. As he started to close his eyes, and as the sounds of the city began trickling back in through his overwhelmed eardrums, Jonas saw the little black arm next to him. Palm faced upward. Intact fingers spread wide and bent to the sky, as if holding a gift, an offering, that no longer existed ...

* * *

Jonas opened his eyes expecting Somali dirt, not a hospital room. He was alone, though in the distance he heard the muted sounds of administration. Someone paging a doctor. Creaky wheels squeaking on a linoleum floor. A rasping cough.

Jonas had been dreaming. Had to be, because his mind simply could not grasp the reality of where he was. It was too unfamiliar.

In his dream, he had been back in the Mog. The images so long ago repressed came back to him in a grainy but pure reality.

A nurse walked by his open door. She was heavyset with a slight limp, her body bowed heavily to the left side as she shuffled. She glanced into Jonas's room and he stared at her.

She stared back and stopped walking.

"Oh my," she said. She shuffled into the room, walking with more purpose now. "You're awake."

Jonas tried to nod but couldn't. It was then he realized he had no power over his muscles. A massive thirst struck him.

"Let me get the doctor."

* * *

"It's a cliché, but you're lucky to be alive." The doctor spoke with a thick Indian accent and his smooth brown complexion was marred only by dark streaks under his eyes. Jonas guessed him in his late thirties – like himself – though hints of gray were already dotting his thick black hair. The doctor had introduced himself but the name had already flown from Jonas's memory.

"In fact," the doctor continued, "it's amazing there isn't more damage done."

"What ..." Jonas murmured.

"Car accident," the doctor interrupted. "And don't strain yourself trying to talk. You are going to be here for at least another day, so you'll have plenty of time to ask questions." The doctor looked down at the chart in his hand. "Long story short – you had a one-on-one with a Chevy Impala. You lost. Somehow you came out of it with a broken wrist, a concussion, and a canvas full of bruises. How you didn't die, I can only attribute to you being a tough son of a bitch. Or just plain lucky."

Jonas felt the words coming easier. "Army Rangers ... don't break," he rasped. "Only dent."

The doctor nodded. "Yes, I heard you were a Ranger in a former life. Well, maybe that's the reason." He paused. "Or maybe the Impala is just a real piece of shit car."

Jonas smiled. A familiar figure appeared in the doorway. The doctor turned to see who Jonas was looking at.

"Hello, Senator."

Senator Robert Sidams offered a thin but warm smile to the doctor. It was a smile Jonas had seen a thousand times before. It said: *you're not the person I'm here for.*

"How's he doing?"

If the doctor was surprised by the presence of the Senior Senator from Pennsylvania, he didn't show it. "He woke up just an hour ago."

"I know. I got the call. Can I talk to him?"

Jonas took another deep breath and spoke. "I'm right here, you know."

They both looked at him, as if his statement was a matter for debate.

"He needs his rest," the doctor said.

The Senator stared him down. "I need my rest, too."

The doctor nodded. "Just a couple of minutes, okay?" Turning to Jonas: "How's the pain?"

"Manageable. How long was I out?"

"Just over a day. Not a coma, but more than just a good sleep. We will need to run some tests just to make sure your brain didn't get scrambled. That's medical speak."

"Yes, sir."

The doctor walked out of the room.

Senator Sidams placed the palm of his right hand on Jonas's shoulder. "Good Lord, Jonas. You scared the hell out of all of us."

"Just trying to be selfish. You know how I need everyone to be thinking about me at all times."

"I thought it was supposed to be all about *me*," the Senator said.

"But you're too fragile to get hit by a car."

"You're saying you're more of a man than I am?"

Jonas smirked. "That's exactly what I'm saying."

Jonas had been Sidams's senior aide before being promoted to Chief of Staff after the Senator's most recent election win. He had known the man for eight years and Sidams was almost a father figure to him, though Jonas would never be ready to let go of his real father.

Jonas sipped on a plastic cup containing room-temperature water. The Senator placed a palm on Jonas's chest, closed his eyes, and bowed his head.

Jonas understood, and closed his eyes as well.

"Bless you, O Lord, and in you we trust to keep your beloved from harm, so we thank you for protecting Jonas from greater injury." He cleared his throat and paused a moment before adding, "And we seek your guidance as how to keep this dumb son of a bitch from being so reckless in the future. Amen."

"Amen to that," Jonas said.

"So what happened?"

"Juliette dumped me," Jonas said. "Thought I would throw myself into traffic to ease the pain."

"Bullshit," Sidams said. "You were helping a stranded motorist. Always trying to save the world, one dumbass at a time."

"That's beautiful. Think I'll put that on my tombstone."

Sidams reached into his jacket pocket. "Brought you a present." He handed the BlackBerry to Jonas. "It's all that's left of your car."

"Thanks." God only knew how many e-mails had gone unread since the accident, Jonas thought. Several hundred, probably.

"I figured you would want some form of communication while you're here."

"Thanks. I miss anything in the last twenty-four hours?"

Sidams nodded. "There's been a killing."

"Figurative or literal?"

"Literal, Jonas. A well-known constituent." Sidams's gaze went to the floor for just a moment. "And a friend."

Holy shit. Jonas tried to sit up.

"Who?"

"Michael Calloway."

Jonas felt the air leave his lungs. Michael Calloway was the CEO of Calloway Manufacturing, a huge distributor of auto parts and one of the largest private employers in Philadelphia. He was also a major financial contributor to and a personal friend of the Senator.

"My God. Killed? What happened?"

Sidams removed his hand from Jonas's chest. "They found him yesterday – it's all over the national news. He was ... crucified."

"Crucified? As in *crucified* crucified?"

Sidams nodded. "It's unbelievable. Found his body in a cave in a state park outside of Philly. Holes in his wrists and feet. Cross was still standing nearby. Blood all over it. Moreover ..." A lengthy pause.

"What?"

"It ... it seems Calloway was soliciting ... gay men on the Internet."

"Are you kidding me? He's married."

"I know, Jonas. I know. The media is just starting to sink its teeth into this, and it won't be going away soon."

Jonas had met Calloway once and had liked him. But the Senator had a long relationship with the man, and Jonas knew they had been close.

"Jesus, Robert, I'm so sorry."

"Turn on the television if you want to know more details, because I don't want to talk about it more. But I needed to tell you."

Jonas didn't know what more to say. *Crucified?*

"I have to stay in D.C. for a vote," the Senator continued. "So I'll miss the funeral. I was going to ask you to go, but you were too busy trying to arrange for your own funeral."

"When is it?"

"Friday."

Three days from now, Jonas thought.

"I can go."

"Can you?"

"No problem. I'll be there."

"Your doctor will let you?"

"Let that be my problem."

Sidams nodded and squinted his eyes in appreciation. "Thank you, Jonas. That would mean a great deal to me to have you there."

"It's my job."

The Senator stared blankly at Jonas's bed, looking through it at something else, deep in his own mind. Jonas wasn't used to seeing that face.

"I don't want to distance myself from him," the Senator said. "Whatever he was doing ... whatever secret life he had ... he was still a friend. You understand?"

"Absolutely."

The Senator seemed lost in thought.

"What is it?" Jonas asked.

The Senator remained silent for a long time. Jonas didn't press him. Finally, Sidams responded.

"His ear was cut off."

"What?"

"His ear. Whoever killed Michael cut his ear off. Postmortem, they think. It's not in the news yet."

Ear.

The word stabbed at Jonas.

"I've actually seen that before, you know." The Senator continued to look through Jonas. "In Vietnam. It happened to one of ours. No one I knew, but we found the body. Both ears cut off.

Rudiger pushes the memories from his mind, knowing they will hover close by, just like they always do. Preacherman is dead now, but never far away.

Rudiger drops the butt in the dirty snow of the parking lot and watches it die. He's in a Cleveland suburb. Long drive from Philly.

Philly was a mistake.

The man – *Michael, not Mike* – was the wrong person. He was not the *One*. All that work done for nothing. Rudiger had watched as the man, naked and bleeding in the near-freezing night air, asphyxiated to death, his body going limp and straining under its own weight. Another hour getting him down and burying him in the makeshift cave.

Then came the day and a half of waiting, with Rudiger sitting next to the body. In the cold. Watching. Wondering. Rudiger, at first so convinced it would happen, finally understood it would not. Not with that one. Not with Michael.

Had to keep looking.

Before Rudiger left the body to the animals, before he covered up the tracks he cared about covering, he'd done one last thing. Cut off Michael's ear.

Rudiger lifts his hand and feels the hardened scar tissue circling his own left ear. Another gift from the Preacherman.

He walks inside the grocery store and grabs a cart, then slowly trolls the aisles. The items he places in the cart are simple and healthy. Enough to last a few days. Nothing that needs cooking. Rudiger only stays in anonymous mom-and-pop motels, and those never have kitchens in the rooms.

God told him to come to Cleveland, just as he told him to go to Philly. *Clean in Cleveland.* That's what the magazine cover told him. Least that's what the letters spelled to Rudiger. Rudiger has a gift, gift of interpretation. God gave him the gift. So God talks to him. All makes sense.

He wonders what he's gonna find in Cleveland.

"'Scuse me," he mutters to a woman standing in front of a sea of canned vegetables. She shifts to the left. Then turns and looks at him as she apologizes.

Rudiger freezes.

She looks *just like her*. Long, stringy hair. Skinny like a dope fiend. Bright eyes that once probably looked hopeful but now convey a touch of crazy.

Preacherman's whore.

The bitch who had laughed when Preacherman had his way with him. When Preacherman was done, the whore had her turn with Rudiger next. She'd been the one who thought the slice around his ear was well-deserved punishment for Rudiger trying to escape that basement. The image of that beast's face was burned into everything that Rudiger was made of, and here was the same face, twenty-five years later, not a day aged, browsing the canned veggies.

Rudiger knows it *can't* be. He can't look away.

She catches his gaze, then offers a weak smile that quickly evaporates.

The resemblance continues to digs its nails into Rudiger's skin.

Maybe this is what he's here for. Maybe it's all a part of what he's supposed to do. Through her, he can help rid himself of his past. Exorcise his demons, some would call it.

He keeps staring. He doesn't want to, but he can't help it.

She is scared. Rudiger knows what fear looks like in the faces of others.

Without taking anything from the shelf, the woman turns away and pushes her cart down the aisle. She doesn't look back.

Rudiger looks at her backpack. It's a cheap kind. The kind a company would give away for free. It's purple, and the image of a steaming cup of coffee is plastered smack in the middle. Beneath, in big, bold letters, is the name of a coffee shop.

Café Rave Niche.

His mind seizes the words in the air and tears them apart, spreading them before him like playing cards. He grabs the letters he needs and stitches them back together, looking for meaning. Then it's there. The anagram is perfect. No wasted letters. What are the odds?

Cave her face in.

Rudiger turns and follows her, leaving his cart at an angle in the canned vegetables aisle.

* * *

He sits in his car and waits. White Buick, decade old, jacked just west of Philly. Stole fresh plates minutes after arriving in Ohio. Anonymous car for an anonymous man.

He watches as she loads her bags into a dated Camry, its paint dulled under several layers of street grime. No child seats.

She pulls out and Rudiger follows her. He keeps a distance. She takes him from busy boulevards into quieter residential streets. He sees her pull into a driveway and he drives past, knowing she can't see him as she pulls into a garage.

He drives another block and parks his car next to a small expanse of dead grass with a play structure on it. Paint faded from age. Too cold for kids to be out.

He walks back toward her house, keeping his head bowed while his gaze remains fixed before him. No one else outside. He checks his watch.

Rudiger looks in the window next to the door and sees a messy house. The woman is unclean. Unclean people suit him not at all. He continues looking and sees no movement. No indication anyone is home except her. No car in the driveway. None on the street in front of the house. Her one-car garage was empty before she pulled in.

She's alone.

Rudiger knocks.

No one comes.

He waits a moment longer. He starts humming.

Rings the doorbell.

Somewhere inside he hears the steps. They grow louder as she comes closer.

Rudiger steps to the side. If she bothers to look through the peep hole, she'll see no one.

The footsteps inside stop. A few seconds pass. Rudiger thinks he might have to force himself in. Then she unlocks the door and opens it.

Stupid.

Rudiger swings into view, smashing his fist into the bridge of her nose before she can even think to react. She falls backwards and lands hard on the floor. Carpet keeps her skull from cracking.

Rudiger shuts and locks the door as he listens to her wheezing and gurgling on the floor. He hums louder, losing himself in the rhythms of a song he can't place. When he turns to her, she is groaning and grabbing her face. He pulls her hands from her face and drags her by the arms out of view from the front door.

He drops her arms and they thud on the hallway floor. Rudiger knows she is done. She can't move. Can't scream. Helpless. He quickly searches the small house. No one else home.

When he returns she stretches her face into terrified protest. *Probably was hoping I was looking for money*, he thinks. Or jewelry. But I came for her and her alone. Now she knows it.

He straddles her body and squats down over her torso. His legs pin her arms to her sides. She opens and closes her eyes, as if eventually she'd open them and he'd be gone.

"Pullee ... pullee ..." Her words are garbled, but Rudiger knows she is saying *please*. He's an interpreter, after all.

She begins to cry, stopping only to choke on the blood draining into her throat.

For a second, he sees something in her eyes, a flash that pulls him back into a void. He sees the whore, standing over him, laughing as the Preacherman starts slicing up the side of his face, telling him he's a dirty fucking boy. A sinning boy. So bad a sinner that he better hope Jesus gives him forgiveness when the Rapture comes. And that whore bitch woman just laughed as the blood poured down his face.

The vision fades.

The woman closes her eyes.

Rudiger begins.

CHAPTER FIVE

WASHINGTON D.C.
APRIL 6

"You're back." Veronica's gaze swept over Jonas, noting the soft cast on his wrist. "Not too much worse for the wear. Didn't get your pretty face too bruised up."

Which wasn't true. He still had a large welt on his forehead. Jonas dropped his briefcase on his desk, looking at the clutter. He'd only been gone for three days, but three days is all it takes in politics to lose your footing permanently.

He turned to his assistant, whom he only ever called V. Tall, athletic. Feminine to the point Jonas assumed that, at any time, only expensive lingerie separated her couture from her naked skin. She was achingly beautiful and inexplicably single, and Jonas had often been tempted to ask her out before his senses got the better of him. It was bad enough his personal life was always fucked-up. He didn't want to do the same with his professional one.

"You didn't come to visit me in the hospital," he said.

"I did. You just weren't conscious." She brushed past him and dropped a stack of papers on his desk without explaining what they were. "It was the only time I've seen you vulnerable."

A dull ache resumed in the back of his head. "Then you haven't been around me enough."

"I'm glad you're okay."

"Thanks, V. Me, too. What did I miss in the last couple of days?"

She shrugged. "Just the normal life-and-death decisions that are made here every day."

"Anything actually interesting?"

"No. Not really." She paused. "Except Michael Calloway. You heard about that?"

"Who hasn't? It's the only thing on the news." Jonas thumbed through the stack of papers she'd given him. None of it could wait, but all of it would. "I'm catching a flight later to go to the funeral. The Senator asked me to."

"Need anything from me?" she asked.

"You mean like a date to a funeral?"

"I have just the outfit."

"I'm sure you do. But I don't think the point of the funeral is to have all eyes on you." Jonas flipped through the first few pages of a brief on a bill to expand coal-mining rights in western Pennsylvania. It'll never pass, he thought. Though if it did, it would mean huge political capital for the Senator.

"Heard you broke up with Juliette. Want to talk about it?"

Jonas finally looked up and sighed. "Yeah, do you have a few hours so maybe we can braid each other's hair and swap stories of heartache?"

"Don't be an ass."

"It's my default position."

"Well, I'm here to talk if you need me."

"Thanks. I do appreciate it. We just ... I guess she didn't see what was worth hanging around for."

"Then she's a fool."

He smiled. "More like an idiot savant."

She offered her own crooked smile and tilted one leg forward. "More fish in the sea?"

"I'm sure there are."

"Good." V crossed her arms. "You get back to work, then. I won't bug you for at least fifteen minutes."

"Thanks," Jonas muttered, finally sitting down. "Actually, V, can you do me a favor?"

She turned. "Of course."

"Grab me a couple Advil, will ya?" He massaged his temples. "Actually, make it three."

* * *

Jonas's visits to his dad were usually reserved for the weekend when he wasn't in the office (at least not all day) and when traffic was more an annoyance than an unyielding force of nature. Jonas didn't know how his trip to Philly would play out and he wanted to see his father before he left. Sooner was always better than later. Later could be too late.

As expected, the rush-hour roads were a snarled mess and the seventeen-mile trip was a combination of misery and boredom, assuaged only slightly by an NPR Podcast Jonas had downloaded and hadn't yet had time to hear.

He walked into the Jefferson Memory Care Residence as he always did, with a mixture of trepidation and sadness. Signed in at reception, gave and received familiar greetings with the staff, and headed back into the north wing of the building. He entered the code into the electronic keypad at the first set of doors and read the sign he'd read countless times before: *WARNING! Elopement risk. Please close door firmly behind you.*

Through the doors and into the hallway. The smell was immediate and familiar. It wasn't decay and it wasn't industrial cleaner, but some mix of the two. Nurses and staff smiled at him as he passed. Residents offered blank stares or looked through him, as if his was just another ghostly presence mixed in with their twisted view of reality. Those with stronger minds sometimes looked at him with pleading eyes. Those people were few. Jefferson wasn't the place you sent Aunt Betty when she could no longer remember how to use the microwave.

Jonas's mother been the caregiver for Cpt. William Osbourne (Ret.) for the first few years. The disease had come suddenly and without mercy, as such things do. The symptoms were mild at first. At first. The worst was the fourth year. Before Jefferson. His dad still understood what was happening. Barely. The man who flew over twenty combat missions over Cambodia and Vietnam slowly decayed into a ghost who shat his pants and couldn't remember who he was.

Then Jonas's mother died of a brain aneurysm. No warning. She simply collapsed one day while giving her husband lunch. A neighbor coming to visit found the Captain (as he'd *always* been called) sitting on the kitchen floor, stroking his wife's hair, as water boiled over onto the stove.

Jonas hadn't wanted to put his father in a home, but with no siblings for help and not enough money to support a live-in nurse for more than a couple of months, he had no choice. The first facility was simple, caring, and covered by the Captain's pension. But it took just two months for the Captain to show enough violent tendencies to be "disqualified" for treatment in a private facility. That's when things went downhill fast.

Jefferson took in the violent cases. It was the bastion of last hope for those with advanced Alzheimer's, hope being a place to die with a slice of dignity rather than a place to recover. Since arriving at Jefferson just over a year ago the Captain had lost all ability to speak and walk, and the best reactions Jonas could expect from his father were open eyes, an occasional nod, and the thinnest crack of a smile. Smiles were rare.

Jonas keyed in the code to the second set of doors and entered the north wing. The Captain's room was first on the right. Jonas checked there first, but he found Carolyn-an eighty-something ex-fashion designer – asleep in the Captain's bed. Carolyn had a tendency to sleep wherever the hell she wanted.

A familiar nurse stuck her head in the door.

"He's in the hallway," she said. "God, what happened to you?"

"Long story." He walked down the hallway, finding his father in the corner at the far end.

In earlier years, the Captain made the Great Santini look like a pussy. He was the warrior who had seldom spoken, but when he did, every word carried the weight of the world with it. He was the decorated soldier. The brother among his fellow soldiers. The dedicated – though distant – husband. The man to whom duty meant everything, before that very idea became a cliché. The Captain was the reason Jonas went into the military. Not to try to please his father. But to try to be his father.

The Captain sat alone in his wheelchair, his chin touching his bony chest, his hands gripping the chair's arms for support. He wasn't asleep because Jonas could hear sounds emanating deep in the Captain's throat. Sounded like humming. Jonas pulled up a cracked plastic chair and sat next to his father, silent in his attention, trying to recognize the song. After a minute he gave up.

"Hey Dad. It's Jonas." He leaned down and looked up into his father's face. The Captain's eyes opened halfway and the humming stopped. "You look good, Dad. Real good."

No reaction. The humming started again.

In warmer weather Jonas would wheel his father outside for some fresh air and sunshine on his milky skin. Too cold for that today, so Jonas picked up one of the Captain's hands and held it tight as he recounted the week's events.

"Big week, Dad," he said. "Got hit by a car. Can you believe that?" He held up his cast to prove it.

More humming.

"Yeah, could've died. But then I figured you would be bored as hell if both Mom and I were dead, so I decided to live." Jonas thought he saw a smile, but couldn't be sure. "Got a pretty bad concussion, though. Real pain in my ass. Threw up like a drunken frat boy last night because of it. And now I have to go to a funeral for someone who was crucified. Crazy fuckin' week."

He looked again. The Captain was a big fan of salty language, and often a well-placed *fuck* or *shit* got a reaction. Not today.

Jonas kept talking and the Captain kept humming, their respective sounds in a rhythm and cadence that somehow worked together, the two men in worlds far apart but still somehow connected. Jonas ran his thumb back and forth over the bones in the back of his father's hand, a gesture he never even would have dreamed of doing when his father was healthy. It was amazing, Jonas thought, how only a disease that rendered the old man demented could allow Jonas to share affection with him.

He even told his father about the flashback he had of Somalia. The explosion. Falling from the building. The little black arm, detached from its owner, lying in the dirt road next to him.

"I wanted to forget," Jonas told him. "And I thought I had, but something made me remember. Maybe it was the accident. Maybe it was just time for me to think of it again."

But there was more, wasn't there? The car accident. The flash of his time in the Mog. They weren't quite separate events. There was a thread between them, one connecting the other, and Jonas understood that thread, because it also passed directly through the man sitting in front of him. It was a window on mortality, a reminder that to dust we all return, and that time is short, and life not to be taken for granted. Jonas had almost died in the Mog that day. He nearly died on the Beltway. And in front of him, the reminder that even those who survive wars succumb to unconquerable foes.

Yet there was something connecting both events. Jonas realized in both of his near-death moments, they were the only times Jonas felt truly and utterly *alive*. It was something beyond the adrenaline rush. Beyond the fear. His mere survival buttressed his ego, telling him he survived for a reason. That, despite all his success in life, he was meant for something *more*.

The Captain tried to say something, but it only came out as a long, anxious warble.

Time went at a different pace when you were the only side of a conversation. After an hour, Jonas had nothing else to say. If the Captain had any idea his son came to visit, the memory would soon be gone, and Jonas could only hope the time he was there gave his dad some level of comfort. Small slice of warmth. Maybe a flash of a happy memory. It all made Jonas want to live only in the moment, because sometimes it seemed that's all there was.

He ended his visit as he always did, with a phrase that was alien to the father and son when Jonas was growing up.

"I love you, Dad."

CHAPTER SIX

PHILADELPHIA

A BRISK WIND caught Jonas as he stepped off the rental car shuttle in Philadelphia. Jonas had been to Philly more times than he could remember – almost as many times as he'd been to Harrisburg, the state's capital. Every time the Eagles lost, a little part of him died. He should have become a Steelers fan, he knew, but he just couldn't do it.

The trees on the side of the interstate whipped by in a flurry of barren branches. The drive took him just outside the city, and the rental car's GPS system told him he'd arrive in twenty more minutes.

Gave him time to think.

His first thought was what the hell was he going to say at the funeral. The Senator had called just before Jonas boarded his plane, informing Jonas he was expected to say a few words at Calloway's service, assuming, of course, he was agreeable to it.

Jonas agreed. He always agreed.

As the drive lulled him into a deepening ennui, Jonas thought about what he wanted, *really wanted*, with all of it. Jonas was on a trajectory, and that path was going to take him far in politics. He thought a House seat wouldn't be too hard, and a Senate slot not beyond question in another ten years or so. And if Sidams kept ascending, Jonas could rise with him. Sidams could one day be President. Jonas could be his Chief of Staff.

But is that what he wanted?

He kept rising because he was good at what he did, and when you're good at what you do, it's easy never to question if it's what you *want* to do. For all Jonas knew, he could have been a great software engineer, or police detective, or even a goddamn rodeo clown. But he always took the path that opened up before him, never bothering to look past the trees on the side of the road, never wondering if something a little different could be found by doing a little off-roading. Jonas's life felt scripted, and even if that script led to success, it didn't always make it fulfilling.

The accident had woken something inside of him. Something raw. That piece of him that was pure instinct, that could smell blood, that could feel danger before it presented itself. It was the piece of him that made him want more.

He hadn't sensed those feelings in a long time. Not since the Mog.

Mogadishu, Somalia.

He'd been an Army Task Force Ranger back then. Nineteen ninety-three. Sent to a starving little country to see if something could be done about the warlords there. Jonas was twenty-three and had been with the Rangers for two years already, a young age for such an elite group. From the moment his transport had landed in-country, things had been both clear and blurry, like looking through a piece of rippled glass. There were days of boredom. There were days of humanitarian assistance. There were days of bullshit administrative duties.

And then there were days in the shit. The kind you trained for, days and weeks on end, just so you could convince yourself not to run in abject terror.

Jonas remembered most of it. Most he had seen though the clear part of the glass. But then something happened. Something very bad. Jonas only remembered streaks of it. He viewed the last days of his tour through the rippled part of the glass, the images vague and unreliable.

He'd shoved those images so far inside his head they hadn't come within a stone's throw of his consciousness in a long time. Until he was hit by a car, that is.

Since the accident, Jonas had started seeing again. Seeing flashes – clear flashes – from nearly two decades ago. They only came in short bursts, mere fragments, but they were real enough to have happened yesterday.

The flashes were during the time of the really bad shit. What he saw scared the hell out of him.

It also excited him.

CHAPTER SEVEN

THERE WAS MORE press at the funeral than Jonas had wanted, but they had been limited to outside the church and were not allowed into the service. Michael Calloway had been more than just an important man. He was the victim of a gruesome killing. *Crucifixion*. Nasty, brutal, symbolic, *personal* death.

Jonas sat in the second pew during the service, watching those around him without turning his head. Every pew was full and those not able to sit stood in the back of the church. Despite strict instructions by Calloway's family, Jonas counted four people who surreptitiously took pictures at various points during the service. Three were men, and Jonas guessed they were all reporters who'd been able to sneak inside. When they weren't taking pictures they were taking notes, or otherwise looking bored.

The fourth was a woman sitting across the aisle from him. A black woman who Jonas guessed was about his own age, maybe a couple of years younger. A long black dress spilled over shapely legs. She sat erect, as if trying to get the best view without standing up. Every now and then she would close her eyes, but not out of boredom. Out of concentration, Jonas thought, as if she might have to recite the words at a later point.

Jonas soon began to focus on her, because it was better than focusing on the headache slowly creeping up on him. He wondered who she was and what she was doing here.

He only had seconds to think about it before it was his turn to speak. Jonas wasn't introduced, but his name was in the program, which meant the Senator had confirmed he would be speaking and that actually asking Jonas to do it was just a formality. Jonas smiled. *Bastard.*

As he rose, the woman in the black dress turned and looked at him, and for a moment the two of them locked gazes. There was a mutual curiosity and interest, Jonas thought.

You wondering about me, too?

His knee had been tight and stiff since the car accident and Jonas limped as he walked toward the sanctuary of the church. The congregation was silent save the occasional stifled cough.

Jonas stood behind the pulpit and looked before him. He felt a tinge of nervousness, but was comforted by an ego that assured him he would be fine.

"Senator Sidams was a lifelong friend of Michael Calloway, and he regrets dearly that he couldn't be here himself today." Jonas was already comfortable in front of the church full of strangers. "I'm sure Michael would have appreciated the Senator staying in Washington for a vote, doing his job for the people of Pennsylvania." He paused and scanned the crowd, then passed his gaze over the woman in the second pew. She had her full attention on him. "I only met Michael once," he continued, "so I can't say I'm the most qualified person to be standing here in front of you. But my one meeting with him was memorable." Weird, he thought. Eulogizing a man he barely knew who was crucified after soliciting gay sex on the Internet.

Jonas spent a few minutes speaking about the meeting with Calloway. He scanned the crowd comfortably, making eye contact with every somber face. Once, as he rested his gaze on the woman in the second pew, she smiled. Just a little.

"As our meeting was ending, Michael focused his attention on me. I was warmed by his smile, and for the first time he directed his words at me and not the Senator. He said he had heard my father was ill and he asked about him."

Jonas looked down and saw the woman had closed her eyes again. He shifted his weight and gripped the top of the podium tighter. He suddenly felt a little nervous.

"I don't know how he knew about him – the Senator, I suppose – but my father was slipping deeper into the haze of Alzheimer's. I thanked him and told him my father was steadily getting worse but that I appreciated his concern."

Jonas looked down again at the woman. Her eyes still closed. Head tilted back at the slightest of angles. Jonas cleared his throat.

"Michael asked me if I ever prayed for him. The easy answer would have been yes, but it wouldn't have been the truth. I'm not a religious man, I told him. He smiled even brighter and took my hands in his. He bowed his head and asked me to do the same. And then this man – this powerful businessman who had a reputation for being a fierce and ruthless competitor to his rivals – said the most beautiful and personal prayer I had ever heard. Thinking about it even now nearly brings tears to my eyes, something not easily done to an ex-Army Ranger."

Smiles across the church. The woman finally opened her eyes and smiled broadly at him, showing perfect white teeth.

"That night I visited my father. He looked the same. In no way did he show any signs he knew who I was. As always, I sat next to him and told him about my day. About my meeting with the famous Michael Calloway. Then, as I got up to leave, he grabbed my hand, something he hadn't done in a long time. He lifted his head and stared at me, and in that moment he *knew* me. His eyes brightened and, if I let my imagination do a little work, I could have sworn he said my name."

A soft murmur of approval across the church, the sound of satisfaction.

"I'm convinced our prayer together helped my father that day. Michael's words and kindness touched *me*, a natural cynic, and though I only knew the man for a few hours, his life affected mine. I can only imagine the joy for those who knew him for years and even lifetimes. He will be missed, but his spirit will continue to affect us all."

* * *

She approached Jonas after the service, gliding toward him in the reception hall. Jonas allowed himself a thin smile as she approached. She reciprocated.

The woman extended her hand. Jonas took it. She paused and held his hand for a moment before speaking.

"I'm Anne Deneuve."

The shake was firm, but still feminine.

"Pleased to meet you, Anne. I'm-"

"Full of shit," she said.

"Excuse me?"

"Was I not clear?"

Jonas took his hand back.

"No, not really."

"Okay, then," she said. "I said you're full of shit."

"In what way?"

"Are there multiple ways?"

"I hope so, because the way I know of would be an insult. And insults at funerals are a real downer."

She tilted her head and studied him as if he were a math problem to be solved.

"The bit about your father. You made that up. Or at least exaggerated it."

"Did I?"

"You did."

"And how would you know that?"

"Because I'm paid to know things."

"Aren't we all? And who pays you?"

She paused, seeming to decide whether to press on.

"The FBI," she said.

Jonas felt a squint take over his eyes.

"The FBI sent you to the funeral of a corporate titan to see if anyone lied during his service?"

"Not exactly."

"So you're insulting me off the clock?"

"Exactly."

He let the moment settle around them.

"Intriguing."

"Can I buy you a drink?" she asked.

He smiled.

"Don't flash those pretty teeth at me," she added. "It's not what you think."

"How do you know what I think?"

"Meet me for a drink and I'll tell you all about my special abilities."

She didn't wait for answer. She didn't need to.

Jonas watched her walk away for about ten steps before following.

CHAPTER EIGHT

THE FOUR SEASONS Philadelphia rose like a grey monolith toward the equally grey sky. Jonas wondered if colorblind people sought comfort in this city. He valet-parked his car and headed inside toward the Swann Lounge, where he'd agreed to meet Anne. The bar was large yet still intimate, with spaces carved out by the studied placement of tables and chairs. You could be loud or quiet in a place like this, Jonas thought. A black baby grand sat unmanned near a wall, gleaming.

He found a chair offering a view of the entrance. A waitress wearing black slacks and an eager smile told him it was teatime and he told her that did him no good. He sent her away with an order for a Grey Goose gimlet. Up.

Anne came into the lounge ten minutes later. Jonas wondered if she was a slow driver or had diverted to her room first to freshen up.

"You made it," she said.

"Were you worried I wouldn't come?"

"I didn't give it a lot of thought."

"That means you gave it some thought."

"Yes," she conceded. "I gave it some."

The waitress came, set the glass before Jonas, and offered Anne the same speech about it being teatime. Anne looked over at Jonas's drink and ordered a gin and tonic.

"Hard to sip tea after a funeral," she said.

"Hard to sip it anytime."

"It's good for you."

"That doesn't make it tasty."

"Are you always this argumentative?"

Jonas picked up the drink with his good hand.

"That's the nicest way I've heard it described."

"And how is it usually described?"

"Depends on who you ask. If you ask an ex-girlfriend, which the streets are littered with, they would call it being obstinate and unwilling to share in my feelings. If you ask my boss, he'd call it being professionally cynical."

She shifted in her seat. "Did you just say the streets are littered with your ex-girlfriends?"

"I did."

"That's a repugnant phrase."

"I mean, not literally, of course. That would just be weird."

She sucked in a shallow breath. Jonas knew the face. It was mild disgust mixed with curiosity. He never knew how that mix would settle in a person's stomach.

"You're wondering why I asked you out for a drink."

"It wasn't my charm?"

"I don't charm easily."

"But you must charm some."

"You are far from discovering that."

He settled back in his chair, enjoying the parry. "In that case, yes, I am wondering why you asked me for a drink."

The waitress came by and placed the drink in front of Anne, where it sat untouched for a few minutes while she spoke.

"You have a connection to what I'm working on. I don't know what it is or if it's even relevant, but I have to follow up on it. Anything can be important, even the slightest lead."

"A connection?"

"Yes."

"And what are you working on?"

"It's confidential."

"And yet I have a connection to it."

"I think so. Yes."

"And how have you established this?"

It was the moment he saw her falter. Her eyes narrowed slightly as she considered her words. Not as confident as she had been just seconds before.

"I'm a contract worker for the FBI, Mr. Osbourne. There are two reasons for this. First, they couldn't possibly afford me on a full-time basis."

"And the second?"

She hesitated. "What I do would be hard to justify to the taxpayers as a legitimate government position."

"It's sounding like you're some kind of escort."

Anne finally reached for her drink. "You're getting closer to charming me, Mr. Osbourne. I can't imagine why any of your exes let go of you."

"How do you know I'm the one who gets dumped?"

She ignored his question. "I'm not an escort, Mr. Osbourne. I'm a psychic criminologist."

"Like a medium?"

"No. Not a medium. A medium channels the dead. I'm a psychic criminologist."

"Like a fortune teller?"

She put her drink down. "Okay, I'm assuming you're a hell of a lot smarter than you're pretending to be right now. So let's lift this veil of bullshit and get to the point."

"Fair enough," he said. The vodka settled in him nicely. "Veil lifted. Here's my perspective. You're a beautiful woman who approached me at a funeral. You have a sharp wit, a sharper mind, and a massive amount of confidence. You come at me with a story that I'm sure has several layers to come. It'll be all thought out to the last detail. Maybe your story's true, maybe it isn't. I don't know, and honestly I don't really care. What I do know is I'm the Chief of Staff for one of the most powerful Senators in the government, and the line of people who approach me with well-crafted stories could easily cover the litter of all my ex-girlfriends." He leaned over the table toward her. "Ninety-nine percent of the time, these people want something from the Senator. Something that wouldn't be in his best interests, and in many cases, illegal. It's my primary job to protect him, so when I act a little stupid, it's a cover for blowing you off."

She blinked a few times. "Yet you still met with me."

"Well, you *are* gorgeous."

"You're that shallow?"

He picked up his gimlet. "Like a kiddie pool left out in the summer sun." A sudden pain rushed through his head but he was careful not to wince or massage his temples, as much as he was tempted to.

"Your head," she said. "It hurts."

"Sometimes I think too much."

"You were recently in an accident," she said. "You were knocked unconscious. You still hurt from it."

Jonas held up his cast. "Wow, I'm drinking with Nostradamus. It doesn't take a medium to read the newspapers, Ms. Deneuve. Or see the bruises on my face."

She looked at him and half-tilted her head. A dog hearing a high-pitched noise. "I'm not a medium. Something happened to you after the accident."

"Yeah," he said. "I stopped getting out of my car on the Beltway."

Monotone voice. "You're having memories."

Jonas was bringing his drink to his lips when she made the pronouncement. He was glad, because he was looking down and she couldn't see the surprise that must have been obvious on his face. He composed himself and looked up.

"We all have memories."

She leaned forward. "But these memories *scare* you," she said.

He gulped down the last of his gimlet and dropped his business card on the table in front of her. "Thanks for the drink."

He figured she would contact him again if she were for real.

And even if she wasn't, part of him still hoped she would call.

CHAPTER NINE

MONONGAHELA NATIONAL FOREST
WEST VIRGINIA
APRIL 15

Rudiger doesn't like a mess.

Sometimes there's gotta be a mess. Can't be helped. But he doesn't like it. Nice and tidy. *That's* how he likes it. Everything in its place.

There's a mess now. The boy's just shit himself, and Rudiger wonders if it's something he should deal with. Blood is one thing. Blood is messy, but pure. And it's all over the place.

Shit is another thing. It's dirty. Foul. Unclean. It causes Rudiger discomfort.

The boy keeps screaming.

Rudiger thinks of him as a boy, though surely he's at least eighteen. Name is Dylan. Freshman at West Virginia University. Rudiger had been traveling south, looking for some clue as to who the One could really be. He read every sign along the highway, every personal ad in every local paper, every bumper sticker on every car in front of him. Rearranged the letters, twisting and turning them, keeping some letters and discarding others, looking for clues. There had been many clues, but none of them had felt *quite right*. Passing near the university, Rudiger picked up a free copy of the campus newspaper. He'd spied an article about campus recycling, written by the boy. Rudiger had quickly rearranged the letters of the article's title.

BRING ME REVEAL CHRIST

Took Rudiger four days for the preparation. Secured the wood to make the cross and found a good location for the crucifixion, a remote area of the Monongahela National Forest. Dug a hole in the moist earth for the cross and a larger one to make what he considered an appropriate cave. Then tracked the boy down.

"What are you doing to me?" the boy screams in disbelief.

It's dark but Rudiger's headlamp spotlights the sweat dripping down the boy's belly. A campfire scatters softer light across the naked torso, painting his agony with an orange hue. Blood flows freely from the holes in his wrists. The shit falls onto the ground in snaky trails. Lakeside breeze carries the stench away.

Rudiger doesn't know how to answer, so he just tells the truth.

"I'm killing you."

Then come the sobs.

Rudiger wonders if the boy is the One. He hopes so. He won't know for another two days.

"No use cryin," Rudiger says. "If you're the One, then it'll be all right. Little pain now. Glory forever."

"Oh God oh God it fucking hurts …" The boy speaks in stutters and stumbles, fragments and spit. There is life still in him, much of it, but the boy doesn't believe it. He thinks he'll die in minutes because he's never felt real pain before. The human body is quite resilient. It doesn't want to give up. But sometimes it has to.

The next part comes with effort. Rudiger's ready. He's strong and powerful. He touches his own left arm and his skin feels like cool stone, hard and unmoving, stretched taut over bulging muscle. Using a rope and a pulley attached to a tree, he hoists the crucifix fully upright. The boy is much lighter than the business-man. Maybe a hundred and fifty pounds total.

The boy vomits as his weight stretches his lungs and restricts his breathing. Howls as legs buckle. The weight pulls him down, but the spikes in his wrists keep him firmly in place.

It's nice here, Rudiger thinks, poking at the fire with a stick. Next to this lake. Peaceful. As the screams fade he hears an owl call to another without any sense of alarm.

"Please ..." Bile drips off the boy's chin. "Please." His breathing is tight and shallow.

"There ain't no please," Rudiger says, surveying his work with the beam from his headlamp. "How can you say please? You know you will die. Jes accept it as did your Savior. With humility and joy."

Rudiger steps back and considers. Both of the boy's shoulders are clearly dislocated. His lungs have hyper-expanded and he'll probably die from asphyxiation. Or succumb to hypovolemic shock. But not for a while.

Preacherman would've been proud, Rudiger thinks. Would've said the boy was a sinner of one sort or another, and done got what he deserved.

Preacherman's face comes into Rudiger's mind, sharp and tight. The crooked teeth. One eye always open wider than the other. The corpse smile. In Rudiger's vision-flash, Preacherman is hold-ing the Book, telling Rudiger he best read the whole fucking thing if he wants some kind of outside shot at salvation.

Preacherman taught him all about the Book in those two months. Preacherman was the one who told him Jesus would come back one day. Sure enough, inside that book, within those torn and greasy pages, in the cold basement, with the smell and the pain and the solitary dirty light bulb that barely gave enough light to read, Rudiger did indeed find the bit about the Rapture. The return. Salvation. In that moment, as he disappeared inside the words of promise and rescue, little twelve-year-old Rudiger thought God's full glory surely must be the sweetest sight in the world, and ever since that day he's been waiting for it to come.

Wasn't long ago Rudiger decided to take matters into his own hands.

He studies the dying boy.

The boy doesn't *seem* to be the One, though there's no way of knowing now. If he isn't, Rudiger will have to set to work again. Have to find the next clue. Build another crucifix. Sharpen more spikes. Select a remote location. Find, catch, and move the target. Crucify him. Bury him in a makeshift cave or tomb. Wait for the third day to see if He has arisen. If not, then Rudiger will repeat the process.

Lot of work. God's work.

Sooner or later he'll be caught. Rudiger's not stupid. He can only hope he fulfills his mission before that happens. He has to trust in the guidance he's been given.

The boy is now shaking. Convulsing. His head is bowed and a long rope of bile dangles from his lower lip.

Rudiger stands beneath him and touches the boy's sweat-stained thigh. "You feel it close now?"

No answer. The boy's long black hair is matted, damp, stuck against the side of his face.

"It'll come all of a sudden. You'll feel cold one moment, but then it's like someone covered you in the softest, warmest blanket you can imagine. I know. I've been there. *Embrace it.* Because when it's seconds away you'll be happy. Happier than you've ever known." Rudiger touches the boy's bare thigh and feels the heat of the skin. Hot like an infection.

The boy opens his eyes. Campfire shows them green. He looks down from his perch and sees Rudiger, and the green eyes are no longer accusing. Not forgiving, either. They only contain wonder. Wonder at all of it. He stares into the next world.

"I don't know you," the boy says.

"No, you don't."

The boy ejects a small cough. Rudiger turns to the fire, where he sets about cooking his dinner. Can of beans and a can of peas. Two-liter bottle of water. He eats and waits, looking up every now and then to see if the boy is dead. Gonna take a while, he thinks. The fire tries to die over the next couple of hours, but he stokes it to life again and again. When the moon finally comes out over the nearest treetop, the boy dies. Rudiger waits thirty minutes before bringing the body to the ground. As he prepares it for burial, he unsheathes the knife hanging from his belt. Military-issue blade, full-tang, blade black and clean. He bends over and slowly slices off the left ear of the boy, places it in a napkin, and puts the appendage in his breast pocket.

Then Rudiger kicks out the fire and uses the light from his headlamp to help him finish his work.

CHAPTER TEN

WASHINGTON D.C.
APRIL 16

SWEAT COVERED HIS face like a swarm of flies. Hot and sticky, tickling his cheeks and forehead. Jonas wiped his face along the linen and flipped the pillow over, hoping the other side would be cooler. The pillow wasn't the problem. The problem was his own body temperature, which seemed to be approaching the temperature of the sun.

He rolled out of bed and stood. Gravity overwhelmed him and a wave of dizziness nearly felled him. He sat on the edge of the bed and held his head. Palms burned into his flesh.

Lingering effect from the Beltway accident? Jonas thought too much time had passed for that. Maybe bad Chinese take-out from last night.

It didn't matter. Jonas stumbled to the toilet and bent over the bowl just in time. He felt better after the first volley of puke. He wiped his mouth, flushed, and remained in position for a bit longer, just in case.

The swirling water in the bowl settled and Jonas saw a ghostly reflection of himself in it. The translucence of the reflection did him good, he thought. He could only see his sharpest features: his tight jaw line, his close-cropped hair, his ears, which did their best not to appear too big. The face in the water was undeniably masculine, one comfortably accentuated by either a military-issue flak helmet or a clean shave and a thousand-dollar suit.

Jonas smiled at his own arrogance.

Only I could admire myself in vomit-tinged toilet water.

He felt safe enough to pry himself away and return to his bed, though his legs still shook and the sweat still beaded his forehead.

He pulled the comforter over him and closed his eyes, thinking about what Anne had said. That he had some kind of connection to one of her cases. Connection to what? Must have to do with the Calloway murder, since she was at the funeral. Nothing made sense, and all the nonsensical thoughts floated and swirled in his mind, trying to fit together into a coherent formulation that never came. For the briefest of moments he envied his father, whose mind was now unable to grapple with complicated thoughts and deeply rooted memories. He quickly dismissed the morbid thought and pulled the covers up a little higher.

Minutes later came sleep. Soon after that came the dreams.

* * *

"Mind over matter, Sonman. It's all up here." Second Lieutenant Jonas Osbourne tapped his helmet with his finger, rapping it twice. *It was an important argument, he thought. One the enlisted soldier would do well to believe, regardless of veracity. Mental preparedness was critical, especially when needed to overcome fear. Fear could explode from any direction ...*

The two soldiers patrolled a neighborhood in western Mogadishu. The unit had split into smaller teams for reconnaissance patrols disguised as humanitarian "meet and greets." Let the locals know of their presence and remind them the Americans were there for relief purposes only. The neighborhood was an Aidid stronghold, however, and the warlord had many supporters, some of whom had weapons. And some knew how to use them.

Jonas eyed the buildings for snipers.

"Yessir." PFC Sonman's eyes darted back and forth. Sonman was regular Army, a grunt, little more than a redneck with a few weeks of training and a vacant stare. "Mind over matter."

"It's true, Private." Jonas wanted to keep the soldier engaged in light conversation while keeping him focused on the task at hand. He would rather have been touring with a Ranger brother and not a grunt, but those weren't his orders. He barely knew Sonman.

"Not that you can necessarily shape all your destiny with your mind," Jonas continued, "but you can control more than you think. If you think negative thoughts, bad things will keep happening to you. Think good thoughts, though, and, well, good things. You know?"

Their boots crunched the pebbles on the dirt road beneath them. "Yessir."

"Focus your mind on the good we're doing. The relief efforts. The fact that we're going to skull-fuck Aidid so some of the mercy food can actually go to the people."

"Skull-fuck. Yessir."

He looked over at Private Sonman.

"Why'd you join the Army, Private?"

A pause. "Needed something to focus on."

"Rough childhood?"

"No real childhood at all."

"Want to elaborate?"

"No, sir."

That wasn't unusual. Many soldiers in the regular Army were looking for an escape. This Sonman was clearly one of them. That was okay by Jonas, who found his own way here via West Point and the desire to emulate a father who was a hero to many in the military. *Truth be told, Jonas loved the service. He loved where he was. Helping through strength. Being a presence. Protecting and defending. He loved the excitement and didn't hate the boredom. And, goddamnit, he was a good soldier.*

Jonas turned and saw Sonman had stopped walking. A hollow stare ghosted his face, as if someone had simply turned him off.

"Private?"

Sonman didn't respond. Jonas followed the soldier's gaze to a rusted tin sign hanging crooked on the building across the street.

Jonas reached out and touched Sonman on his shoulder. "What is it, Sonman?"

Then Sonman slowly came back to life, turning to Jonas. Jonas could barely hear his words.

"Nothing, sir."

"You read Somali?"

"No, sir."

Jonas wanted to ask another question, but then he felt something. Maybe it was a change in the air pressure. Maybe the noise on the busy street abated for just a second, as if a rift in time rolled through the urban market. Whatever it was, it caused Jonas to turn his head. The street teemed with locals darting in and out of buildings. No one strolled. No one seemed eager to spend too much time out in the open.

A dirty white taxi rolled by, its wheels kicking dust off the unpaved road. No passenger.

"Heads up," Jonas said. He took a step forward, allowing separation between the two men.

"It's here," Sonman said, quiet enough Jonas barely heard.

"What's here?"

"I don't know," Sonman said. "But it's gonna change things."

Jonas looked over at him and wondered what the hell the soldier was talking about. He decided not to dig deeper at the moment.

Across the street, two Pakistani soldiers looked over. They were part of the United Task Force, who, along with U.S. Forces, were all part of Operation Restore Hope. They were there to secure an environment the U.N. could no longer contain. It was the Wild West out here, Jonas thought. With automatic weapons.

Jonas had seen the Pakistanis earlier, walking through the heart of the market. They were professionals. Well trained. They kept their space between them and treated the locals with respect. The larger one gave Jonas a slight nod. Brothers in arms.

That single nod took away Jonas's momentary apprehension. Whatever had raised his hackles was soothed by the sight of the other soldiers.

Sit norm.

Jonas nodded back.

As the Pakistani turned to his comrade, a shot cracked through the air.

The Pakistani crumbled, and Jonas saw the reason. Clean shot through the front of the throat. Blood sprayed from the wound as the soldier collapsed onto the dirt of the street.

Sniper.

"Take cover!" Jonas shouted.

Sonman fell back and secured a position against the chipped wall of the building adjacent to their position. He called in for support as Jonas raced across the street.

"Get back! Get back!" Jonas shouted at screaming pedestrians. The Somalis scattered everywhere, disappearing into buildings in seconds. The cab driver spun the wheels of his car, which took a few rotations before gripping firmly and shooting the car in a spray of dust and dirt down the street.

The second Pakistani soldier froze. He stared at his fallen comrade with wide, panic-laden eyes.

Bad place to freeze.

The second shot cracked through the air just as Jonas reached to pull the soldier to the ground. The bullet smashed into the Pakistani's face, exploding skin and bone into a spray of pulpy mist. The impact snapped his head back violently before the rest of his body collapsed only feet from his comrade's own pool of blood.

There was nothing he could do for the men, and Jonas questioned his decision to run into the line of fire. He crouched, spun, and used his M16 to quickly scope the windows in the three-story building across the street.

Nothing.

He looked at building's entrance and motioned to Sonman, who leaned against it, shielded from above by a rusted tin awning. He pointed up and gave him the signal to wait.

They could do a room-by-room search, covering each other along the way. More troops would be on scene to assist in moments, but they couldn't afford to waste any time. Jonas prepared to burst to his feet and sprint across the street.

Then Sonman ran.

He didn't run away. He ran into the building. Without waiting for his commanding officer. Directly against protocol and any sense of logic.

He just fucking ran.

"Wait!" Jonas shouted as he leapt to his feet.

An enormous lead fist punched him in the chest.

He'd been hurt before, but this was different. This was like a car hitting him, slamming him into the ground. His mind spun but his training took over, and he knew exactly what had just happened.

The sniper had just shot him in the chest.

Jonas knew enough to roll away from his position and hurl himself through the open doorway of the bullet-pocked building next to him.

He could still move, and that was a good sign. With luck, his Kevlar stopped the bullet, though a sharp pain when he tried to breathe told him he wasn't unscathed.

Before he assessed his own injury, Jonas grabbed his radio.

"Two-five this is two-six. Two-five this is two-six. Over."

Painful seconds passed until a static-laced voice crackled through.

"Two-six this is two-five. Over."

"Two-five I have sniper fire in the Huriwaa market. We are three blocks east of the Nafari Hotel. Two U.N. troops DOA, and I've been hit. Over." He struggled to catch his breath.

"Roger that, two-six. Assessment of your condition. Over."

Jonas wondered the same thing. He ripped the Velcro straps of the flak jacket open, giving just enough space to run his hand inside and feel for blood. More sharp pain, but no liquid.

"Think the flak stopped the round. Maybe a broken rib. I'm fine. Over."

"Roger that, two-six. Sending in additional response. Can you sit tight? Over."

Jonas took a deep breath, winced away the pain in his chest, and raised himself enough to peer through a dirty window. Except for the two dead Pakistanis, the crooked street was empty.

"Negative, two-five. PFC Sonman went after the sniper. Solo. I need to provide backup. Over."

"Are you mobile-ready? Over."

Jonas stood and leaned against the wall, the pain from his chest searing. But he could move.

"Roger that, two-six. Leaving my position now. Send support ASAP. Guessing one sniper but could be more. Two-five out."

"Copy two-five. Two-six out."

No time to waste. He had to run across the street, hoping the sniper wasn't waiting to take another shot. In all likelihood, the shooter was long gone, having secured three hits, two successful. Private Sonman would likely break into an empty room. *Fucking regular Army piece of shit,* Jonas thought. It would be a shame not to kill the sniper, but it was better than a green PFC trying to play Rambo and getting his skull separated from his body.

Jonas moved to the open doorway and readied himself for the sprint, hoping he could still run in his condition. He began counting in his head, preparing to run on three.

One.

Squeezed his eyes shut.

Calm yourself. You can do this.

When he got to two he heard the screams.

CHAPTER ELEVEN

WEST VIRGINIA
APRIL 17

RUDIGER CHANGES CLOTHES inside the van. Turns and takes one last look out the open back doors at the body. The boy is naked, nearly folded into a ball. Body wedged into a hole in the ground. Face staring up at pine needles and slices of sky.

He is not the One.

There is meaning, Rudiger thinks. All death has its purpose. I am learning.

Preacherman speaks to him, and the voice makes Rudiger want to gag. *You jes keep fucking up, don't you, boy? Can't do nothin' right.*

Rudiger pushes the voice away, a skill he has improved upon but never perfected after all these years.

He drives the van over brittle ground, leaving the woods. In the rearview mirror he sees the cross, erect in the dirt, its arms soiled with the evidence of its use. It's not a symbol. It's a tool.

Won't be long before he gets caught. He's only as careful as he needs to be, and nothing more. Doesn't matter. He has a purpose. What happens to him means nothing.

He drives to a decaying suburban mall. Parking lot mostly empty. No exterior security cameras. He wipes down the interior of the van with his dirty clothes. No way he can fully erase all traces of his DNA. Not possible.

Walks the parking lot, checking for unlocked vehicles. Only a matter of moments before he finds one. No keys. Not in the next one, either. On his third try, he finds a shit-colored Accord with the keys safely wedged in the passenger-side visor.

Gone.

Two miles on, a brief stop at a strip mall yields new license plates. Should be enough to get him to Virginia, long as he minds the laws.

Virginia.

He doesn't know what's waiting for him there. Doesn't even know why he's going. But after seeing a billboard (*Virginia Is For Lovers*), Rudiger's mind exploded with the possibilities:

Virgin

Sin

Risen

Revival

Savior

He can't use all the letters to make one sensible clue. Doesn't matter. Doesn't bother him neither that the phrase also has lots of bullshit words. Words like *ravioli* and *airfoil*. These are to be discarded from the deck, the low cards. His mind only clings to those words saturated in meaning. Makes things cleaner. Easier.

He'd been able to make the letters dance ever since his time with the Preacherman and his whore. Maybe he even had the ability before then, but Rudiger remembers just about nothing of the time before. His childhood was gone, a twelve-year chunk of life that was only shown in photos and video but little of which dwelled inside Rudiger's mind.

Mom left when Rudiger was fifteen. She didn't understand why Rudiger would never talk about what had happened to him, or how he escaped. Or what had happened to the person who stole her baby boy for two whole months. Or why Rudiger read the Bible every day, spouting quotes from Revelation at every opportunity. Or how he could rearrange letters so quick in his head. Rudiger was a freak, and Mom couldn't take it no more. Maybe there was a little guilt there, too. She was the one who told him it was okay to ride his bike after dark, after all.

Rudiger looks at the map on the seat next to him, searching for the closest chance to turn east. Virginia just feels *right*. He pictures long fingers of grass growing around the moss-covered trunks of black alder trees. The spotty winking of firefly light in the thick dusk. He smells air draped in moisture. Hears cicadas humming like power lines.

Cars begin to pass him. A few drivers offer sidelong glances as their cars whisk by. Rudiger rolls down his window and spits into the world.

He wonders how long it will be before he finds the One. And why, if God wants him to succeed, has he only found failure?

How many people must he kill before his work is done?

Rudiger doesn't like to kill unless he has to. Seems odd, he thinks, considering some of the things he's done. Considering how easy killing comes to him. Still, needless slaughter makes no sense. Why step on a spider when you can walk around it?

Maybe God doesn't think I'm ready, Rudiger thinks. Maybe all the killings are just practice, dry runs to make sure I don't mess it up when it comes to the real thing. Maybe it's not a question of my faith in God, he decides. Maybe it's about God's faith in *me*.

He squeezes harder onto the faded and peeling steering wheel.

Sees a sign for Interstate (*earnest tit*, his mind reads) 64. That'll take him into northwestern Virginia. He stays firmly in the right lane of traffic and minds the speed limit.

An hour passes and Rudiger's mind drifts to other things. Billboards get scarce. Soon Rudiger's bracketed only by the trees that loom along the interstate. They seem proud and defiant, as if they serve as the first line of defense against the assault of concrete and asphalt. The air in the car grows warm as the sun continues to pour through the dirty windshield. He cracks the window again. Smells nothing.

Whoosh whoosh whoosh

Sounds lull him. The tires find the groves in his lane and the car rolls on by itself. He notices a red sedan in the lane next to him, passing him so slowly the cars seem to stay aligned. He looks up and sees a white pickup in his rearview mirror, coming fast behind him. Single occupant. White male. Rudiger keeps his speed steady as the truck hurls toward him.

The truck jerks to the left, its intent to pass. But the red sedan is in the way. The truck yanks itself back into Rudiger's lane. The driver slams on his brakes to avoid careening into the back of Rudiger's shit-colored Accord.

The truck's horn blares behind him. Rudiger looks in the rearview. The driver is flipping him off with both hands, leaving none to steer. Rudiger doesn't understand. He isn't driving below the speed limit. Doing nothing wrong.

He releases his foot from the gas pedal. The Accord slows.

The pickup driver leans on the horn, letting it blare. Red sedan spooks and slows down at the same time. Pickup is stuck behind both cars. Through the dirt-streaked back window Rudiger sees the man's face fill with red.

Man's looking for blood.

Red sedan picks up speed and finally pulls ahead of Rudiger. The pickup swerves into the left lane and pulls alongside him. Rudiger chances a direct look. The man is screaming, his bushy moustache wriggling along his lip like a caged ferret. Fuck you, his lips say. Fuck you and fuck your mother. *Motherfucker.*

Rudiger wonders at the rage. What does *that* feel like?

Red sedan gains more ground but stays in the left lane. The pickup rides him hard, waiting for an opportunity to cut Rudiger off. When the driver makes his move there isn't enough space, and the back of the pickup clips the front left quarter panel of the Accord. Rudiger hears his headlight shatter.

He grips the wheel and steadies the car, slowing the Accord to a crawl. Pulls onto the shoulder. The pickup swerves over directly in front of him, skids to a stop. Rudiger wants to drive off, but that's too risky. Need to avoid the cops. Gotta deal with this in the here and now.

Pickup driver screams as he heads toward Rudiger's car.

"Are you fucking *kidding* me?"

Rudiger takes a deep breath as he measures the man. He's younger – maybe late twenties. Wears a tight grey t-shirt that shows little muscle and a preference for Skoal tobacco. Long, stringy hair curtains a skinny neck. Posture suggests little or no training in formal combat fighting. Weapon of choice is an aluminum baseball bat, clutched firmly in his right hand. Kid-sized bat.

Rudiger steps out of the car. The man storms towards him but slows down a few feet away.

"Hey, fuckstick," the man says. "You fucked up my truck. Now what you gonna do about it?"

Rudiger thinks the man has the same accent as himself. He takes a step forward. The man doesn't expect it. Man expects him to cower and submit, so Rudiger does the opposite.

"Put the bat down," Rudiger says. Voice low and controlled. He struggles to make eye contact. "Then we can talk."

The man raises his bat. "Oh, we're gonna talk all right. We're gonna do a shitload of talking right now. You better have some fuckin' cash to pay for this."

Rudiger notices a rectangular impression in the man's front pocket. Cell phone. Doesn't want the man calling anyone.

"Get back in your truck and drive away," Rudiger says. He glances up and down the highway. Only a couple of cars and a semi.

The man laughs. "Like hell I will."

Man's an idiot, Rudiger concludes. Temperamental and used to getting his way. But not smart. Rudiger tries another tactic. He removes his shirt.

"Look at me," Rudiger says. He looks at his own body and sees the scar tissue from an old bullet wound rise like a crater rim over his muscled left shoulder. "I can kill you with my hands." He takes a step forward. "Do you believe me?"

The man says nothing. He spits on the ground and takes a half-step back.

"You some kind of fuckin' loon?"

"Yes," Rudiger replies. "I am *exactly* that."

The man walks back to his truck, never taking his eyes off Rudiger. As Rudiger watches him get inside, he puts his shirt back on and walks back to his damaged Accord. Damage is minimal. Crisis averted.

He sits back behind the wheel and starts his car.

The man reemerges from the pickup.

Baseball bat is gone. Now there's a gun.

Idiot.

Rudiger retrieves his own handgun from under his seat and holds it in his lap. He waits for the man to approach. Man will get close. Won't shoot from a distance. He'll want to scare and threaten Rudiger, empowered by his weapon. Wants to be the stronger one.

Rudiger waits. He looks forward down the highway and checks the rearview mirror. This time, no cars.

The man raises his gun and points it at Rudiger though the windshield.

"Get out of the fuckin' car."

Rudiger waits. *Come closer.*

He does. Two steps forward. "I said *get out* of the car. We're going to settle this the way I say so."

Rudiger nods. As he opens his door, he checks the highway once more. Empty. God is smiling on him.

As he stands, he squeezes off two rounds from his hip. Not his shooting position of choice. Aim is faulty. One round misses completely and the other catches the man in his left arm, spinning him around.

It's enough.

Rudiger raises his gun and fires again. The nine-millimeter round catches the top of his skull, slamming the man onto the ground. Body crumples a few feet behind the back of his truck. Blood creeps from his head and mixes with bits of gravel and dirt.

Rudiger lifts the corpse. The dead man is light. He heaves it into the bed of the pickup. Blood from the head wound spills against the side of the pickup – red blossoms on dirty white paint. No time to clean it. A plastic painter's tarp sits crumpled beneath a cinder block. He uses it to cover the body. That'll buy him a few extra minutes. He considers the prints he may have left on the tarp. Doesn't have the time to do anything about it.

He wonders if this was all supposed to happen. Maybe this is his next clue.

He walks around to the front of the pickup and stares though the open door. The cab is an explosion of American filth: discarded candy wrappers and potato chip bags on the seat and floor. Open beer can wedged in a broken cup holder. Porn mag open to a centerfold on the passenger seat. He smells pot, heavy and sweet, the scent embedded in the frayed cloth of the seats.

He looks up briefly as a white Dodge speeds by. Driver barely turns his head.

Rudiger sticks his head inside the cab.

Something's gotta be here, he thinks. This must *mean* something.

Then he sees it. This time, he doesn't even need his gift. The words he needs are *right there*, clear and crisp on the front of a *Soldier of Fortune* magazine. The cover shows two eyes glowing bright and green through the canvas of a face covered in moss-colored camouflage paint. Heavy typeface paints the bottom quarter of the cover:

Rangers - 400 Years of Pride

His mind flashes back. He knew a Ranger once, so many years ago. A Ranger who had tried to stop him from doing what he had to do. A Ranger who had shot him.

It all makes sense. Virginia isn't supposed to be his destination. Supposed to be Washington D.C. *That's where the Ranger lives.* The Ranger is the one person Rudiger's mind draws to, now and then, sticking to his memory like the traces of a vivid dream. Rudiger had followed the man's career over the years, always sensing there would be a time when the two of them might need to meet once again.

Rudiger believes that time is now.

CHAPTER TWELVE

WASHINGTON D.C.
APRIL 18

THE SHRILL RING of his cell phone angered him. He closed his eyes as he reached for it. "Osbourne."

"Hell, son, it's almost seven. Thought you would be in the office by now."

The Senator. Shit. Jonas realized he forgot to set his alarm.

"Rough night, sir. I'm heading in soon."

"You tie one on last night?"

"Feel like I tied an anvil on."

"You should know better."

"Yeah, you would think so."

"Listen, get yourself cleaned up and get in here. I need that brief on Denver by noon. Gonna float it to a couple of friendlies this afternoon."

"Jackson?" Jonas asked.

"Yeah, him. And Montgomery."

Jonas stifled a yawn. "You're hoping they'll pull in Wyatt, aren't you?"

A heavy exhale. "Need support from the right on this one."

"It's not a bill. There's no vote."

"Need all sides on board, Jonas, you know that. If the Israelis or the Palestinians smell uncertainty, they'll walk away from Denver with nothing. And the President will look stupid. Now get your ass in here."

"*Oui, mon capitain.*"

"And cut the French."

"Yes, sir."

Jonas closed the phone and almost cracked a smile. Work was just what he needed.

The cell rang again. This time Jonas looked at the caller ID, expecting to see the Senator's office number.

Private.

It gave him pause.

"Osbourne."

"Wow, you sound like shit. Rough night?"

The woman's voice was unmistakable. It wasn't just the pitch. It was also the soft, smooth cadence, the kind that could hypnotize. Or lure ships toward jagged rocks.

Anne.

"I can't stop thinking about you," he said. "It's making me lose sleep."

"Yeah, I have that effect on people."

"How did you get my cell-phone number?"

"Remember who I work for?"

"Oh, yeah. Stupid question. What do you want?"

"I want to talk to you," she said

"Isn't that what we're doing?"

"I want to interview you. Formally."

"Formally?"

"Yes."

"About what?"

"About Michael Calloway's murder."

Jonas hesitated.

"I figured that's what you were working on. You think I had something to do with it?"

"If I did, you wouldn't have gotten a call from me. You would have received a visit from much stronger and more unseemly people."

"So, what do you think I know?"

"I'm not sure. I don't think you have any clue. But I think I can coax it out of you."

Jonas looked at his pillow longingly.

"What did you have in mind?"

"Hypnosis."

"There are easier ways to get me into bed," he said. "Like asking."

He heard her exhale in frustration. "Look, Jonas, I'm just asking for a little bit of your time and cooperation. It's ... it's hard to explain, but I can feel relationships between things."

"What the hell does that mean?"

"It means I'm good enough at what I do to know when I get a strong sense about something and when I'm just bullshitting myself. I went to that funeral hoping the killer would turn up. If that happened, I think I would've known for sure who he was. He didn't show up, but *you* did."

"But *I'm* not the killer."

"I know that, Jonas. But I still got some kind of sense from you that day, a trace of something. Think of a bloodhound given a piece of clothing to smell before he's unleashed to find a victim. I can sense traces of *connection*, and the sense was stronger the second we shook hands. I can't tell you what that sense means, but I haven't gotten it from anyone else on this case."

Jonas didn't quite know how to respond.

"I realize what I do is unorthodox to you," Anne continued. "But just ask around the Capitol about me. You'll find out my reputation is solid. I think you can help me, and I'm hoping you will." She told him her phone number. "Call me, okay? I don't have a lot of time to burn on this one."

Anne hung up before Jonas could say another word. He stared at the phone as if it would give him advice. It didn't.

But it did ring again. Three times in as many minutes wasn't unheard of, but it wasn't how he wanted to start the morning. He looked at the screen.

Private.

Anne again, Jonas thought. Maybe she felt like she hadn't sold herself enough and needed to give Jonas some references to call.

"What now?" Jonas asked.

But the voice wasn't Anne's, and it wasn't even female. It was vaguely familiar, like the wispy memory of a decades-old nightmare, one without detail but still with an intangible sting of fear. The caller only spoke one word before hanging up.

"*Hooah.*"

CHAPTER THIRTEEN

A COOL BREEZE swept around Jonas's legs as he climbed the southwest steps of the Russell Senate Office Building. He looked up and saw the building's American flag whipping in the wind, its red and white stripes shimmering against a brilliant blue morning sky. Springtime in Washington, his favorite season. The misery of the frozen months was just distant enough behind him, and the misery of the sweltering summer was just far enough ahead. He pushed open the entrance door and felt the building's staleness replace the fresher air just feet away.

"Morning, Mr. Osbourne."

Jonas nodded at the security guard. "What's happening, Roger?"

The man shrugged. "Nothing exciting."

"Then you're doing your job."

"Yessir."

Jonas pulled out his cell phone and put it in the white plastic tray, checking for any new calls before doing so. The earlier phone call had given him a jolt. He'd received strange phone calls before – even threatening ones – but those were always on his office line. Not many people had his cell number, but this morning two new people had called him on it. Anne, and whoever had said *Hooah*.

Hooah. It was the Army battle cry. It pretty much meant anything except "no." Jonas hadn't used the term in years.

Why someone would call him and simply say one word before hanging up was unknown to him. The voice had been monotone and threatening at the same time.

Most of the threatening calls were about Denver. Senator Sidams was to be a major player at the Denver Peace Accords, and even the most fragile of agreements would cap the already distinguished career of the Senator and Chairman of the Foreign Relations Committee. Could even be a springboard to a presidential run in seven years. But Sidams's angle for the Accords was controversial, as were all things concerning a truce in the Middle East.

Truce, not peace.

Hatred was a learned thing, and elders in that region of the world would be teaching it to their children for endless generations to come. There would never be peace. Just fleeting moments of quiet while everyone reloaded.

Hooah.

Jonas passed through the marble rotunda and saw an Army Staff Sergeant walking with brisk purpose toward the elevator. The man's posture was extreme enough to seem robotic, and Jonas could see discipline and strength chiseled into his face. In that moment, as in many of his moments, Jonas missed the Army. He missed the camaraderie. The discipline. Even the fear. At least he was in as good as shape now as he ever was thanks to a fierce regimen of boxing and mixed martial arts. He sparred frequently, fought occasionally, and rarely found himself on the losing side of a decision. Once a Ranger, always a Ranger.

He pushed his shoulders back and walked a bit taller as he jogged up the stairs to office 301. He never took the elevator.

Jonas could feel the energy behind the door before he walked into the Senator's offices. It was often like this, the kinetic pulse of politics. Once inside that office, there would be little time to relax. There were the endless meetings. There were the agendas to follow, then change, then abandon completely out of futility. There were the requests to see the Senator, the requests from the Senator to see others, and the requests from both sides to cancel for fear of actually seeing each other. There were the promises and the lies, often mixed together into a smooth cocktail of delusion and hope. And, once in awhile, if the country inched forward into the right direction, there was the satisfaction.

Those days were rare.

He opened the door and felt the energy wash over him, sweep him up, and beg him to get on the raft before the big rapids came up.

V whisked by and Jonas caught the soft wind of her perfume. She smelled like the right kind of morning.

"You look like shit," she said, walking by, a coy smile on her face.

"Thanks. That's what I was going for. Hang on a sec, V."

She turned and smiled. "Yes, boss?"

"You know anyone at the FBI?"

"I had a brief fling with a Special Agent last year. Verdict? Not so special."

"You still in touch with him?"

"Did I say it was a 'him'?"

The comment stopped Jonas for only a beat.

"That's hot."

"Pig."

"Listen, get a hold of *her*, or anyone of a decent rank over there. They use a contractor named Anne Deneuve. She's a medium."

V pulled a notepad out of nowhere and began writing. "Medium what?"

"Like a psychic. Psychic criminologist, I think it's called."

"The FBI uses psychics? I thought that was only on TV."

Jonas ignored the comment. "I need to know if she's legit."

"A legit psychic?"

"Yes."

"Don't you think –"

"Just do it, please. Okay? She wants to meet with me and I'm trying to decide if I should take the time to do it."

V spun and kept walking. "Maybe you should just ask the psychic," she quipped.

Jonas headed toward his office, knowing V would have good feedback within the hour. That's what he loved about the people he worked with. Despite all the different personalities and attitudes, everyone did their work to the best of their ability. Senator Sidams had been in the Senate for over twenty years and he did not believe in rewarding mediocrity. Jonas had seen him fire longtime friends and bring on board political rivals. No one who worked for the Senator took his or her job for granted, not even Jonas, who, as Chief of Staff, would be the hardest to replace.

The Senator paged him the second Jonas's ass touched his chair. Jonas made a beeline for Sidams's office.

Robert Sidams looked up from his desk, which was a massive chunk of cherry built around the time Edison was first toying with filaments. The Senator's white hair was fully intact, despite the stress of two decades in Washington. His lean, clean-shaven face showed the hint of a tan and a scowl, making him look like a Midwest rancher reluctantly dressed up and shipped to D.C. Behind him was a wall of photos, most of the Senator shaking hands with heads of state from both friendly and belligerent nations. Sidams wore the same smile in every photo. It wasn't fake, but it certainly didn't tell you the cards he was holding.

"You look like shit," he said to Jonas.

"So I've heard."

"You want to talk about it?"

"I'm trying to reconcile familial issues and my obsessive need for constant approval."

"Seriously, Jonas. I need to know you are at a level of high functionality."

Jonas shifted his gaze to the carpet for a second. "My head is still a bit out of whack from the accident. And I ..."

I'm remembering things from the service. Things I had completely blocked out. Now I want to know more.

"You what?"

"I'm fine. Ready to roll."

Sidams assessed Jonas with eyes that had once stared down Kim Jong Il.

"Fair enough. I need to see the Denver brief."

"Can you give me an hour?"

"Will it be in better shape than it is now?"

"Infinitely."

"Fine. Have it by then. Make sure to check the wire for anything current. I don't want to find out Hamas has done something stupid in the last few hours that will screw everything up."

"Define 'stupid.'"

"Like kidnap more tourists."

When Hamas kidnapped a busload of Israeli tourists who were on their way to a weekend of fun in Eilat the previous year, it represented a major shift in tactics for the Palestinian organization. The abduction was done on Israeli soil, not within the Territories. The tourists were blindfolded and whisked away in secret to Gaza, where they were held for six days. Though Israel launched a few rockets in retaliation, no one knew where the hostages were, so open attacks were dangerous. On the sixth day, the hostages were driven back to the open highway and released, unharmed.

Hamas didn't want to hurt them. Hamas just wanted to show Israel they *could* have.

The brazen act increased already elevated tensions in the region. Sidams had just proposed his bill at the time and the kidnapping had almost torpedoed it. The Denver Peace Accords were just months away. The President would be there, but Sidams was going to be involved in every meeting. Every conversation. Every handshake. Which meant Jonas would be there as well. It could be a monumental moment in history or just another failure in a long succession of fizzled peace attempts.

"I'll check," Jonas said to the Senator. Jonas remained standing in front of Sidams's desk.

"Something else, Jonas?"

"This ... this is stupid. But I wanted to get your opinion."

"What?"

Jonas told him about Anne Deneuve.

"And she wants to interview you? Officially? In connection with Michael's murder?"

"There's nothing official about it. The FBI can't claim her as a credible source, even though they pay her. But I think they can use her for leads."

"What do you have to do with the murder?"

"Nothing. But she thinks I have some kind of connection."

Sidams squeezed his jaw. "Why don't you just tell her no?"

"I'm highly tempted to."

"Except?"

"Except I'm kind of curious to see what she does."

The Senator stared at him through long seconds of thick silence.

"And she's gorgeous," Jonas added.

"Christ, Jonas. For someone with the mental and physical discipline you possess, you sure do melt at a pretty face."

"No argument there, sir."

Sidams waved him off. "Fine. Go see her. Doesn't hurt to cooperate as long as it's unofficial. I just don't want to read anything in the papers about this, you understand me?"

"Yes, sir. Perfectly."

Jonas was deterred by the smell of over-brewed coffee on the way back to his office. He stopped in the small kitchen and poured the remaining trickle of brown liquid from the pot into a Star Trek mug.

V walked up behind him.

"Did you take the last of the coffee?"

Jonas took a sip. The bitter liquid slithered down his throat. "Trust me, I'm doing you a favor. Can't we get an espresso machine in here?"

"Some of our constituents might find that elitist."

"Better tasting coffee is elitist?"

"Better *anything* is elitist, you know that. Staff meeting in five," she said.

"Shit." Jonas looked at his watch. "Short today, okay? Gotta finish the Denver brief."

"OK, boss. And I have information for you on your lady."

"Really? That was fast."

"You sound surprised."

"Thought you would need longer."

"I'm good."

"You *are* good."

She stared at him with either *fuck me* or *fuck you* eyes. His inability to distinguish the two was one of the many reasons he was often single.

"The FBI denies using psychic criminologists as an official source," V said, "which is what Ms. Deneuve is. Not a medium. Regardless, my person there tells me Ms. Deneuve is bonafide."

"Your person knows her?"

"Knows of her. I guess she's a pretty big deal. The *Post* even did a profile of her about a year ago." V handed him a printout from the *Post's* website. The article was titled "*The Art of Science.*" He scanned the first paragraph.

"She worked that Anderson kid killing a few years ago. Remember – in Orlando?"

"Yeah, I remember. Big story. The mom did it, right?"

"But they couldn't try her without a body, and then the Feds found the boy out of nowhere."

"That was Deneuve's work?"

"That's the story. Again, off the record."

"Got it. Thanks. Good work, V."

"That's what I do. Have fun on your date with her."

"It's not a date."

"Is she cute?"

"Cute isn't the right word."

"What's the right word?"

Jonas thought about it.

"Intriguing."

V smiled. "You know, Jonas, something tells me you won't need a psychic to be able to read your mind." With that, V walked away, quickly disappearing amid a small flurry of anxious-looking aides carrying stacks of papers.

Jonas stopped by his desk for a quick check of his e-mail before going to his staff meeting. He reached for his mouse and only then did he notice the envelope on his desk.

Jonas's name was on the front. Unsealed.

Jonas opened the flap and pulled out the shiny pamphlet from inside.

It was proselytising literature, the kind you might be handed by an Evangelical on the Vegas strip immediately after being handed a flyer showcasing local hookers.

There was no note. Only the four-page pamphlet. On the cover was a 1950's-style drawing of a man covering his face and screaming as flames leapt up and scorched his skin.

The typeface was bold and large.

"Confess your sins ... or else!!!"

CHAPTER FOURTEEN

RUDIGER ACHES FOR a smoke. He thinks of cigarettes as his one vice. Goes against the discipline he commands over his body in every other way. But he loves the feeling of smoke snaking through him, like a rush of warm air over chilled skin. He's mindful not to smoke too much. No more than three cigarettes a day. He's only had one so far. The night will make him soon yearn for more.

So Rudiger waits. Waits and thinks.

The Preacherman's voice scratches against his brain.

Kinda stupid, dontcha think? Goin' to all that trouble to place a fuckin' pamphlet in his office? Not to mention calling his private cell phone. You got somethin' to prove, boy?

Rudiger concedes the ghost his point. It hadn't been easy to accomplish both those tasks, after all. Not easy by any stretch. Rudiger answers out loud to no one: "Has to be open-minded," he says. "Jonas has to see me comin'. I don't know why, but it's important."

He ain't the One.

"I know. That's why it's important."

You ain't makin' sense.

Rudiger brings his fingers up to his mouth for a moment and then lowers them, smoking a cigarette that doesn't exist. He lowers the window next to him. The rumble of his idling car grows louder. This part of Washington D.C. is dirty, but Rudiger likes its energy, so he has stopped here, waiting. Filthy streets washed clean by the nightfall. Housing projects only silhouettes of the desperation they shine in the morning light.

"He's connected to me," Rudiger says. "And because we're connected, he might direct me to the One. Maybe Jonas is the final clue. If so, I need him thinking about me."

The silence in his head is almost dizzying. Then:

Well, I think you're jes goddamn showboating.

Rudiger turns his head and watches a young black man approach his car. Hands shoved deeply in the pockets of a thick red coat. Black wool cap.

Rudiger stares straight ahead.

"Help you?"

Rudiger exhales more invisible smoke. "No."

The man sniffs. "You looking for a little somethin'? Got what you need. Got it *all.*"

"No." Rudiger puts his hands in his coat pockets.

The man is silent for a moment.

"Who the fuck were you talkin' to in the car?"

"Talking to?"

"I heard you. You were talkin' to *someone.*"

"No one you know."

The man's eyes widen a bit. "You a cop?"

"No."

"Then maybe you should get the fuck out of here. Not exactly your kind of place, 'stand me?"

Rudiger feels the gun in his coat. Unnecessary. His other hand fingers a folded 3.5-inch tactical Buck knife, its anodized aluminum handle cold and assuring against his fingertips. Also unnecessary. It would be so easy to kill this man, but it would be a mistake.

He knows what the Preacherman would say. Would say the nigger should die, as should all of them. Preacherman's whore would've laughed and agreed, repeating her man's racial diatribe through alcohol-strained wheezes. Preacherman had very specific ideas about who should live and who should die. Funny thing is, Preacherman was the one who ended up with a knife stuck in him. Same knife that nearly took off Rudiger's ear. Rudiger didn't know if that was irony or not, but it sure made some kinda sense.

"OK," he says to the man. Rudiger pulls his car into drive and eases away from the curb. He leaves the depressed neighborhood and heads toward the Capitol. The streets grow familiar as he gets closer. He's been driving them all day.

He finds the place.

Rudiger circles around the block and waits until his target leaves the parking garage.

CHAPTER FIFTEEN

JONAS LEFT THE garage just after seven, earlier than usual. The Capitol shone brilliantly against a starless sky. It took years for Jonas to stop being impressed by the view, but it finally happened. Damn shame, he thought.

He missed his Audi. The poor thing was towed to the junkyard after the accident and Jonas had settled for a rental while he waited for the insurance check to arrive. He arrived at Anne's house four miles and twenty minutes later, about par for D.C. traffic. She lived in a modest row home, probably built sometime before WWII.

"Thanks for coming," Anne said. She was still in professional attire, her black suit pants blemished only by an errant pet hair. Cat, Jonas guessed. He heard jazz bleeding from inside as she opened the door for him.

"My office is back here." She led him through a living room that was well appointed but sparse, as if Anne and clutter didn't much care for each other. "You want some wine? I normally don't offer it during professional visits, but I'm guessing it might help in your case."

Jonas followed and scanned the room for any photos. Nothing. "What case is that?"

"A reluctant interviewee."

"And getting me drunk will help?"

"Immensely."

"In that case, I'd love some. Red, if you have it."

"Sangiovese?"

"Perfect."

Her office was like her living room. Modern. Comfortable. Devoid of much personality. There were few personal touches providing insight about who Anne was or what she was all about. Maybe that's how she wants it, Jonas thought. Maybe that makes it easier for her to do what she does.

He sat on a stiff black leather couch while she poured the wine.

"You keep the alcohol in here?"

"It's where I spend most of my time. Makes it convenient."

"I figured you were out in the field most of the time. On location."

"Do you even know what I do?"

"Not really. But my ignorance pictures you brushing your hand over a piece of dirt and telling some wide-eyed cop, 'This is where he was taken.'"

She narrowed her eyes. "You're quite the wiseass."

He shrugged.

She handed him a glass. "I have something called Receptive ESP. There are a few different types of this. Mine is clairvoyance."

"You can see the future?"

"Not at all. It just means psychic seeing. Clairaudience is psychic hearing. Clairaroma is psychic smelling."

Jonas thought clairaroma sounded like a very disappointing psychic power. "How does your ... ability work?"

"It's usually tactile. Usually I need to touch something that belonged to the victim, and sometimes I get a trace of where that object has been. Flashes. Sensations. Sometimes I just need to be near something that resonates for me to get a sense."

"You can see the perp?"

She shook her head. "Rarely. Think of it this way. We all have limited degrees of psychic abilities. One common ability is déjà vu. An overwhelming sensation of familiarity with a place. You can't explain it, but it's real when it happens. The sense is tangible. My clairvoyance is like that, but I sense where the object I touch has been, not where I've been."

"I gotta say, it sounds cool, but it still seems like bullshit."

Anne smiled. "A lot of it is. Most self-called psychics are frauds." She sat on the couch next to him and sipped her wine. "In the 80's, a serial killer was killing young black men in Atlanta."

"Wayne Williams."

"That's right. The police received over 19,000 letters and 2,000 sketches from psychics. Not a single one said the killer was black, which he was. It's for reasons like that any testimony from psychic criminologists isn't allowed into evidence at a court proceeding."

"But the FBI likes you."

"Because I'm right more than I'm wrong. But a lot of times I don't even make a guess, because I don't see anything at all. They like me because I don't bullshit. I don't waste time."

Jonas wondered if all this was exactly that.

"So you want to hypnotize me. How does that play into your ability?"

"Because a person in a hypnotic state often channels my clairvoyance much more purely than someone who is throwing off all sorts of defenses."

"Like quippy remarks and round-about answers?"

"Exactly."

He let a few drips of wine linger on his tongue.

"Why don't you just ask me what you want to know?"

"Because I think you don't even know what you know."

"That makes me sound like a genius."

"Don't flatter yourself."

"It's what I do best."

She shook her head. "Now you're being borderline annoying."

He set down his wineglass. "First of all, I'm doing you a favor by being here. I've got enough work to keep five of me working until midnight, but the Senator asked that I cooperate as long as it's unofficial business, which, by the way, I assume this is."

"It is. I won't reveal you as a source unless you give me permission."

"Good. Second of all, there's no way in hell you're hypnotizing me. So why don't you ask me what you want to ask me."

She nodded in the way someone does who is used to being confronted. Calm. Patient. "Very well, Jonas. I do appreciate you coming tonight, so we'll do this any way you want."

Jonas was immediately placated, which annoyed him.

"Let me tell you what I think," she said. She reached over and grabbed his hand. Jonas knew she didn't do it out of affection, but rather to try to voodoo herself into his psyche. Still, the warmth of her skin was not unwelcome. "I get a sense from you, a sense of connection to the Calloway murder. It might just be that you had met with the victim before. Trust me, many if not most of my ... intuitions ... wind up amounting to nothing. But I have to try, don't I? And I get something from you that's stronger than just a casual connection. There's something about Michael Calloway's death that connects you to it. Tell me something, Jonas." She seemed to search for her words, but maybe she was just trying to control the pace of the conversation. "What did you think when you heard about the second crucifixion?"

Jonas bristled. The news of a second brutal killing had occupied countless hours of reporting, speculation, and shameless fear-mongering on every television news outlet. Serial killers were usually enough to get the public salivating. Original ones really commanded attention.

Jonas shrugged. "To be honest, I'm fascinated by it," he said. He remembered first seeing the breaking news on CNN, then the aerial footage of the cross, the hole in the ground with the bloody sheet draped over it. Jonas had watched the coverage well longer than he would normally pay attention to anything on TV, and he couldn't shake the feeling of *There but for the grace of God go I* ... "Maybe it's because of ... the type of crime itself. Or just the seeming randomness of the two victims. Or maybe it's because I had met one of them."

He felt himself being studied.

"Do you feel a connection to the second victim?"

"The student? No. Not at all. Should I?"

"I'm just trying to determine if your connection to the first killing has a relationship to the second. Whoever killed Calloway likely also killed that student in West Virginia, so I'm looking for more than a murderer here. I'm looking for a serial killer. And maybe your connection isn't to Calloway. Maybe your connection, if there is one, is to the killer."

Jonas could feel his forehead heating up. He hated feeling like he was hiding something, especially if he didn't even know what he was hiding.

"I don't know who killed Calloway."

"I didn't say you knew who killed him. Just that you might know the person who did. Big difference."

"This is weird."

She released his hand. "And we're just getting started."

Jonas thought of something. "When you get your senses, is it from people or things?"

"Both," she said. "Though people give off stronger indicators than objects."

Jonas reached into the pocket of his jacket and pulled out the pamphlet he'd found on his desk.

"What is that?"

He handed it to her.

Anne's hand began to shake.

CHAPTER SIXTEEN

"Who gave this to you?"

"How do you know someone gave it to me?"

She ran her fingers over the glossy paper. "This is something you didn't ask for."

Jonas studied her face and tried to read how much of Anne Deneuve's power of perception was training versus talent.

"I found it on my desk this morning."

Anne's gaze remained steady and firm on the front of the pamphlet for at least a minute. Finally, she opened it and read the inside. When she was done, she put in on the floor rather than handing it back to Jonas.

"You need to find out who gave that to you," she said.

"Why?"

"I'm not ready to tell you the answer to that."

Jonas felt his patience asking for the check. "Are you fucking with me?"

"Trust me, Jonas. You would know it if I was."

"So what now?"

"I want to talk to you. The real you."

"Anne ..."

"Jonas, let me hypnotize you. There's something going on inside your head that I need to get to. I don't know what it is or if you even know what it is, but it's important."

Jonas remained silent. The idea of opening up didn't scare him. It terrified him.

"Anne, I really don't want to do this."

"That's obvious, but it's not all about you."

"Yes, it is."

She brushed an imaginary piece of lint off her knee, making him focus momentarily on her legs.

"Tell me something, Jonas. Have you been ... remembering things lately?"

"Remembering things?"

"Yes. Things from your past. Things you've been suppressing coming back into your consciousness."

Jonas felt his breath sharpen, and to the extent his heart ever beat faster from anxiety, it did so now. The more he spoke with Anne, the more he believed her credentials. And the more he wanted to run from her. He was uncomfortable with another person peering through the layers he chose to present.

Still ...

There *were* the memories. In that, Anne was right. Things *had* been coming to the surface lately.

"How did you know that?"

"So you have."

"How did you know that?"

She leaned forward and placed her hand on top of his. He felt her warmth flow through him, "Jonas, it's what I do. You can choose to believe or not."

He heard her refrigerator humming in the silence after she spoke.

"I ... yes, I have been remembering things. Since my accident, I've had some ... I'm not sure what to call them. Flashbacks?"

"While you were awake?"

"Sometimes. Sometimes during sleep."

"Okay."

"But ... they aren't pleasant things."

"I know."

"I don't know how much I want to keep dragging them up again."

She ignored his request.

"I need you to tell me what happened. What you're suddenly remembering. I think it's important to my case."

"But how can that be?"

Anne stood and walked a tight circle in the room before ending behind him. Her voice draped over him like a heavy, comforting cloak.

"I stopped asking myself that question a long time ago, Jonas. I just know that it *can* be. Things can *be*, Jonas. And once you start accepting that, there's almost no limit to what you can discover." She placed her hands on top of his shoulders and brought her lips next to his ear. "Let's do this and see what we can discover."

Jonas felt himself nod, lured more by her voice than her words. He would do it, but he knew it was only to convince a beautiful woman he could relinquish control if he had to. He didn't think hypnosis would help her case, and it was certain to be unpleasant for him. Whatever it was swimming just below the surface of his memory would soon be coming up to feed.

And it was hungry.

CHAPTER SEVENTEEN

RUDIGER PEERS THROUGH the window. A man and woman inside. On the couch.

The beam from a nearby streetlight cuts into him, spotlighting him against the old row home. Not smart, he thinks. Should be in the car, waiting for Jonas to come out.

But he can't help himself. Lets himself believe the risk is worth it.

God wants me to see what's happening.

He gazes through the slats of the wood blinds and into the room. The woman is beautiful. Strong. She reaches out and touches Jonas.

Jonas Osbourne.

Rudiger hasn't seen him since the time in the Mog. Since the day he almost died. Rudiger found out Jonas had survived the attack that day. In fact, Jonas had always been in the back of Rudiger's mind over the years, enough so that Rudiger even tracked his progress as a successful politician, knew he was in D.C. Now Jonas Osbourne is sitting twenty feet away from him.

Rudiger feels the connection, feels it deep in his bones. It would have been easy to simply take him, but instead Rudiger gave Jonas some warning. First the phone call. Then the pamphlet.

He needs Jonas's mind lubricated, wondering what is happening. Open to all possibilities. Just like Preacherman said. Open minds bring open hearts.

Listen, boy, Preacherman had said, *open up your mind to what's out there. Open up to all I ken give you. Open up to my flesh. Receive me as the One. Feel my heat pass through you. Feel the pain and the glory. The blood and the spit. The hair and the skin. Feel it all, because there is no redemption without sin. You can't be saved if you have nothin' to be saved from, boy, don't you see that? What me and the woman do to you – that ain't no punishment, don't you see that? It's a means to eternal glory.*

Rudiger tries to shake the image of the Preacherman's teeth puncturing his thighs and focuses instead on the couple inside the row home.

Jonas isn't sleeping, but his eyes are closed. The woman moves from the couch and sits across from him, leaning forward. She speaks, but Rudiger can't hear her. Probably has a deep voice, he thinks. Deep and smoky.

He pulls back for a moment. Looks behind him. Street is empty, but two cars have passed in the last minute.

Rudiger leans forward a last time and looks into the house. Jonas is talking now. Eyes still closed. The woman looks uncertain, the confidence in her face replaced with hesitation. She begins to speak but stops. Jonas keeps talking. The woman shifts back in her seat. Away from him. Doesn't like what she's hearing.

Rudiger pivots and walks back to his car. Flips the collar of his black peacoat up against the cool night air. The street is quiet. Rudiger slides into the driver's seat of his car, which is parked behind Jonas's car.

Jonas could be inside for minutes or hours, but it doesn't matter. Rudiger waits.

CHAPTER EIGHTEEN

MOGADISHU, SOMALIA
1993

Fucking regular Army piece of shit, Jonas thought. It would be a shame not to kill the sniper, but it was better than a green PFC trying to play Rambo and getting his skull separated from his body.

He moved to the open doorway and readied himself for the sprint, hoping he could still run in his condition. He began counting in his head, preparing to run on three.

One.

Squeezed his eyes shut.

Calm yourself. You can do this.

When he got to two he heard the screams.

* * *

Jonas sprinted across the street and ran straight into the same building where PFC Rudy Sonman had disappeared. Once inside, his brain registered that the sniper hadn't taken a second shot at him.

So far, so good.

The building was a three-story concrete shell, its exterior unpainted and scarred by time and violence. Rough layers of mortar scabbed over random parts of the façade, and hand-cut fenestrations served as windows, protected by neither glass nor shutters.

It was dark and dusty inside. To Jonas's eye, it was an abandoned building, though he knew the Somalis abandoned nothing except hope. Probably a residence, he thought.

The scream came again. A woman. Then shouting. A man. American. *Sonman.*

Jonas took the first flight of uneven concrete stairs with ease, his adrenaline overpowering the pain in his ribs and the fifty pounds of gear on his body. At the top of the steps he crouched and aimed his rifle into an empty corridor extending fifty feet in front of him. Halfway down, a small black face peered into the hallway from a room. Just a boy, Jonas saw. Probably no more than ten.

But even boys carry guns in Somalia. And they used them.

"*Hoyadaa futada ka was!*" the boy shouted.

Jonas had been in the Mog long enough to pick up some of the choice local phrases. He knew what the boy had said. *Go fuck your mother in the ass.*

The boy disappeared back into the room. Seconds later, the barrel of an assault rifle inched its way into view. Jonas sighted the weapon and considered firing as a warning, but then decided against it. An open hallway was not a place he wanted to be during a firefight.

More screams erupted from above him, this time followed by three shots. The woman stopped screaming. Seconds later, Jonas could hear the cries of a baby.

"Sonman!" Jonas shouted. "Sonman, what's your situation?"

No answer.

The rifle barrel floated in the doorway in front of Jonas. Inside, the boy laughed, and then taunted Jonas in heavily accented English.

"American. *Here*, American."

Another door opened, directly across from the boy. Another rifle barrel emerged. More laughing.

"Come *death*, American."

Jonas felt the situation growing out of control. He had no idea how many armed Somalis were inside this building, and he started to realize that running in here without support was a mistake.

Fuck the sniper, he thought. Get Sonman and get out. Stupid place to die.

A flash before him.

The boy took a shot without exposing anything but his arms. The shot was wildly inaccurate, driving deep into the concrete ceiling far from Jonas, but there would be more. Jonas had no choice. He aimed at the exposed flesh and fired a single round.

The boy screamed as the bullet tore through his forearm. His weapon crashed onto the hallway floor.

The baby kept crying upstairs.

"Sonman!" Jonas shouted.

No answer.

Jonas remained in position. The screaming boy-soldier howled from within his room.

"Asad! Asad!"

The voice came from the other room off the hallway. From the holder of the second rifle.

"Asad!"

Jonas assumed Asad was the wounded boy's name.

Asad kept screaming.

The baby upstairs kept crying.

Jonas saw what would happen next. It was too predictable, and it was a fucking shame.

Asad's friend would go to help Asad. But by running across the hallway, he would expose himself to the American, which was a great risk. His only hope to help his friend was to kill the American and then comfort Asad.

Jonas waited for it. It would happen. He wished it wouldn't. He wanted to walk away, but that wasn't protocol.

The boy jumped into the hallway. He was about the same age as Asad. Just a kid. Just a fucking kid. With an assault rifle pointed directly at Jonas.

The boy let out a howl of rage, his brilliant white teeth shining against his coal black skin.

Jonas fired once.

The bullet hit the boy in his shirtless chest. He collapsed in a lifeless heap before firing a shot. Instant death.

Asad screamed louder.

"Nadif! Nadif!"

The baby no longer cried upstairs.

Nadif was motionless. Blood pooled on the concrete beneath him.

"Fuck," Jonas muttered. It was his first kill in-country. It was his first kill *ever*. And it was a boy. "*Fuck.*"

Go, he told himself. Place could be swarming with belligerents in a matter of seconds. Get the hell out of here.

First get Sonman.

Jonas grabbed his radio.

"Two-five this is two-six. Over."

"Two-six I read you. Over."

"In pursuit of sniper and receiving resistance. I'm anticipating more soon, so I'm going to find Sonman and fall back until support arrives. ETA? Over."

"Roger that, two-six. Fall back as necessary. Support is on foot about seven blocks west of your position but are encountering their own resistance. ETA within fifteen. Am requesting bird support and will let you know. Over."

Asad's screams were now whimpers. Jonas saw his twitching arm reach into the hallway.

"Roger, two-five. I also have a wounded boy here on the second level of this building. If possible, medical support requested." *That's not going to happen*, he thought to himself. "Over."

"Copy, two-six. Out."

Jonas clipped the radio back to his shoulder. Hot dust sparkled and danced in the hallway, illuminated by stray beams of light from cracks in the walls. He turned and headed up the stairs behind him, knowing violence could come from any direction. He kept his gun trained in the direction he walked: forward and up.

It was library-quiet now; even Asad ceased his suffering wails. Probably succumbed to shock, Jonas thought.

He climbed the stairs quickly but not carelessly. The stairs gave way into another empty hallway, the top floor of the small building. Like the floor below, the hall extended for about fifty feet, with two doors on each side of the corridor. Enough for four small apartments, which in the Mog was a concrete room with no kitchen or running water.

Jonas crouched and leaned against the corridor wall. He had no idea what room, if any, Sonman was in. He also didn't know who else might be waiting in the rooms for him. Waiting to kill.

"Sonman!"

The shout ricocheted off the concrete walls. Silence.

Jonas shimmied along the wall until he reached the first door on the left. The sniper would have shot from one of the two rooms on this side of the corridor, he knew. He also knew the unpainted, brittle wood door would give little resistance against his Army boots.

He kicked in the door and readied his rifle.

The room was empty save a balled up blanket sitting in the middle of the dirty floor. Closed wooden shutters adorned the far wall of the room. No shell casings on the ground. If the sniper had been in this room, he'd bothered to clean up before leaving. Possible.

He considered yelling Sonman's name again, but decided against it. The first shout was loud enough for the soldier to have heard. Sonman was either no longer in the building or was incapacitated. Giving away his own position wouldn't do Jonas any good, so he remained quiet as he crept to the next door.

The second door on the left was similar to the first. There was one difference with this room, however: Jonas heard something inside. The sound was neither loud nor constant, but someone was definitely inside. It sounded like ... like an animal. Growling.

Jonas squeezed his eyes shut for a second, steadying his nerves. He then took a deep breath and counted to three in his head.

He kicked in the door, which splintered as it flew open.

Jonas immediately crouched and aimed his rifle, but he couldn't understand what his targets were supposed to be.

In fact, his brain couldn't process what he was seeing at all.

"*Sonman ...*"

Jonas breathed the name, but he didn't hear himself. He didn't hear anything. There was too much already in his head, overwhelming his senses. He felt his brain wanting to shut down, to reverse the last few seconds and replay it with a new ending. But the human machine is a wondrous thing, and Jonas's was particularly fine-tuned. Despite what he was seeing, Jonas was able to take command of himself and function with the training drilled so deeply in him.

"Sonman! Drop your weapon!" Jonas pointed his rifle directly at Sonman's helmetless skull. Willfully aiming a loaded weapon at a fellow soldier was something that you never, ever did, unless the situation was so out of control that the safety of other members of the unit or innocents was in immediate jeopardy.

Sonman, crouched on the floor, twisted his head toward Jonas and exposed his teeth in a snarl. Maybe it was a smile. It was hard to tell with all the blood covering his mouth.

And there was something –

In Sonman's mouth. He was biting it, and his crimson lips parted up and around it, exposing his pink teeth.

"Jesus Christ, Sonman ... *what did you do?*"

Jonas took a step forward. A man and woman lay in the northeast corner of the room, their awkward positioning and pools of blood beneath their heads enough clue to convince Jonas they were dead.

Jonas trained his weapon tighter on his target, but then was momentarily distracted by something on the floor just a few feet to his right. He stared at it for a split second and knew the image would haunt him the rest of his life.

A baby, or what was left of it, was on its stomach, its naked skin seeming to melt into the concrete floor. In the single second Jonas had spent looking at it, half of the time was consumed by the thought that it couldn't be a *real* child. It was a toy, wasn't it? A doll of the most horrifying kind, the kind that rose from the depths of sweat-filled and drug-laden night terrors. In the last half of that second, Jonas told himself it was real, because it was bleeding, and dolls don't do that. Bleeding from the stump of a tiny black neck that had once and for too short a time held a head to it. A flick of his eyes was all Jonas needed to find the head, just a few feet away, its eyes still open and mouth pursed in an eternal suckle. Jonas didn't know if it was a little boy or little girl, and he didn't want to know.

Sweat poured down his face and he felt bile rise in his throat as he looked back at Sonman. The man was growling.

Time slowed. Jonas's peripheral vision disappeared, but what he could see directly in front of him he did with almost supernatural ability. He could see the gleam of the sunlight in the individual droplets of sweat peppering Sonman's face. Jonas could barely get out a whisper.

"Sonman ... fuck ... what did you do?"

Sonman spit at Jonas, and out from his mouth flew a small black chunk, which slapped against the floor near Jonas's feet.

Jonas looked down.

An ear.

A girl – no older than five, Jonas guessed – was pinned beneath Sonman, and from all visual evidence the soldier had just bitten her ear off. She didn't move. Jonas didn't see any other obvious wound on her, though the blood pouring from the hole on the side of her head made that kind of assessment almost impossible.

Her eyes weren't just open. They screamed, stretched to the point of bursting. *Why is this happening to me?* her look said.

"It's what I'm supposed to do," Sonman sputtered, his words stifling what almost sounded like a laugh. "The sign ... outside. It was a message."

Jonas's hands felt numb from the surge in adrenaline. He struggled to steady his rifle. "Disengage, soldier. That's a direct order."

But Sonman was too far gone, Jonas knew. The soldier had detached, like an old frayed shoelace pulled just a bit too hard. He had heard such stories, of course. It was all part of warfare. Guys go crazy all the time, and their craziness takes all sorts of shapes and sizes. But he had never heard of anything like this. And this ... it was just sniper fire. Certainly enough to stoke large flames of fear and adrenaline, but *insanity*? As Sonman breathed heavily through wet, bloody lips, Jonas tensed his finger on the trigger of his weapon.

"Now, soldier."

"Not done yet." Sonman slowly reached for the large knife on the floor, the one that already had blood on it. Baby blood.

"Don't you grab that knife, soldier." Jonas realized he wasn't calling Sonman by his name. He was already disengaging from the relationship, because he knew that, in the next few seconds, he was going to shoot him.

The girl wasn't dead, but she wasn't moving. Paralyzed from fear, Jonas thought. He could see her chest moving up and down in short, tight bursts as she breathed like a rabbit caught in the jaws of a coyote.

Sonman's wet fingers squeezed the handle of the blade.

"Disengage, Private!"

Sonman paused, his eyes wide.

There was a moment, a fraction, an opportunity. Jonas could save him. Goddamn it, he could save him.

Jonas could barely hear his own voice. "Don't do it. Jesus Christ, don't do it. We can stop this now." He tried to steady the frenzied rhythm of his heart. "Let me take you back. It doesn't have to happen like this."

And for a moment, Jonas thought it would happen. Sonman's eyes widened even further, as if something Jonas said resonated. But the moment didn't last. The detached mind serves only itself and doesn't bother with things like reason. It only had one direction and one speed, and logic wouldn't veer it off its course. Sonman pushed himself a few inches off the floor. Not to get up, but to give him more power to bring the tip of the Army-issue fighting blade into the chest of the little girl.

That's when Jonas fired.

He felt no shame or fear from doing so. He didn't want to kill his fellow soldier, and in fact aimed his rifle so he likely wouldn't, but if Private Rudy Sonman did happen to perish in this room, Jonas was okay with that.

Sonman's body pitched sharply to the right as the rifle round slammed into his left shoulder. The flesh was unprotected and the bullet would do damage, Jonas knew. But it wouldn't kill him.

Jonas ran over and kicked the knife out of Sonman's hand. From his position, Jonas could now see from the window and down into the street. He saw the two dead Pakistani soldiers, the blood from their wounds seeming to cradle them as if they were merely sleeping on top of large rose petals. One block away a company of U.S. soldiers was advancing. The situation would be fully under control in a matter of moments.

Jonas turned his head to Sonman, who was face down on the floor, his right hand squeezing his left shoulder. Low, guttural moans came from beneath him. Jonas then knelt by the girl. Her wide eyes moved to meet his, but that was the only indication she wasn't catatonic.

"You'll be okay." He knew she didn't understand, but he hoped his tone would comfort her. He turned her head and saw the gaping hole where the ear should have been. He squinted in disgust and then spoke into his radio.

"Two-five this is two-six. Private Sonman is wounded, and a little girl here also needs immediate medical assistance. I'm on the top floor of –"

Jonas fell silent.

A grenade rolled up next to him and rested against the leg of the little girl.

There was no pin in it.

Jonas saw his death, and he even had time to look over at Sonman, who now stared at him with a wide smile – *clown smile* – red and grotesque, the kind that said the *real* good jokes were only seconds away. Sonman's outstretched hand was empty save the grenade pin, which was hooked around his dirty thumb.

There was just enough time to do *something*, to move, to make a life and death decision.

"Two-six, please report. Two-six, please report."

With the two seconds he was afforded, Jonas pushed himself off the ground and lunged as hard as his legs could manage toward the open window.

Jonas flew. He soared as would a bird, but only because the explosion in the room sent shockwaves through his body, propelling him as though he had wings.

He stared down at the corrugated tin canopy three stories below, the one he would soon smash through with all hundred and eighty pounds of human weight and fifty pounds of gear.

CHAPTER NINETEEN

WASHINGTON D.C.
APRIL 18

THE FIRST THING he noticed was the heat. Seeing the candle flames, he thought for a second the room was burning.

He jolted in his chair before he saw Anne, who spoke to him in a tone not quite soothing.

"It's okay, Jonas. You're here with me. I was hypnotizing you, remember?"

With those words, he did remember. He remembered it all, and he knew he would never be able to push it all away again. He sank back into his chair and tried to control his breathing. "People pay you for this?"

"It was important for that to happen," she said.

"Was it?" he shot back. "That's supposed to cure me of something? I'm supposed to be able to have closure now or something?"

She shook her head. "Don't mistake my intentions, Jonas. I'm not a psychologist. I'm not here to help you. I'm only here to help my work."

He stared at her through the diffused light. "You're cold."

"I'm professional."

"And how did it help *you*?"

She crossed her legs and leaned forward toward him with excitement, as if finally revealing a secret stored for years. "I got an imprint from you. An image. A feeling of intense familiarity in things you have been a part of. When you were under and as I touched you, I saw Sonman – not clearly, but clear enough. I felt him, a sense of his presence in your life. It's the same imprint I received shaking your hand at the funeral, the connection with Calloway. The same imprint I received when I touched the pamphlet. I think Sonman is who we are looking for. Sonman put that pamphlet on your desk. I think Sonman is who killed Calloway. And the student."

Jonas wanted to protest, to tell her that her powers of intuition were nothing but imagination left unharnessed by logic. He wanted to tell her PFC Rudy Sonman had died that hazy afternoon in the Mog. He wanted to tell her that Sonman's body, already wounded by an M16 bullet, was torn apart by the grenade blast.

But he couldn't tell her that, because Sonman's body had never been found. The girl was found, or what was left of her, as were the remains of the girl's mother, father, and baby sister. But there was no evidence Sonman had even been in that room.

"I need to leave," Jonas said.

"No, Jonas. Not yet. I have more questions."

Jonas stood. His legs felt weak, as if he'd just finished a long sprint in a shallow tide. "I know you do, which is why I'm going to leave now. Call me in a few days. Maybe we can continue then. For now, I just want to sleep." He turned and walked toward the door. "Hopefully without dreaming."

She followed him, and as he opened the door she opened her mouth as if to offer one more protest to get him to stay, but she caught herself and closed her lips.

Then she leaned forward and kissed him on the cheek, allowing her lips to skim a few extra inches on the side of his face. Her breath was warm and inviting, and when she pulled away, she did so only partially, staying close enough for Jonas to see tiny flecks of gold in her otherwise brown eyes.

"Be safe, Jonas."

* * *

Outside the night was cold and still. Jonas pulled his keys from his jacket pocket and pressed the button on the remote. The rental car winked at him from across the street. The sweat on his face cooled.

He crossed and went to open his car door. It was then he paid closer attention to the car parked twenty feet or so behind his. It was unremarkable – a Honda Accord, he guessed. Shit brown. But it was the only car parked remotely close to his own, and there was someone sitting inside.

Waiting.

Jonas could only see the faintest of silhouettes, which made the figure look like a black paper cutout taped to a chalkboard. A small orange glow blossomed and then faded, and Jonas knew the man – *it was a man, wasn't it?* – was smoking.

Smoking and waiting.

The figure turned his head and blew smoke out the cracked window. The smoke billowed in a stringy cloud for just a moment before fading into the night air. Jonas was close enough to smell it.

Jonas didn't feel threatened, yet he waited a few seconds before getting in his car. There was something just *not quite right* about the person waiting in the car. Jonas didn't know why, but he had trusted his instincts enough times to know they usually pointed him in the right direction. So Jonas stood outside his car, waiting, and offered the occasional glare at the Accord to let the driver know Jonas knew he was there.

Instinct usually not being enough, Jonas finally left, pulling away from the curb and looking one more time at the Accord in the rearview mirror. Nothing suspicious. Just some dude smoking a cigarette. That's all.

Jonas drove a few blocks toward home before deciding to make a quick loop and drive back by Anne's house. He couldn't stop thinking about the one possibility that made the least amount of sense: the man in the Accord was Sonman. Jonas knew it wasn't true and the idea wouldn't even have had a home in his mind had he not just spewed the whole story to Anne just moments before.

But what if Sonman was alive? Jonas thought. Don't I have a duty to at least look at the guy in the car?

Duty, Jonas thought. *It's always about fucking duty with me.* Maybe I need to see a shrink about that.

He turned onto Anne's street and discovered his sense of duty would not be appeased that night. The Accord was gone, and the still-smoldering remains of a cigarette on the cold asphalt were the only traces of the stranger in the car.

CHAPTER TWENTY

JONAS WASN'T READY to go home. He needed answers, and in D.C. answers were readily available if you had the time, patience, and contacts to be able to ask the right questions. What Jonas lacked in time and patience he more than made up for in contacts. He scrolled though the contacts on his BlackBerry as he drove downtown.

"Yeah," the gravelly voice said on the other end of the line.

"Chuck, it's Jonas."

"Yeah?"

"You sleeping?"

"Yeah, Jonas. I'm sleep-talking."

"I mean *were* you sleeping?"

"Does it fucking matter? I'm awake now and I'm talking to you. What do you want?"

"I need to know about Rudy Sonman."

The pause was too long. "Who?"

"Don't shit me, Chuck. You know exactly who that is."

"Yeah?"

"Yeah."

The silence could have settled in nicely on the moon.

"How bad?" Chuck asked.

"How bad what?"

"How bad do you need the info? Would this take care of my chit with the Senator?"

Jonas considered. Sidams had done the Major General and his boss a nice little favor two years ago by leaning heavily on a Pennsylvania defense contractor who had demanded a five hundred percent markup on Kevlar body armor.

"Yeah, we'll call it even. Where?"

"Hay Adams. Give me a half hour."

Jonas hung up and pressed down on the accelerator, thankful for all the beautiful back channels that came with his job.

* * *

It was late, but not too late for Off the Record, the hotel bar of choice for hushed conversations among the Washington elite, questionable, and unabashedly criminal.

He walked through the lobby of the Hay Adams hotel and into the lounge, immediately spotting an aide to the Senior Senator from Texas. Jonas loathed the Texas Senator and felt only slightly less antipathy for the aide, a churlish man in his mid-forties who would lobby for oil drilling within the asshole of his own grandmother. The aide was sitting next to someone Jonas didn't know, and the men seemed to barely hold each other's attention. Jonas nodded as he passed them.

Major General Charles Ogilvy was already there, a feat that seemed impossible. But he was, and if Jonas had awoken the man it wasn't obvious. He wasn't in uniform, but the creases on his slacks could have cut diamonds. His bald head was smooth and black, and only the freckles of grey in his eyebrows belied a few decades and wars in his service to his country. Jonas had met the Vice Director of the Joint Staff through Senator Sidams, and the hardened veteran had softened to Jonas when he found out Jonas was a Ranger. The two men shared a friendship that consisted of the occasional drink and jokes at the expense of Navy pukes, and years ago Jonas shared with the Major General what had happened to him in Somalia. His memory of events had been sketchy then – not like the details he could suddenly recall in the past two weeks – but he remembered Private Rudy Sonman. Ogilvy said he'd look into what happened to Sonman, but he'd never called Jonas back about it. Once, when Jonas pressed him on it, the Major General had said only this: *Leave it alone.*

Ogilvy wasn't smiling when Jonas sat across from him.

"How long's it been, Chuck?" Ogilvy was two decades older than Jonas and outranked almost every person in the military, but Jonas never called him *sir*. It went against every instinct Jonas had, but Ogilvy had always insisted on it.

"Least a year. You look like shit."

"I get that a lot."

"Heard about your Beltway heroics." The Major General shook his head. "Dumbass."

"I get that a lot, too."

"Bet you do. You all patched together again?"

Jonas no longer wore his wrist cast. "Good as new. You drinking?"

"Let's see. It's eleven at night and my wife is wondering what the hell I'm up to. Got to be at work at oh-eight-hundred. Hell yeah, I'm drinking."

"Nice to hear." Jonas signaled the waitress.

"Grey Goose gimlet, up."

Ogilvy looked up. "Two fingers of Wild Turkey."

"Rocks?" she asked.

"Not even if my life depended on it."

"Sure thing."

As she walked away, Ogilvy turned to Jonas.

"So, Sonman. Thought you buried him a long time ago."

"I thought so, too," Jonas replied. "But recent events caused me to do a little grave robbing." He told Ogilvy about the memories he had since the car accident. Then he told him about Anne and what happened during the hypnosis session. He ended with Anne's hypothesis about the serial killer, the religious pamphlet on Jonas's desk, and the smoking man in the car just an hour earlier. Through it all, Ogilvy soaked in the information with little more than a few slight nods of his head and the occasional widening of his eyes.

"Let me get this straight. You think the man who tried to kill you in Somalia is not only alive, but is the same person responsible for the crucifixion murders?"

"I just –"

"Shh," Ogilvy cut him off. "Let me finish. And this same person, one Rudy Sonman, has come to Washington to do the same thing to you?"

Jonas was silent.

"OK, you can talk now."

"I don't know," Jonas finally conceded. "I have nothing to go on, I know. Nothing real. *No actionable intel.* But ..."

"Not true," Ogilvy said. "You have the advice of a palm reader."

"Psychic criminologist."

Ogilvy rolled his eyes enough to see out the back of his head.

"She's well respected," Jonas said. "She does work for the FBI."

Ogilvy leaned forward. "My kid works for the FBI, and he sucked on so many paint chips as a kid I'm surprised he can find his own dick."

"Wow. That's kinda harsh."

"Doesn't make it less true. My point is she's grasping at straws, and she's got you doing the same thing."

Jonas closed his eyes for a moment and hoped he would find the answers he wanted written in neon letters on the inside of his eyelids. He didn't.

"It just seems like ... it's just odd that I started remembering these things and she picked up on it. It makes me want to know more."

"More?"

"About Sonman. I know you know something. You looked into it, didn't you?"

"Why didn't you? It wouldn't have been too difficult for you to research if you really wanted to."

Jonas thought about it. "I think I wanted to forget all about it. The injuries took me long enough to heal from. I just wanted to get healthy and move on."

"That's not it," Ogilvy said.

"No?"

"No. I read your debriefing from that day. I read word for word your detail of what happened in that building in Mogadishu."

"Yeah?" Jonas had never seen that file.

"Yeah. Your problem wasn't what happened to that family. Soldiers in hot zones see shit like that, even worse, all the time. You were mentally tough enough to be able to handle that. *Your* problem –"

"Yeah, tell me my problem."

"*Your* problem was *one of your own men* deliberately tried to kill you. Not a mistake, no friendly-fire bullshit, but a deliberate attempt to kill a comrade. I don't think your training allowed you to contemplate that, and your brain couldn't reconcile it. I'm not sure any Ranger could."

Jonas sipped his drink but didn't respond. "Shit, Chuck. I don't know. Maybe ..."

"Maybe my ass. It's exactly what happened."

"OK, then. That's what happened. That was then. Now I want to know."

Ogilvy leaned back in his chair, his broad frame consuming every square inch of the leather. "What do you want to know, Jonas? What is it that'll help you sleep at night?"

"Is he alive?"

Ogilvy sighed, the kind of sigh that a doctor might make before confirming a patient's worst fears.

"No remains were found in the vicinity of the incident. You know that."

"But ... but remains *were* found."

"Yes. The girl. Her family. What was left of *you*. But no trace of Sonman."

"Ever?"

"Ever."

"How is that possible?"

"You didn't ask me here to interpret the facts, Jonas. Just to report them."

"So, if he somehow lived, he never reported back to duty."

"Nope."

"How the hell would he get out of the country?"

"No idea. Best guess is he was grievously injured in the explosion and crawled off somewhere to die. He was also wounded from your rifle round. Some Somalis probably found him and threw him into a garbage fire."

"Sounds like interpreting facts to me."

Ogilvy tipped his drink. "Touché."

"Or he lived," Jonas said. "Somehow got himself out of country, and went AWOL."

Ogilvy nodded. "Not completely out of the realm of possibility. But pretty damn close."

Jonas felt the vodka just starting to kiss his brain. "But more importantly, why did he do what he did?"

A shrug. "Why did Mark David Chapman kill Lennon? Who the fuck knows?"

"You're saying Sonman was mentally imbalanced."

"I think that's a safe assumption."

"Then how did he get into the Army?"

Ogilvy stifled a laugh then sucked down the last of his Wild Turkey. "Look, the kid was probably borderline bat-shit loony as it was. Probably just sane and ripped enough to look like a good specimen to the recruiting pukes. Does great in Basic and moves on. Looks good all around and now there's real fucking action to deal with, so maybe the admission standards drop a little. Then he's shipped to Somalia and gets assigned to you. He's pumped up, excited, ready to lay down the shit, right? See it all the time. Maybe he's a little jacked on ephedra, or, who the hell knows, even 'roids. He's excited. Wants to be alert. Impressive. Aggressive."

"That's not what I remember," Jonas said. "I remember him being detached. Quiet. Nothing at all pumped about him, except his physique. That, and he had a hell of a scar on his ear."

"Detached and quiet? Sounds like a real winner. So he's out with you and what happens? Sniper. Real bullets. Two dead Pakistanis. Blood all over the place."

Jonas felt himself drifting back in time. "All over ..."

"And he isn't a coward. A coward runs away. He's the exact opposite, but maybe even more dangerous. He charges straight into the shit, throwing away every second of training he's ever received. He goes Dresden on everyone's ass – complete firebomb. Women, children. No matter. They're all hostiles."

Jonas was seeing it all again, though this time the colors were different. It was like watching an old movie of the events, the film faded by light and time.

"He cut the baby's head off," he whispered. "With his field blade."

Ogilvy lost some of his momentum. "I know, Jonas. I know. I can't imagine what you saw."

"He bit the girl's ear off."

"He what?"

"The ... little girl. He bit her ear off. I saw him spit it out on the floor."

"You sure?"

"Absolutely."

"It wasn't in the report. Which means you didn't tell them that during debriefing."

"I don't remember any of the debriefing. But I'm telling you that's what happened."

Ogilvy did the closest thing to furrowing his brow. "Which, in the mind of your palm reader, ties him theoretically to the two crucifixion victims, both *sans* one ear."

"Maybe."

"It's better than having nothing. I'll concede you the point."

"Much appreciated."

Ogilvy signaled the waitress, and with the deft hand gestures of a third-base coach, ordered each of them another round.

"Look, Jonas, I came here to get out of debt and give you some peace of mind. Not sure if I gave you that, but I promised to tell you what I knew. Truth is, I pretty much know jack shit except for the fact that, as far that the United States Army is concerned, Private Rudy Sonman disappeared off the face of the earth. Which, I might add, is not unheard of in the military. But ..."

"But?"

"I know one other thing. Something else was in his file. Something recent. Came to my attention last year."

"What?"

Ogilvy seemed uncomfortable, as if bringing it up would only cause harm. "I don't even know how verifiable it is. Personnel files get full of rumor and innuendo. Happens all the time."

Jonas felt his jaw tense. "What is it?"

Ogilvy let out a long breath and looked longingly toward the waitress, who wasn't there in time to rescue him with more bourbon. "There was another person. You remember a man named Cohen? Isaac Cohen? He was in your unit at deployment. He was one of the first on-scene after your attack."

Jonas hadn't thought of that name in years, but hearing it now brought back good memories. "Cohen? Hell, yeah. Good guy."

"That's right. Honorably discharged nineteen ninety-five. Became a school teacher in SoCal."

"What about him?"

"Cohen was in touch with the Army less than a year ago."

"That so?"

"Indeed. Seems he contacted some lifers he knew. He said he had something to report."

"Which was?"

The waitress arrived and Ogilvy settled back into the chair, the fresh drink nestled between his hands. "Cohen told his lifer friends an interesting story. Said he was on vacation and he spotted Sonman. Said he recognized him by the scar on his face."

Jonas sat up straight. "Jesus."

"You got that right. More right than you know."

"Even after all these years? He recognized him?"

"According to his report, Cohen never forgets a face. He even approached Sonman and repeated his name over and over."

"And?"

"And he said Sonman denied knowing him."

Jonas didn't know what question to ask next. But, against his normal backdrop of skepticism, he was willing to believe. He *wanted* to believe.

"Where ... where were they?"

Ogilvy sipped his drink, letting it settle before speaking again. When he did, his voice was raspy with the tendrils of alcohol.

"Jerusalem."

"Jerusalem?"

"More specifically, the Church of the Holy Sepulcher."

Jonas was suddenly frustrated by his own ignorance. "What is that place?"

Ogilvy polished off the rest of his drink, about twice as fast as it took him to down the first one. "*That place*, according to all good Christians, is where Jesus-fucking-Christ was crucified."

CHAPTER TWENTY-ONE

Jonas's gaze flicked back and forth between his BlackBerry and the road as he pulled up Anne's cell number. He swerved back into his lane as the phone rang.

Despite the hour, her voice sounded alert. "What's wrong?"

"Why do you think something's wrong?"

"It's late."

"But you're awake."

"What is it, Jonas?"

"They think he might be alive," Jonas said.

"Who?"

"Sonman?"

"Who thinks so?"

"A contact from the military. High up. He's read Sonman's official file."

"The file said he's alive?"

"No. But his remains were never found, and a reliable witness claims to have seen Sonman in Jerusalem last year?"

"Jerusalem?"

"Yeah, the Church of the Holy ... something or other."

"Sepulcher."

"That's it. You know it?"

"Yes, Jonas, I know of it."

Jonas swerved around a jet-black BMW.

"You know that's where –"

"Yes. I know exactly what happened there. And what that means about Sonman."

"You think he's the one, then?"

Anne was silent so long Jonas thought the call had dropped.

Finally: "I don't like assuming too much, Jonas. But I think it behooves me to involve some people I know. First thing we need to do is get a hold of your witness and try to get a sketch out of him. Do you know where to find this witness?"

"I can find out. No problem. Call you tomorrow when I get that info."

"Okay, Jonas." Her words were coated in a tinge of nighttime rasp. "Be careful."

Jonas hung up before responding.

"Hooah," he said to the windshield.

Ten minutes later he was in Georgetown. His was a quiet neighborhood where most of the residents arrived home at a reasonable hour, and Jonas had to circle around before finding a spot a block and a half away from his apartment. He slid out into the cold night, grabbing his wool coat and black leather briefcase from the back seat before crossing the cobblestone street.

Streetlights lined the sidewalks like sentries, their beams overlapping into a continuous pool of orange and yellow haze. The row homes loomed three stories high to his left, each a different color and set back behind waist-high brick walls, over which ivy spilled toward the ground. Jonas listened to his footsteps and his own breathing.

In the far distance, cars hummed.

A child yelped from inside a home. *Doesn't want to go to bed,* Jonas thought. Then he looked at his watch.

Almost midnight.

Maybe a nightmare.

He felt his pace slow, his normal reaction when he wanted to better sense his space. Walk too fast and you miss too much. Maybe you don't hear something you're supposed to hear.

Then time seemed to stop.

It had happened to him before, but not very often. When it happened, it was almost always bad. The air would go still and all sound was sucked away by some invisible force.

Everything just stopped.

It hadn't happened in a long time. The last time was in the Mog, right before the face of the Pakistani soldier disappeared in a red haze of blood and bone.

Jonas immediately crouched and pretended to tie the laces of his shoe, which didn't have any. He looked down and then behind him, sensing no movement. An SUV was parked to his immediate right and the ivy-choked brick wall to his left. Strategically, Jonas was in a very vulnerable position. Not the kind of thought he would normally have walking down the street to his home, but considering the circumstances of the day ...

Stop it, he told himself. You're overreacting. Your adrenaline is flowing from what Chuck told you at the bar, because, let's face it, you don't live in a world of excitement, do you? You have a great job, but you're not in the shit shooting things up anymore, and you miss it. Getting hit by a car was the most exciting thing to happen to you in years, and now your brain is trying to keep the adrenaline high going.

So you make ghosts out of night air. Goblins out of ivy.

Jonas stood and squared his shoulders. He then turned in a full circle, letting anyone who might be watching him know he was *aware*. Because, despite his common sense trying to get the better of his intuition, time *had* stopped for a reason.

He slowly resumed his forward progress, and as he moved the sounds of the evening returned. He heard his feet rising and falling against the cracked concrete beneath him. A car door closed in the distance, far enough away for Jonas to give it little thought. A dog barked three times inside a row home, then no more.

With each step closer to his home, Jonas felt a growing suspicion his intuition had atrophied over the years.

Then he smelled the cigarette smoke.

Faint at first, like a smell within a dream. Jonas stopped and tried to detect what direction it was coming from.

Doesn't really matter. Cigarette smoke doesn't travel far. Source must be close.

He clutched the handle of his briefcase, wishing it were the butt of a gun.

Then a thought occurred to him. Jonas pulled out his cell phone and dialed Anne. She answered on the first ring.

"Something wrong?" she asked.

"I don't know." His voice seemed to echo on the empty street. "That's what I was hoping you could tell me."

"What do you mean?"

"Do you ..." Jonas considered if someone was waiting for him, his words belie his suspicions. Then he decided he didn't care. "Do you get a sense about me right now?"

"Sense?"

"Can you ... sense if ... if something is about to happen?"

"What's going on, Jonas?"

"I was just wondering if your ... *intuition* ... could work through cell phones."

Her voice was calming but not calm. "It doesn't work like that, Jonas. Are you in trouble?"

Jonas looked over at a dirty white van parked next to him, its back windows taped over with newspaper from the inside.

"I'm not sure."

"What do your instincts tell you?"

Jonas didn't hesitate. "Yes."

Her words were controlled but came quickly. "Listen to me, Jonas. What I have. *My ability*. We all have it. I just happen to be able to channel it better than most people. But I'm telling you right now, don't ignore what your senses are telling you. Hang up and call the police."

"I'd have nothing to tell them."

"Where are you?"

"A block from home."

"Are you in your car?"

"On foot." Jonas thought he heard movement inside the van. Maybe it was his imagination. Maybe it wasn't.

The cigarette smoke became stronger.

"Gotta go," he said.

"*Jonas –*"

"I'm fine," he said before disconnecting the call. Then he chanced a distraction. He deftly punched at the keys on his BlackBerry, sending Anne a text.

Calling now, but won't talk. Keep the line open and listen. If you hear me yell, call police and tell them corner of Potomac and O St.

He sent the message, waited a few seconds, then dialed her number. Without listening for her answer, Jonas slid the phone back into his coat pocket.

A breeze swept the street. Something caught the corner of his eye on the sidewalk next to the van's front tire.

A cigarette rolled in the breeze. It wasn't even a butt. There was at least half of it left.

Jonas put his briefcase down and took a step forward, leaning slightly toward the cigarette.

The tip was still smoldering.

Then he looked up and noticed the car parked directly in front of the van.

Honda Accord. Shit-brown.

Jonas immediately shifted his footing, placing his left leg forward and putting most of his weight on his bent right leg.

A force from behind slammed into him. Jonas sprawled to the concrete.

"Fuck!" he yelled, thinking of no better signal to Anne.

His assailant leapt on top of him, pinning Jonas's face down on the rough concrete.

Jonas knew his attacker would go for the head. He remained still, playing possum.

Soft fingers reached beneath his chin. Leather gloves.

Going to twist the neck.

Jonas reached up with his right hand and pushed the gloved fingers up toward his face. They moved a few inches, just enough to get an index finger next to his mouth.

Jonas bit as hard as he could.

It was like biting into a hot dog that was concealing a pencil. First leather, then flesh, then a solid and sickening crunch as his teeth approached bone.

A grunt but no scream. Jonas released and the hand was suddenly gone. The weight on him shifted, just enough for Jonas to free himself. He swung his elbow in a tight arc as he twisted his body, slamming it into his attacker's ribs.

The weight rolled off him and Jonas sprang to his feet.

The man stood in the streetlight. He wore all black, his face only a ski mask. His clothes were tight and flexible, revealing a lean and muscular frame.

It could be anyone, but Jonas knew exactly who it was.

Sonman.

The man in black attacked with speed.

Jonas parried the first blow and sidestepped to his right. Sonman corrected and pivoted, but did not attack. Fists controlled. Balance perfect. Neither man moved, as if knowing intimately the training of the other.

Steady. No movement. Locked gazes.

Waiting.

Jonas crouched and attacked, sweeping his leg.

Sonman countered perfectly, punching the right kneecap.

Searing pain. Jonas pulled away before a second blow could land.

Jonas shifted more weight to his right leg and assessed the damage. Sore, but nothing critical.

Jonas stared at the man as he controlled his breathing.

Sonman waited.

Jonas pushed off his back foot and reached with a jab at the same time.

Sonman swatted the fist away, countering with an upward thrust with the base of his palm. Jonas leaned back before contact and dipped beneath a second strike coming from Sonman's left hand. Jonas wove, and as he came up on the other side, locked his left arm and slammed his fist into Sonman's exposed side. Kidney punch.

Sonman staggered. Jonas couldn't let him regain composure. He doubled on the left hook with a blow to Sonman's head.

The impact was crushing to Jonas's knuckles, softened only in the slightest by the thick cotton of Sonman's ski mask.

Sonman sprawled to the ground, rolled, and then bounced to his feet almost as if nothing had happened. A quick shake of the head was the only indication to Jonas his punch even registered.

Attack, Jonas told himself. *Don't let up.*

Jonas moved forward, crouching, looking for an opening. His target would be the man's throat or the nose. A singular crushing blow. He needed to end this.

Then Sonman reached into his waistband and pulled something out. Something black. After a flick of the wrist and push with his thumb, Jonas saw it was a knife.

Not a small one.

"I don't mean to kill you. I just need you close to me. But dead ain't good."

Jonas knew it was true. If Sonman had wanted him dead, Jonas would be dead. Sonman would've taken him out immediately rather than risk a fistfight. But being "close" to Sonman – whatever the hell that meant – didn't sound much better.

Jonas moved back. The situation had changed. The knife would restrict Sonman's ability to fight, but a single connected blow could be lethal.

He continued increasing the distance between them and scanned the ground, looking for something – anything – that could serve as a weapon. Even a stray rock would work, but there was none.

Sonman advanced, knife in front, held tightly, dagger-style. Steps small and fast, a scorpion descending upon its prey.

The distance between them was closing.

Jonas considered his options. To his left was Sonman's car, parked alongside the curb. The waist-high brick wall was to his immediate right.

He might be able to turn and run away before Sonman reached him. But he didn't want to.

Then he remembered the BlackBerry in his pocket. It was an older model. Older, larger, bulkier. Jonas grabbed it.

When Sonman was less than ten feet away Jonas threw the BlackBerry at him, hurling it as hard as he could, spinning it with his forefinger like he would a skipping stone.

His aim was perfect.

The BlackBerry slammed into the dead center of Sonman's forehead, hard enough that Jonas could hear the shattering of its plastic case before the pieces scattered on the sidewalk.

Sonman grunted and dropped to one knee. He quickly got back to his feet, but Jonas could see the man's balance was off.

Jonas pounced.

He lowered his head and charged into his attacker, slamming the top of his head into Sonman's breastbone. Sonman flew backwards and sprawled onto the sidewalk, losing his grip on the knife.

Cold steel skimmed the concrete.

Jonas pushed backwards and lunged toward the knife. He grabbed it and turned back to Sonman, who was now back to his feet, standing motionless fifteen feet away.

Jonas advanced, his arm raised and locked in a tight L in front of him, the knife blade now a part of him. He didn't have to remember his hand-to-hand combat training. It had never left him.

Sonman took a step back, but did not run.

Then the sirens came. Distant at first. In seconds the flashing red and blue lights were visible, bursting down the street behind Sonman, backlighting his silhouette. Jonas cursed the timing. He knew the police were responding to Anne's call, and when Sonman had the knife he would have been far happier to see them arrive. But this would be a confusing scene to the cops, and Jonas would soon have to drop his knife. And he didn't think Sonman would be the type to stay put.

Sonman risked a momentary glance behind his back before leaping up the brick wall to his left. Jonas pivoted and cursed as he saw Sonman propel himself past Jonas and back down onto the sidewalk. He didn't look back – Sonman tore down the street with a speed that amazed Jonas.

Jonas dropped the knife and started pursuit.

"Stop! Metro police!"

The shout came from behind him. Jonas spun and held up his hands, not at all surprised by the sight of a cop with a nine-millimeter aimed directly at his chest.

"He's the one you want," Jonas said. He tried to keep his voice firm but calm. "Don't let him get away."

"Shut up and get on the ground. Now!"

Jonas did as he was told, except for the part about shutting up. "I work for Senator Sidams and I'm telling you right now letting that man escape will be the worst mistake of your career."

It was only seconds before he felt a knee in his back and his arms pulled behind him. It didn't escape Jonas he had been in almost the exact same position just a few minutes before with Sonman.

As he felt the cool steel of the handcuffs strangle his wrists, the cop breathed in his ear.

"I don't see no one else here, buddy. Just you and a knife."

CHAPTER TWENTY-TWO

THE CONCRETE FEELS good to Rudiger, and his feet bound off it as he sprints down the darkened street. The sprint turns into a run. No one behind him. He's careful. Crosses the street, scales the wrought-iron fence of a small urban cemetery, and dodges tombstones as he makes his way to the other side. Cemetery lights soften the granite of the grave markers, making them look like giant teeth. Crooked smile.

Rudiger weaves through them. Climbs the fence on the far end and finds himself on a busier street. Some late night strollers. A couple far ahead, one on the other side of the street, a man with his poodle. No one pays attention to him.

Good.

His run trickles to a walk as he removes his ski mask and gloves. Buries them in a nearby trashcan.

Checks his finger. Already swollen with two bite marks just above the second knuckle. Skin is broken but he doesn't think the bone is. Hurts though. Face hurts, too.

His forehead throbs.

Think. Don't feel. Just think.

Won't be going back to the car. Doesn't matter. He can steal a car anytime. Nothing in the car to find neither. The gun they'll find won't trace.

Can't walk the streets all night. Wishes he had his gun and cash. He can get more, but not tonight. Gotta stay quiet tonight. Down the street he finds a homeless shelter. No one waiting outside. Rudiger tries the door and it swings open.

Steps inside. Rudiger sees no one. The lights are bright. He wants to shrink inside himself. A woman turns the corner of the short hallway and approaches him. Pretty young thing. Not too young to be unsure of herself. Not too old to have given up hope. She exists in that narrow slip between promise and disappointment.

"Do you need a bed tonight, sir?"

"Yes, ma'am," Rudiger says, his voice softened by her politeness.

"You're new here," she says.

"Yes."

"Are you hungry?"

Rudiger shakes his head. He doesn't want her to look at him.

"You're hurt." She moves to touch his face but he pulls away. "Your face."

"Ain't nothin'."

She says nothing else about the knot on his head, which must be swollen and red against the death-kissed pallor of his skin. When she turns, he reaches up for the first time and touches it. Skin feels like fire.

He follows her. They pass down the short corridor and through a set of double doors. Small gymnasium. The place maybe once was a school. Cots lined up in neat and orderly rows. Rudiger counts thirty-three of them in total. Only seventeen are occupied.

The woman points to a cot farthest from the other guests, as if she knows that would be best.

"Blanket, pillow here. There's a toothbrush and toothpaste and some other articles in the baggie for you. Showers are down the hallway if you want, and we have a clothing bin if you want us to find you anything new to wear."

"I'm fine," Rudiger mumbles. "Thank you."

"My name is Mary. What's yours?"

"Peter," he says, wishing it were true.

"Well, Peter. I'm glad you came in tonight. Let any of us know if you need anything."

He nods and tracks her steps with his eyes as she walks away. They're not so different, Mary and him. Both doing God's work, in different ways and all.

Rudiger sits on the cot and considers how long he'll stay. Police will keep looking for him. Maybe search here. They'll ask Mary about him. She'll speak of a man wearing black clothing with injuries on his face. Have to keep moving. But he's tired and ... confused. He decides to stay, leaving his fate in God's hands. If God wants him to succeed, then the police will stay away. If they come and arrest him, then God wants him to fail.

A deep-tub sink stands in the corner of the gym. It looks out of place, an afterthought, perhaps a place to hand-wash some clothes. Rudiger walks past his row of cots toward it. He keeps his gaze firmly ahead, ignoring those who might be watching him. At the sink, he opens a bar of hotel soap-Comfort Inn, the wrapper says – and lathers up his hands. He watches the grime from his fingers swirl in a cloudy pool down the drain. He brings the water to his face and cleans himself, feeling the sting and the throbs from his injuries. The water is good, purifying. He pushes his tongue out to taste it. Soapy and warm.

He opens his eyes and notices the cross for the first time. Small, wooden. Hangs on the wall instead of a mirror. Not the traditional cross design. But Rudiger is familiar with it. Two equal lengths bisecting in the middle, like two capital letter "I's" on top of one other. Four smaller crosses embedded in each quadrant. Sometimes called the Crusader's Cross, but Rudiger is more familiar with its more common name.

Jerusalem Cross.

It's a sign, and it comes at the perfect time. A time when Rudiger is close to questioning his cause. Jonas was supposed to lead him to the One, but he slipped away. Rudiger doesn't understand why God would ask him to do something and then not let him do it.

He closes his eyes and tells himself his life is a story, though he doesn't remember much of his childhood before the time of the Preacherman.

He remembers riding his bike after his paper route, because his momma told him it would be okay. *You ken*, she said. *Not that dark out yet. Summer still got hold of us.* He'd been coming home after delivering the three sacks of papers he was responsible for, and his momma was wrong. It *was* dark out. That night had been warm – soft summer night in the Appalachians – and as he rode he noticed the dirt-grey Lincoln trailing him, following like a pack of coyotes waiting to surround an old dog. Rudiger didn't know why, but he didn't try to ride away. Just let that car come right up alongside, just as fate intended it to. That was the first time he saw the Preacherman. Saw the gray stubble on pasty cheeks, the long face leaning out the cracked and dirty car window. The black hat with the round brim, sharp enough to cut. And later, under the haze of the single light bulb in the basement, the smeared dirt and filth on the Preacherman's white collar.

The time between the Preacherman and the Army was supposed to be a time of healing, of new-born hope, but it wasn't that at all. It was a time of withdrawal. Isolation. He'd never told no one but his sister what had happened in the two months he was gone. He saw his momma and daddy split up, unable to reconcile their baby boy with the thing that came limping back home, bloody, torn, and silent. It was also a time when his ability grew, the way he could see letters in a way no one else seemed to. And it was a time of the Bible, of understanding the one lesson Preacherman taught that Rudiger believed. That there would be a Judgment Day, and, glory to all, that day would be the end of all his pain.

And then there was the Mog. This part of his life Rudiger remembers well. He killed that family in the Mog, for they were unclean and impure, but, moreover, the Somali street sign told him to. Doesn't regret the sacrifice, but he didn't fully understand it until the next part of the story: the *transformation*. The transformation happened only last year. The last time he saw a Jerusalem Cross was at his transformation, when the doctors in the Israeli hospital told him he had the Syndrome. Jerusalem Syndrome.

As the surviving rivulets of water creep down the side of his face, Rudiger thinks about that day – the day he was told what to do. He wasn't crazy, like they said.

He was the sanest one of them all.

CHAPTER TWENTY-THREE

JERUSALEM, ISRAEL
ONE YEAR EARLIER

THE STREETS ARE narrow and clogged, the arteries of an old man waiting for his heart to finally stop.

Rudiger separated from his group, though he was told not to. He didn't care. Groups are for safety and protection, neither of which he needs. Jerusalem would protect him. He carried his backpack loosely over his right shoulder as he walked through the Jaffa Gate. His guide had told him that, at the time of the Second Intifada, a non-Muslim would not dare pass through this gate to the Old City.

A man hoisting a slaughtered lamb barked in Arabic as Rudiger passed.

Red. Blue. Blazing yellow. The fabrics hanging in the stalls ghosted from the breeze of passing humans; the outside air was only a visitor down in the tangled streets of the ancient city and had no bearing or direction. Smell of spice and meat. Vendors shouted, mostly to each other. To get lost in the Old City was an expectation, but Rudiger knew where he was going. It was where he was always going. It was why he booked the trip. Why he decided to fly halfway around the world.

It was too easy to say he was looking for answers. He'd reached a point where answers didn't matter anymore. He had a new last name. New documents. A job. A small apartment, where he kept quietly to himself. Private Rudy Sonman was killed in Somalia. Rudiger Mortisin was alive and living in Salt Lake City, earning twenty dollars an hour as an independent building contractor. He didn't speak to many people, but to those who asked, Rudiger received the jagged scar on his ear from a job-related accident. Sometimes they asked for more details. Rudiger never gave them.

The trip to Jerusalem was his first time outside the country since the military. As in all things, he traveled alone, though he was part of a tour group for pilgrims coming to the Holy Land. Even now, as he walked the streets of the Old City, he did not fully understand why he had come, but he had learned to trust the direction of his instincts.

For years Rudiger sought to end his pain. This pain that could only be eased by the something far greater than suicide. Ever since Rudiger learned of the Rapture under the tutelage of the Preacherman, he was convinced that only the judgment of the world would end the degree of suffering within him.

A flyer for the trip to Jerusalem had initially caught his attention. He knew he had to go. He would go to where it all began, and he would find answers.

Go find an answer. Go find salvation. Bring it all about, and end the pain. The confusion. The thoughts and the void. Pour it all into a new world, where he didn't have to be Rudiger anymore.

Here, in the din of the merchants and the smell of animal flesh, Rudiger wound his way past throngs of tourists. He turned one corner, then another, the space above him alternating between corrugated steel rooftops and open sky. Stone street smoothed by the footprints of millions before him. Black with filth. Rudiger veered right, up a grade of steps, lost but certain. History surrounded him, buried beneath capitalist catcalls and promises of salvation.

He was closer. He looked up at the limestone building next to him, and saw the letters carved into the rock.

Via Dolorosa.

Way of Suffering.

He had memorized the maps weeks before his trip and knew he was on the west end of the eastern fraction of Via Dolorosa.

There. On the right. Barely marked on the exterior of the Polish Catholic Chapel, but unmistakable.

The third station of the cross.

Where Jesus fell for the first time.

The lashes had bled Him. The cross too heavy a burden. As they watched, as they all watched, Jesus fell, the massive cross surely crushing His lungs, perhaps causing internal damage that sped His death.

Rudiger touched the wall. A man next to him snapped a picture, more interested in proving he was *there* than understanding what it was he documented. Rudiger stared at him, his hand still outstretched, his fingers spread wide on the cool rock. The man backed away.

Rudiger hurried for no reason. No reason except the twisting thing inside him telling him the message was soon.

The voice was the Preacherman's. Raspy and old, scratching like a cat.

He will tell you

He speared past an elderly couple. The man shouted something. Rudiger ignored him. Up the narrow road, weaving through humanity, ignoring trinkets thrust in his face. The connection was closer now, promising him information. Promising truth, dangling it just out of his reach, teasing him.

Chapel of Simon of Cyrene. Fifth Station.

Simon had aided Jesus here, and, for a short distance, helped to carry His cross. A man dressed in all white stood against the face of the chapel, his eyes closed. Long, dirt-smeared toes crept out the front of his leather sandals. A Bible clenched in his right hand. He opened his eyes and nodded at Rudiger. Rudiger nodded back.

go further

Rudiger left him. Moved on. Faster. Closer. He didn't understand his exchange with the man, but there was little he understood about any of this.

Seventh Station. Franciscan Chapel.

The remains of a tetrapylon stood against time on the lower level. Here, Rudiger knew, Jesus fell a second time, His agony only beginning.

The crowds thickened. Rudiger pushed and shoved through them. The heat of flesh swirled about him, the smell of unwashed skin heady and brilliant. A woman snapped her head around and her hair whipped against Rudiger's face. Smelled like earth. A group of Americans spoke in loud and intrusive English. Rudiger shoveled through them, glaring. Then one of them stared so deeply at him Rudiger feared the man would attack. Then:

"Sonman?"

Rudiger squinted and looked at him. Familiar but loose. Intangible. His gaze fell to the ground.

"Sonman," the man repeated, shouting over the crowd. "It's me, Cohen. From the Tenth Mountain Division – Somalia? Holy shit, is it really you?"

The memory reformed in his mind and Rudiger saw Cohen as he had known him, back in the dust and the dirt and the heat. Both men knew what had happened then and that Rudiger was presumed dead. He couldn't be anything else right now, not to anyone. Especially now.

Rudiger was pulled from his focus, his vision. Cohen was part of his past. Cohen *knew* him, and that made the man a liability.

If Rudiger had a knife, he could have easily slid it between Cohen's ribs, and in the crowd Rudiger would have had time to move on. But he had no weapon. He could not kill this man, at least not now.

Rudiger instead pulled himself close to Cohen, invading the centimeters of private space left to anyone in the throng of people. Cohen tried to pull his face back, but Rudiger pressed forward. With their noses almost touching, Rudiger said:

"I don't know you."

Cohen blinked but did not pull back. "Jesus, Sonman. It's you. Did you really do what they said?"

Sonman raised his hand and put it on the back of Cohen's neck. Someone from a distance might have expected the men to kiss, but Rudiger instead squeezed the back of the man's neck and repeated what he had said:

"I don't know you."

He held for a second longer, released his grip, then assessed the look in Cohen's eyes. It was the look a sane person gives the second they realize the person in front of them is not.

Rudiger said nothing else as he then pushed past him, still looking down. Cohen had no chance to follow – the crowd closed in behind Rudiger like water filling the wake of a boat.

He looked up. He had arrived. It would be here. Where he was meant to go all along.

This was *the place*, though many argued one could never really know. Constantine's mother was certain, so she had a church built here.

Ninth station. The third and last time Jesus fell. The remaining stations would be inside.

Rudiger looked up. The ladder was there, immovable, just as he knew it would be. Just as it had been for so long.

Church of the Holy Sepulcher.

It was known to many. Nothing more than a tourist site to some. Something holy to others. Something unique to Rudiger.

He stepped inside the Church.

Darker now. Quiet.

The sweat from his brow dribbled down his face.

To his right, a steep series of steps curved upwards, each step rounded, decreasing in width with ascension. It was not inviting, but all were welcome. Rudiger knew.

Golgotha

It was where he needed to go. The message was closer. The connection was here. As he climbed he shut his eyes.

At the top now.

Soon.

and they brought Him to the place called Golgotha

The words came to him easily.

At the top of the steps an expanse led to a shrine, gleaming in the muted light. It could have been the altar of any church, glorious and reverent, but it was more. Rudiger knew exactly what it was, and his breaths came in shallow bursts. A statue of Christ was suspended from an arch. A glass floor revealed the untouched rock beneath. This was the earth above which the Church had been built. A small gold disc marked the exact location.

I thirst

Where it happened. Where the Roman centurions had driven the piece of wood deep into the ground, where two other crosses stood close by.

Dismas and Gestas

Criminals nailed to them. Here it stood.

it is finished

He breathed His last gasp. Even there, a small fissure in the naked rock showed proof of the quaking earth that rocked the land upon His death.

Rudiger knelt.

Despite the hour, despite the throngs of people streaming through the small streets of the Old City, despite the waves of pilgrims here to pay respect, for a moment, this moment, Rudiger was alone. This, this place where Christ the Holy died, Rudiger was the only one at Golgotha, an impossibility it would seem to most, but a miracle to Rudiger. It was a sign. He wanted him alone. To pray. To send a message. It would surely only last seconds, so there was little time. For it must happen, and it must be now. Rudiger, eyes closed, hand on his forehead, head bowed before God, did not pray. Did not speak. Did nothing but open his mind, offered a receptacle, hoping so desperately for a reason, for a purpose. Waiting. Waiting. He would not be alone long. He heard steps on the stairs, muted chatter in foreign tongues. Heat on his face. Not air. Breath. Breath of something there, but distant. Then it spoke.

Into your hands I commit my spirit.

Eyes open. The words were real. Spoken. Now. It was time to receive.

"Yes," Rudiger said. "Tell me."

Voice of Preacherman. Commandments of God.

Listen, my son.

"Yes."

You know you are special.

"Yes." Heat flashed through him. The universe disappeared. Only this moment existed.

You are not alone in your suffering, and for your pain you will forever understand Glory.

"I am yours."

You must unveil Me. You must bring about what you have dreamed of for so long. For an end to the darkness.

"Anything."

I am in another ... I must be from them ... and then I will be All.

Rudiger no longer knew if he spoke aloud. "Who?"

Use your gift. It will guide you.

"What if I'm wrong?"

Let Me guide you.

"How do they release You?"

They must be as I ... suffer the Glory.

"Suffer." Rudiger's dirty fingernails dug into the palms of his hands. The pain was enlightening. Glorious.

Release Me from their death.

Dying is nothing. "Where do I start?"

Your mind will command you ... you will find the One through your own abilities.

"I don't understand ..."

It will be your last act, my son. It will be your final crossing. And from that all will be righteous. All will be saved.

Final Crossing.

A sound behind Rudiger. Footsteps. At the top of the stairs, a priest appeared, hands folded behind his back, a long, ash-white beard dripping like candle wax from his chin. He nodded at Rudiger and gave him a quizzical stare, one asking: *How are you so fortunate to be up here alone?*

Then pain ripped through Rudiger's head, a kind of pain unknown to him. It tore through his skull like a spear, twisting a gnarled and barbed tip as it scorched from the front to the back. In its wake, something tore, and that tear brought with a blinding light.

You go get it all done now, Preacherman said. *You get it done and then you ken be rid of me forever. That's what you want, ain't it? You want me in Hell? Well, boy, then I say it again. You go get it done.*

He collapsed to the floor, his body thudding against the cool stone, just a few feet away from where the Cross had stood, where Christ's lifeless form had been lowered from the instrument of His rebirth. The priest rushed to Rudiger, who barely noticed the man hovering above him, speaking to him in a language he did not understand or even care to.

His hands squeezed his head. The light grew brighter. He could shield himself from it no more easily than he could wring the pain from his skull.

The priest shook him.

Rudiger screamed. Howled. Tore against the pain and fear.

Then the light dimmed. The pain subsided, its waning traces as relieving as morphine. The light vanished.

When it was over, Rudiger opened his eyes. Sweat glazed him. A viscous tendril of saliva quivered from his lower lip as the priest continued to shake Rudiger's shoulder.

The priest switched to heavily accented English.

"Medical help is coming. You will be all right."

Rudiger looked at him. "I don't need help, Father. I'm more saved than even you."

The priest blinked, then removed his hand from Rudiger's shoulder.

"Do not get up," the priest said. "Rest."

By now, other tourists had started to fill the small gallery, and many gathered around the fallen man and whispered in myriad languages and tones. The priest pushed them back with a flick of his hands and a gruff diatribe.

Rudiger rose. The priest stepped back.

"Please wait. You need to be examined."

Rudiger scanned the small crowd and let his gaze fall on the priest.

"I am chosen," he said. "It is done."

He stood straighter, he thought, than he had in years. He felt strong, but he knew he would need more strength for what he needed to do.

Two Israeli soldiers appeared before the paramedics did, and they spoke in very controlled and patient English. They had asked what had happened and Rudiger told them a fractured truth. They asked him who he was traveling with, and why he had left his group.

Rudiger stopped talking at that point.

One of the soldiers accompanied Rudiger to the hospital when the paramedics finally arrived.

He became a guest of the State of Israel for the next six days, housed in the psychiatric wing of a hospital just outside the city proper. A Jewish doctor with sad eyes and uncontrolled eyebrows asked him many questions before telling Rudiger he was suffering from *Jerusalem Syndrome*. The condition was rare, he said, but not singular. In fact, there had been several thousand cases through the years. The Syndrome was the only psychological explanation any-one had for those persons whose brain simply couldn't handle the religious and historical significance of Jerusalem. Many patients had no background of mental instability. Their brains simply overloaded when visiting the sacred city. Most were Christians, and popular "breaking" points were along Via Dolorosa and within the Church of the Holy Sepulcher. Rudiger fit the profile perfectly.

"You'll be fine soon," the doctor told him. "By the time you get home, you will be back to normal."

Rudiger smiled at the man.

CHAPTER TWENTY-FOUR

WASHINGTON, D.C.
APRIL 19

"YOU WANT TO talk about it?" The Senator's gaze burrowed and wormed its way into Jonas.

Jonas felt his knees wanting to buckle as he stood in front of his boss's desk. Despite the early morning hour, a heat rose in the Senator's office. "Talk about what?"

"It's not really a question. It's an order."

"That sounds more like you."

"What the hell happened, son? First you end up in the hospital because you decided to take a stroll on the Beltway at rush hour –"

"I was helping someone."

"– and now I get a call from a staffer in the middle of the night telling me the police were holding you after a street fight?"

Jonas held his breath for a moment.

"I'm a thrill-seeker, sir. It's in my blood."

"*Jonas.*"

His mind raced. It would be so easy to tell his boss everything, and the bond between the two men screamed for the truth. But his professional loyalty to Senator Sidams meant Jonas couldn't yet have the senior lawmaker tied to anything this sensational.

"Guy wanted my wallet. I didn't want to give it to him."

"Yeah." The Senator pushed his glasses up the bridge of his nose. "That's what you told the police."

"It is."

"But I don't buy it."

"Sir?"

"I've been around liars for a long time, Jonas. Some of the best in the world, in fact. I've learned how to smell the shit beneath the roses."

"Senator, I –"

Sidams raised his hand, silencing Jonas. "Whatever is going on with you, I presume it's going to end. I also presume you're protecting me from something, which I admire. But you're my goddamn Chief of Staff and I expect you to use good judgment in all your decisions. There's a very thin wall between you and me, and a thinner one between the public and me."

"Yes, sir. I understand."

"The Denver Peace Accords will be my legacy, good or bad. More importantly, these people deserve our full focus and effort. I need you *here*, Jonas." Sidams rapped on his desk with his long index finger. "Mentally and physically. Once the Accords are over, I don't give a shit to glory and God if you go naked base jumping off the Washington Monument in full daylight. Until then I need you to be a good boy."

"Yes, sir."

"No more thrill-seeking."

"No, sir."

The Senator pushed his chair back away from his desk and moved his gaze up and down Jonas.

"That your best suit?"

"No, sir. I have one just like it, but without the stains."

"Good. You'll need it for tomorrow."

"What's happening tomorrow?"

The Senator looked down at his desk and began editing the document in front of him.

"You're briefing the President."

CHAPTER TWENTY-FIVE

THE CAPTAIN WAS asleep in his wheelchair when Jonas found him, his chin touching his chest, wisps of long white hair falling forward over his forehead like a cheap Santa Claus wig. Jonas took a knee on the linoleum floor of the north wing and tried to tune out the muffled shouting from behind a nearby door.

"Hi, Dad."

No reaction. The Captain could have been dead if not for the just-noticeable rise and fall of his sunken chest beneath a faded ruby sweatshirt. Jonas rubbed the man's bony shoulder.

"It's me, Dad. Jonas. Do you want to wake up?"

The Captain grustled and grumbled, mumbling something incoherent. His head slowly rose from his chest but his eyes remained closed, and for a moment Jonas was sure his father was going to go back to sleep. But then his eyes opened, not slowly, but sudden and wide, the crystal blue of his irises the color of glacial ice. There was fear in his stare, fear of the unknown, of the what and why of existence, and Jonas could read the questions in the Captain's panicked gaze, questions like *Who am I* and *Where am I* and the always gnawing *What's happening to me?*

Then the Captain's eyes seemed to finally focus on Jonas's face, his expression softened, and the corners of the old man's mouth slowly turned up into something that was almost a smile. It was enough for Jonas. It was enough for him to know that, for at least another day, the father recognized the son, for at least another moment.

"You look good, Dad. Real good."

The Captain closed his eyes and began humming. The melody wasn't anything Jonas recognized, though it rarely was, but it seemed to be from *something*.

Jonas broke off a piece of a chocolate-chip cookie he'd brought. The Captain was a sucker for Chips Ahoy, and even with closed eyes the old man knew when the piece was close, for his lips opened before Jonas touched the cookie to his father's lips. Small crumbs fell onto the Captain's creased trousers as he ate.

"Got in a knife fight," Jonas said, breaking off another piece of cookie.

No pause in the humming or chewing. Jonas stood and pushed the wheelchair down the corridor until they reached the small outside courtyard. The sun felt good on his face. The Captain recoiled from the sun as if someone threw water on his face, but moments later the smile reappeared and Jonas knew his father was soaking in the freshness of an outside world he rarely experienced.

Jonas spoke as he wheeled his father. "Yeah, and it wasn't a mugging like I told the Senator. It was the guy who tried to kill me in Somalia. You remember that, don't you Dad? When I came home with cracked ribs and a concussion? His name is Rudy Sonman, and everyone thought he was dead."

The Captain hummed and rolled his head back and forth. Jonas leaned forward and gave him the last of the cookie.

"The motherfucker's alive and he tried to kill me last night."

An almost-laugh from the Captain. Jonas smiled.

"It's true – swear to God. I don't know why he wants me dead, but this woman – I told you about her last time, I think – she thinks he might be connected to a case she's working on. Serial killer who crucifies people."

As he said the last sentence, a woman with a walker standing near a small grouping of red and yellow rose bushes looked up.

"Oh, my," she said. "That sounds simply awful."

Jonas nodded to her. "Morning, Bennie." Bennie was one of the more functional residents, which wasn't saying much. "Yes, it is awful."

She looked at him sternly. "People have enough troubles in this world without having to worry about being crucified."

"Amen to that." Jonas leaned down and snapped off the top of a yellow rose and handed it to her. He then took a red one and stuck it into a crack on the top of his father's wheelchair. It was very therapeutic, Jonas decided, visiting his father. He could say whatever he wanted and not be judged or blamed. Jonas was the type who liked to vent now and then, but wasn't necessarily looking for advice. An Alzheimer's facility turned out to be the perfect venue.

"Want to walk with us, Bennie?"

"Oh, yes. That would be lovely."

Jonas kept strolling at a snail's pace, pushing his father, while Bennie kept up in her walker, which clunked along the stone path. There was no one else outside.

"I'm sorry, dear. What's your name?"

He had met her at least twenty times.

"Jonas."

"I'm Bennie."

"Hi, Bennie."

She nodded politely as she leaned over the walker. "I used to dance. New York City, of all places."

Jonas nodded at his father. "He was a captain in the Army."

"Yes," she said, her eyes belying a sadness that seemed to have settled in out of nowhere. "I know that."

"Does he ... does he ever say anything? To you?"

Bennie grunted as her walker caught an edge of the stone path. She corrected it and continued forward. "Oh, no. He doesn't say anything. Other than humming, he's a quiet one. Quiet like the night."

"He always was."

Bennie stopped and stared at the Captain. "Yes," she said finally. "He still knows. He's still in there. Some are too far gone, but he still knows."

"Knows what?"

"Knows the world. Knows things. Knows just enough."

"Enough for what?"

A thin sheen of moisture glossed over her eyes. "Knows enough to be scared. Like me. I know too much. I'm here too early, but I guess there's no other place for me. I'm waiting to forget, but it hasn't happened yet. Only spots are black to me, here and there. But time will change that." She looked up at him. "Jason?"

"Jonas."

"Jonas. Of course, dear. Do forgive me."

The Captain changed his tune, the humming taking on a slower and more sorrowful cadence. As his head sunk against his chest, sunlight highlighted the patchwork of white stubble on his ruddy cheeks.

"Do you have a wife, Jonas?"

Jonas laughed. "God, no. I don't know who would put up with me."

Bennie smiled but looked confused. "But you're such a handsome man. Do you have a girlfriend?"

"Not at the moment."

"Maybe you need a better job," she said. She nodded to herself. "Women like a man with ambition."

Jonas considered this. "I'm briefing the President tomorrow."

"Oh. Oh, my. Good for you."

Jonas reached the end of the path and stopped pushing the wheelchair. "There *is* a woman. Not my girlfriend. I think she doesn't even much care for me."

Bennie leaned in with a conspiratorial grin. "But you're *sweet* on her."

Jonas smiled. "Maybe I am."

"Is she pretty?"

Despite the freedom of confiding in someone who wouldn't remember him next time he came to visit, Jonas had to push through an ingrained reluctance to share. "Yes, Bennie. She is. She's beautiful." He turned the wheelchair around and Bennie deftly adjusted her walker behind him, following Jonas back toward the building. "She's a medium," he said.

"I was always a small," she replied after some thought.

The wheels of the chair crunched as they rolled over pea pebbles, and Bennie's walker thudded in the packed dirt of the pathway. The sun felt hotter now and the Captain seemed to fade, as if the brightness of the day wilted him. The three of them remained in silence on the short trip back to the ward – even the humming from the Captain faded into a long and singular note until it died completely. Back inside, the air was antiseptic and cool, refreshing and depressing.

He parked his father's chair at the end of a quiet hallway. It seemed almost heartless, like leaving a baby in a stroller in some abandoned building. But the Captain, when he was able, usually steered himself to this same place before falling asleep, so Jonas could only assume he liked it here. Maybe it was quieter here, away from the anxiety and fear that rippled through much of the ward. Maybe it provided the only sanctuary of peace the Captain could scratch out in a world of internal chaos. Whatever it was, Jonas wouldn't ever know, and the mystery that was his father continued on, as it had since Jonas had first been able to say, "Daddy."

Bennie continued on to her room without a goodbye or even an acknowledgement Jonas had been her date, if even for just a few minutes. Jonas was convinced his father was now asleep, and he leaned over and kissed the old man on top of the head.

"Bye, Dad. I'll be back again soon. I love you."

Jonas brushed the back of the Captain's hand with his fingertips, and his father's hand suddenly seized Jonas's and held tight. The squeezing continued with unexpected force for a few seconds before slowly fading into the gentle grip of an old married couple holding hands as they walked down a city street. Jonas stood there, content with the touch, and waited until the Captain was the first to release the bond.

It took nearly ten minutes.

CHAPTER TWENTY SIX

WASHINGTON D.C.

"YOU THREW YOUR BlackBerry at him?" Anne flipped the cracked phone over in her hand, trying to turn on the lifeless device.

"It was all I had. Hit him pretty good. Middle of the forehead."

"Nice," she said. "That must've been when the call disconnected. I didn't hear the police arrive." She handed the phone back to him and tilted her head to the side. "That call scared the hell out of me. I didn't know what was going on."

"Sorry I couldn't call you sooner than I did. The police weren't too keen on letting me get near a phone."

"Would it make me look weak to say I was worried sick?"

"Do you care about looking weak?"

"A little."

"It doesn't make you look weak."

Dusk slowly succumbed to night as Anne leaned back on Jonas's couch and swirled her fingertip along the rim of her wine glass. Jonas was exhausted from the day – the adrenaline from the night before had seeped from his system, leaving behind only a massive desire to sleep. Though he still had work to do before tomorrow's briefing, Anne had insisted on coming by the scene of the fight to see if any residual evidence spoke to her special gifts. Jonas found himself eager to see her.

"I didn't know much of what was happening either. He's a strong motherfu – ... *bastard*. Really strong. When he pulled the knife, I thought I was done for. Thank God you called the police."

"Why does he want you?"

"No idea," Jonas said. He held up the broken phone. "Did you get ... anything from this? Did it tell you anything?"

"Just that you need a new phone."

Jonas leaned forward. "I'm beginning to think you call yourself a medium just to get attention."

Anne gave him a stupefied look. "I'm not a medium. And look at these legs," she said, drawing the tips of her nails along the back of her calf, which spilled out beneath a thin black dress. "Do you really think I need attention?"

"Point taken."

"Not everything leaves a signature with me," she said.

Jonas held up a Ziploc bag. Inside was the butt of a cigarette. "How about this?"

"Is that from him?"

"Not sure. But I think so."

"Shouldn't the police have that as evidence?"

"Evidence of what? A mugging? Somehow I don't think it would receive real high priority."

She reached out and Jonas handed her the baggie. She turned it over in her hands. "Can I take it out?"

"Sure."

Anne opened the top and carefully lifted out the butt between two fingernails. She then placed it in the palm of her left hand, where she cradled it like a newly hatched bird. She closed her eyes.

"Anything?" Jonas asked.

"Shhhhh."

Jonas waited and watched, the weariness of the day crawling slowly along his body like a sunbeam moving along the floor of an empty room. He needed to sleep. He needed to prepare for a presidential brief regarding the Peace Accords. He needed so many things that had nothing to do with the previous night's events. But he couldn't let it go, because it meant *something*.

Anne lowered her head and her lips moved, quickly, quietly, speaking half-words understood only by her. She clasped her hand around the cigarette, gently at first, then squeezing until her fingernails dug into her palm. Jonas leaned forward, wondering what it was she saw. He wanted to ask, but he remained silent. He could hear the wall clock in his nearby bedroom faintly ticking away the seconds.

Anne opened her eyes. Her clasped hand opened, and she dropped the cigarette butt back into the baggie.

"It's his," she said.

"You're sure?"

"I'm sure."

"What did you see?"

"I didn't see anything. I *sensed* things."

Jonas felt his patience slipping away. "Like what?"

She drew in a long breath. "You said he was strong. He *is* strong. I can feel it. But there's something more about him. Something different."

"He's a serial killer, Anne. Of course there's something different about him."

"That's not what I mean. What I mean is I sense some kind of ... I don't know ... disability maybe?"

"What kind of disability?"

"I'm not sure. Not physical. Mental."

"You mean he's bat-shit crazy? That's not a big leap."

Her eyes flashed frustration. "Jonas, would you shut up for a second?"

"Sorry, I can be an ass."

"Yes, you can be." She looked back at the cigarette butt in the bag. "I don't know what it is, but I get the sense he believes he's doing the right thing. Which, of course, isn't unusual for either serial killers or mass murderers. He's not killing out of joy but out of ... *duty*."

"Duty? There was no duty in him when he killed that family in Somalia."

"Maybe his motives have changed. Maybe he's more ... focused now. His need to kill is no longer just a base desire – he's given meaning and purpose to it. I think he feels justified in what he's doing."

"So there's a connection between a successful businessman in Pennsylvania, a student in West Virginia, and me?"

She shook her head. "If there is I have no idea what it could be. But I think he's trying to find something. I think he's on some kind of a mission. Religious killings often suggest some kind of goal is being sought."

"So when he reaches that goal he stops killing?"

"Probably not. His mental illness will likely never let him think he's reached whatever goal he's set for himself."

"Is that the disability you sense? Mental illness?"

She didn't answer for a few moments as she considered the question. "I don't know," she concluded. "I think it's something more than that. A condition. Some kind of mental illness that still allows him to function in society, but is directing him to kill. He ..." She started to say something else but stopped, allowing herself instead another sip of wine and a moment of silence.

Jonas stared at the floor and tried to file everything Anne just said in a place that would make it make sense. He had to believe in her abilities, which was not easy.

"Why would he want me? To finish what he failed to do in the Mog?"

"I don't know. But you're connected to the murders through him. It's what I sensed in you the first time I saw you in the church. He tried to kill you once, and he tried again last night." She leaned back on the couch, her hair spilling over the top of the cushion, and gazed at nothing. "You're personal to him, which is why I get an imprint from you."

Jonas stood and walked to the kitchen, where he refilled his wine glass. "Do these 'imprints' tell you where he's going next?"

He could hear the sigh from the other room. "No."

Jonas walked back into the living room and dimmed the lights, thinking the glare too harsh for the moment, though he didn't really know what the moment was. He stood behind the couch, holding his wine and soaking in what Anne had just said. With her head tilted back on the cushion, Jonas could see the outlines of her face, the simple arch of her nose, the smooth curve of her forehead that had yet to develop creases of worry and time.

"So what do we do now?" he asked.

She pushed her head back more, connecting her gaze with his.

"Nothing," she said. "Not now. It's too easy to over-think, and then we'll make a mistake."

"I don't think we have enough information to avoid mistakes. I think –"

"Jonas?" she interrupted.

"Yes, Anne?"

"Sometimes you talk too much."

Jonas had at least a half-dozen responses, some of them funny, but he held back. She smiled as she watched him struggle.

He took a step toward the couch, and Jonas now stood directly over her. He thought about how little he knew about her, and yet the sense of comfort and familiarity was so strong that this was the first time he had even reflected upon it. It was rare for him to feel so at ease with a woman. Maybe rare wasn't the right word. *Different.* He approached his relationships much the same way he approached everything in life: defensively. He would skim the surface of the water at high speed, enjoying the ride but always looking around for the direction to turn once something got in his way. Sometimes he would turn and leave it all behind, but usually the obstacle popped up too suddenly, too soon, and he would smash into it, disintegrating into a million bits of excuses and anger. In either case, it never ended well.

But Anne was different. He wasn't even *in* a relationship with her, but he didn't feel the need to look too far ahead with her. Perhaps it was because she could already do that, so he could settle back and let the other person do the navigating. Whatever the reason, Jonas was content to stop wondering and just let things happen.

"Now you're *thinking* too much," she said, looking up at him. The V of her dress tightened against the inside of her breasts as she arched back into the couch.

"I'm not allowed to talk or think?"

She smiled. "You've changed," she said.

"Changed? You barely know me."

"Your accident on the Beltway. It changed you, didn't it?"

He felt his defense mechanisms screaming to be unleashed. "I don't stop for stranded motorists anymore."

She didn't chide him for avoiding the subject, but she didn't back down either. "You're fascinated by him."

"Sonman?"

She nodded.

"Fascinated?" Jonas looked down at her, but looked away as he decided to tell her the truth. "Maybe I am. Maybe I'm fascinated by someone who just doesn't care. By someone who just does whatever the hell he wants to do. No moral boundaries. It's in complete contrast to what I was raised to be."

"Do his ... his moral freedoms make you jealous?"

"What kind of question is that?"

"It's just a question, Jonas. Do you wonder what it would feel like to do whatever you wanted to do, regardless of societal laws?"

He took a deep breath. "Doesn't everyone wonder that at some point?"

"Maybe," she said. "And maybe he's out there, wondering what it would feel like to be normal."

"I have no idea what he's thinking."

"I'm not trying to make him sympathetic, Jonas. I just think it's okay to try to understand monsters, even as we work to destroy them."

Jonas pictured himself sitting with his father, talking to him, letting himself be open and honest. Dropping his shield. He closed his eyes and began to speak.

"I *have* changed. The accident made me think of ... of all the memories I told you about. Of what I saw. Of how I nearly died." He felt himself disappearing deeper within his words. "It was the one moment when I experienced an evil that very few people get to see. And that moment, that *one moment* in that apartment in Mogadishu, I realized for the first time my life deviated from some kind of script."

"Script?"

His eyes remained closed. "Everything I've ever done seems according to some kind of plan. Some kind of linear progression, a roadmap to achievement. Good childhood, good schools, military service, good career. I've always gone according to plan." Jonas licked his lips. "But the horror that day, it was as if there was a break in the plan. A tear in my life, where something completely raw and evil and ... *real* ... leaked in."

"And how did that make you feel?"

Jonas paused for nearly a minute, knowing the truth but not wanting to say it. "I didn't realize it until I started remembering it all again, but ... I don't know even how to say it. It *excites* me."

Her tone didn't change. "Excites you?"

"In a way, yeah. The thrill of being faced with such horror, and battling to overcome it. It *is* exciting, even as fucking horrible as it all is."

"Are you unhappy with the way your life turned out?"

"Not at all. But ... goddamnit, this is going to sound really arrogant, so I'm just going to say it. I feel like I'm meant for greater things than being a Senator's Chief of Staff."

She was silent for a moment. "Maybe you have a hero complex. You always want to save everyone. The problem is that most people don't need saving, or at least don't want to be saved. That kind of complex wreaks havoc on relationships."

Well, shit, that would explain a lot, Jonas thought.

"Is that it, Jonas?"

His eyes were still closed but he sensed she was closer. He felt her looking up at him from the couch.

"Do you want to save people?"

"It's not so much that I want to save people," he said, his voice barely above a whisper. "Sometimes I feel like I'm *supposed* to save people." He finally opened his eyes. "Does that make sense?"

"Do you think you're supposed to be the one to stop Sonman?"

He looked down at her, as she looked up at him. In that moment, in that light, and in that blink of unguarded honesty, she seemed perfect to him. "Maybe I do. Does that sound stupid?"

She smiled, genuine and inviting. "Yeah, you sound a little stupid."

Jonas laughed, louder than he expected, but it felt good. Everything was new with Anne. Everything was fresh, pure.

"I'm okay with that," he said.

"Good, because I've always had a thing for dumb jocks."

"That I doubt. So what now?"

She reached back with her right hand and brushed her fingertips against his pants leg before moving up and grabbing the bottom of his tie.

She pulled on the tie.

Jonas leaned and hovered over her face, their lips inches apart, reversed from each other.

"You don't have to be a mind-reader," she said. He could smell the wine on her breath mixed with a trace of perfume that still sprinkled her long neck.

His lips just brushed hers at first. Back and forth, not for fear of committing, but for savoring that very first contact, the headiness of nascent intimacy. Her hand moved from his tie and then slipped behind the back of his head. She pulled him against her, and they finally kissed, fully, their mouths pressing, their tongues tracing outlines on each other's lips.

Jonas set his wine glass on the floor as he broke from her. He kept his fingers on her shoulder and walked around the couch, wanting to share the space next to her.

"No," she said, holding a hand up.

"What?"

Rather than answering, she rose and came to him instead. She clasped his hand and brought herself toward him. Standing, he could feel all of her through the thin fabric of her dress. She draped both arms behind his neck and his hands instinctively slipped around her waist. As she leaned in to kiss him, he pulled her closer, feeling the curves of her waist and fullness of her breasts. She tasted like summer, he thought, not even knowing what that was supposed to taste like. It was the taste of sun on your face.

"You're thinking again," she said, her words twisted by his lips.

He moved his head and kissed her neck, tracing the curve up from her shoulder with his tongue. "But I'm thinking good things."

She tilted her head to give him more access, breathing out a long sigh as she did. "Then I suppose I'll allow it."

He continued exploring her skin with his lips, wanting more with every taste. After a moment, Anne put her hand on his shoulder and took a step back from him. Then she reached up and hooked her thumbs under the straps of her dress, pulling them over her shoulders. She unzipped the back of the dress and shimmied out of it, revealing to Jonas a tight-fitting black chemise underneath.

His urges told him to grab her and consume her, but his mind argued for allowing the vision of her to settle in just awhile longer. Several seconds passed as Jonas remained speechless in front of her.

"What's the matter?" she teased. "Scared?"

"A little bit," he said, drawing a laugh from her. "You always wear something like that under your dress?"

She took the first step, draping a hand over his shoulder. Her smile glowed in the soft light of the room, and her kinked hair bounced off her naked skin, almost floating.

"Let's just say I get a sense about when I might need to."

His hand found the small of her back and his fingers pressed into her.

"I think I'm becoming a believer," he said.

CHAPTER TWENTY-SEVEN

WASHINGTON D.C.
APRIL 20

RUDIGER WALKS INTO the church, hoping for solitude. He wants to leave Washington. Not much time. Wants to be away from those who might now know who he is, who might be looking for him. They talked to Mary by now. The shelter worker. Her description of him would be in the hands of every cop out there.

But he can't leave. Not yet. He's close to understanding. He can feel it. If he leaves now, his purpose will die.

The feeling is *strong* here.

The church is Catholic, which means nothing to Rudiger. It smells of books, he thinks, walking through the narthex and toward the nave. Old books, left to settle in collecting dust, unopened for years at a time. The church is vast but empty. Hole of solitude from the streets outside the heavy wooden doors.

He doesn't know what to do. He thinks about sitting in a pew. Would the message come to him then? The answers he needs, would they transmit like some kind of holy radio wave from the statue of Christ that hangs above the altar? Or would they be written in a puzzle he could solve by rearranging the letters in his mind?

Vibrant colors. Red and green and blue. Light bursting through stained glass. Haze of dust.

Then he sees them to his right, three in a row. Confessional booths. Never been in one, he thinks.

He hears a cough, faint and brief, muffled behind more than just a hand. In one of the booths. It's the first sign. First directional arrow.

Rudiger walks over, his footsteps soundless despite the vacuum of noise. He opens up the first door and peers through the wooden slats separating the chambers of the booth. He sees a silhouette.

Good.

Rudiger closes the door behind him and sits on the wooden bench. Cold and hard.

"Hello, my son."

Rudiger feels uncertain.

"Hello."

"And how long has it been since your last confession?"

The priest's voice suggests a young man, certainly too young to address Rudiger as *my son*. The tone of it suggests eagerness. Perhaps someone new to the business. Someone thankful to help.

"Never been."

A silence settles between the two men.

"Very well. Are you familiar with confession?"

"No."

"It ... it is a process by which you can heal your soul and regain the grace of God."

Rudiger considers this. "I do believe I've never lost God's grace."

A pause. "Are you Catholic?"

"I don't know what I am. Christian."

"Why do you say that?"

"Because Christ commands me."

A longer pause. "As He should, my son. He commands all true believers."

Rudiger doesn't believe this.

The silence becomes thick and the priest adds: "Are you unwell?"

"Unwell?"

The response is carefully measured. "Confession is … not to be taken lightly. It is important the penitent be of sound faith and … mind."

Rudiger digests the words. "You think I'm crazy?"

"No … just concerned. You're unsure of your own religious history, and that *is* somewhat unusual."

Rudiger slowly scratches his pant leg with a long fingernail. "For our purposes here, *Father*, let's jes assume I'm suited."

The priest coughs. "Very well, then. Let us continue." Rudiger hears the man's voice crack on the last words. "Do you have mortal or venial sins to confess?"

Rudiger understands the words. "Mortal, Father, but I don't come seeking absolution. I jes need advice."

"Advice will come after confession, my son. Mortal sins need to be confessed in order to save your soul."

"My soul ain't in jeopardy."

"I don't believe that's for you to decide." Rudiger could hear the impatience creeping into the priest's voice. "Please confess so that we may continue."

Rudiger's scratching is audible and small frays from the denim of his pant leg are now visible. He wonders if this is a test – would God make him confess out loud what he has done in order to receive his next instructions?

"If my sins involved a crime, do you have to tell the police?"

Rudiger sees the silhouette lengthen, as if the man just sat up a little. "No," the priest says. "The veil of the confessional disallows it. But I would likely encourage the penitent to turn himself in."

Rudiger feels a sense of freedom creep over him, the shackles of discourse removed. "My crimes are done for God, for He has directed me so. Man cannot punish me."

The priest leans closer to the wooden slats.

"Tell me your sins."

"Where do I even begin?"

"The most grievous."

Rudiger sits back and thinks, for "grievous" is certainly a matter of opinion. He feels the stones in his throat as the words roll out in a slow, gravely tone. "I killed a family. Shot a man and a woman, then, with my knife, removed the head of a baby. I held a young girl down and bit her ear off. I was going to stab her, but I wanted her ear first. Don't know why. I think it's because of the Preacherman, and what he did to *my* ear." Rudiger reached up and feels the rough scarring of his left ear. "I remember the taste of her blood. The texture. Thin, almost like water. Sickly."

Rudiger stops speaking. There is silence on the other side of the booth.

"That, Father, is my only grievous sin I can remember, for I committed it without any reason I can speak of. But I think it was a test. A test to see if I could do what was required of me next."

Rudiger stops talking. He stops scratching. All he can hear is breathing through the wooden slats. The breaths are more rapid than before.

"What you have told me is indeed a mortal sin, my son. I must ask you: is it true?"

"You think I'm lyin'?"

"Is it true?"

"It's only the beginning."

The man's voice begins to shake. "You need more than help

from God, my son. We will finish here, and then let me take you to some people that can help you."

"The police?"

"You need help."

"I need *answers*. I'm not crazy. There is a reason for what I do, and I can stop doing it all if I just find the One."

"I want to help you. Do you want to tell me your name?"

Rudiger doesn't want to give a name, even a false one. His fingers instinctively reach under his shirt and find the knife sheathed against his skin.

"He told me to. In Jerusalem. He told me to release Him."

"Who did? Who told you?"

Rudiger looks at the rosary hanging from a dull metal hook inside the booth. "The only One who could give such an instruction."

The priest's voice lowers to a near whisper. "I don't understand."

"Then I guess you can't help me." Rudiger begins to stand.

"Wait. Don't go."

Rudiger flicks the snap of his sheath open with his thumb. His fingers caress the handle of the blade.

"I want to hear more," the priest adds. "I *can* help you." His voice continues to shake and Rudiger can hear the priest breathing faster.

Rudiger sits and considers. The conversation can only go so many ways, and one way ends with the priest bleeding silently to death, waiting for the next parishioner to discover him. Rudiger doesn't want that. He wants answers. He considers the options and decides he has little to lose.

He leans back and pulls air through his nose.

"First man I killed was the Preacherman," he says. "I was twelve, 'bout a month shy of thirteen. He nearly had me, too. Nearly captured my soul and tucked it away in his pocket, forever his to keep. Preacherman raped me. His whore raped me. Beat me. Starved me. Not that I'm looking for pity here, jes telling you what happened is all."

He pauses. The priest says nothing.

"The third day he had me, after he fucked me, he beat me in the face with an old Bible. Smelled like sweat, that book. Sweat and use. Pages wet with my tears. He threw it in my face. Told me to read it, to *believe* it, that it was the only thing gonna save me. Belief in something better coming. Told me I best read that book if I want to understand the difference between good and bad. So I laid there on those dirty sheets and I read it, interrupted only by the two of them comin' in the room when they felt their urges comin' on."

He never even told his parents what happened to him. But now he has to tell the story. It's what's required.

"So I read. I read the whole thing. And it was the best thing that ever could have happened to me, because I knew the Rapture would save me. No matter what happened to my body, the Rapture would free my soul, so it didn't matter what Preacherman or his woman did to me. Earthly pain. Eternal salvation. Goddamn. Preacherman destroyed me and saved me at the same time, is what he did. You believe me, Priest?"

The priest was quiet for a moment. "Yes. I believe you."

"In the first month I tried to escape, but didn't make it. Preacherman sliced my ear open for that one, nearly taking it off. Then he stitched me back up, kissing my head the whole time. Kissing my bloody hair. Tellin' me he was sorry and whatnot. His whore even gave me a little extra food for three days after, told me I needed to get my strength back."

Rudiger laughs. He doesn't remember the last time he did that.

"She gave me strength all right. Strength of *resolution*. Strength of *belief*. Because that day I knew it, jes knew it. Knew no one was coming for me. Knew I had to do it all myself. Bring it all about myself. And then I finally got around to doin' it."

"Doing what?" the priest asks.

"Waiting for the moment he finally let up his guard. Then shovin' that knife down Preacherman's mouth, splitting his throat open. Taking his ear off, as he had nearly done with mine. He wasn't expecting that. No, sir. Not at all. He got relaxed. Thought I was forever weak. He got lazy. Got careless. And you know what, Priest? If he hadn't given me that book, well, maybe that's just what woulda happened. Maybe I woulda been his forever. But that book told me better things would come, so I made it happen. He bled all over that concrete floor, and his body shook like a million volts were going through it as he died. Fishlike. Eyes wide open, staring to nothing. Would've killed the whore, too, but she wasn't there. And that day I upped and walked out of that little house and found my way back home, slow but sure. Resolute."

Another laugh. Feels *good*.

"I never told nobody, 'cept my sister. They found him, of course. I buried his ear and the knife I killed him with, but everyone just about knew I did it. But no one ever made me talk. They tried. They *all* tried. But I never told. My parents couldn't understand, so they took it out on each other, which is what I suppose married people do. Never found the whore-woman. She just disappeared like those kind of people do. Back into the ashes and some such." *Though I swear I killed the ghost of her in Cleveland*, he didn't add. "But I tell you this, Priest. From that day on I had purpose. Rapture is coming, and I am ready. Ready for the end. So close. *So close*. Which is why you have to help."

The church grows old as the two men sit in silence.

Rudiger then tells the priest of Jerusalem, and the words Christ spoke to him.

"You say you were institutionalized in Jerusalem?"

"I was held for ... observation."

"Is it conceivable that ... forgive me ... is it conceivable that you are one of many who have been merely overwhelmed by the spiritual significance of the Holy Land? That what you thought you heard was nothing more than your own faith transcending logic?"

Rudiger slips the knife from the sheath and turns it over in his hand.

"Don't matter," Rudiger says. "You can choose to believe or not believe. What matters is my purpose, and how you can direct me in it."

"What is your purpose?"

"To find the One."

"Why hasn't Christ told this to you?"

It's one answer Rudiger doesn't know. The source of his love and his frustration. It is the reason he's here. "I ... think He wants me to grow in this journey," Rudiger answers. "Wants my faith to grow by finding my own answers, and only in doing so will I be successful. I've killed three people in my mission. They were all wrong."

"You've killed *three* other people?"

"Killed two men because I thought they were the One." He pauses. Looks at his knife. "And a woman. Jes ... because I was supposed to."

"The ... the men." The priest's words were slow and controlled. "Did ... did they die the same way Christ died?"

"Yes they did."

Rudiger realizes his error. His killings have made national news. The priest now knows he's sitting inches away from a man hunted across the country. Rudiger squeezes the grip of his blade and wills himself not to be impulsive.

"Have to leave now," Rudiger says. "Need to finish up my work."

"No. Don't go. Let me help you."

"If you could help me you would've done it by now."

The priest's silhouette shakes slightly, a quiet tremble. His words strain to reach Rudiger's ears.

"Please. Not yet."

Rudiger leans toward the slats. "You want to help me? Tell me why God doesn't let me succeed. *He* told me to do these things. I didn't want to. It's all because of *Him*. But now He won't let me finish."

The priest remains silent.

Rudiger's voice becomes harsh, the frustration and suppressed rage leaking out in a hiss. "That's what I thought. I'm running out of time. Don't you see that? Here. Here. In *this* city. I'm close. Jes need more guidance. Tell me. Who is it? Who's next?"

The priest is silent for so long Rudiger wonders if he'll ever speak again. Finally: "I can't tell you who to kill next. You and I need to go to the police together, son. You can be helped. It's the only way you can save yourself."

Rudiger spits on the floor in anger. His knuckles strain from the grip on the blade. "Don't need help. I need *direction*."

"You need to find peace. And you need help to find it."

Rudiger is struck by the words.

Find peace.

Something so familiar about the words, and he senses of all the words exchanged in this shanty of wood and hope, these are the ones he's supposed to hear.

Find peace.

"Thank you, Father. You've been most helpful."

Before the priest can answer, Rudiger pushes open the door and walks out of the church, his feet taking him through a winding series of streets and alleys and back into an anonymity that serves him better than any weapon.

CHAPTER TEWNTY-EIGHT

"CHRIST, JONAS, YOU look like shit."

"You know, sir, I never tire of you telling me that."

Jonas kept stride with the Senator as they reached the initial security detail outside the White House. A bird chirped somewhere in the distance, and Jonas thought about how that bird had no fucking clue its nest was right next to the home of the most powerful person in the world.

"You stay up late preparing for this?"

That, Jonas thought, and some other extracurricular activities. Jonas had worked through the night as Anne slept peacefully in his bed. For the first time in a long time, Jonas found it difficult to leave a woman in the morning.

"Yes, sir."

"So you're not just going to wing it?" the Senator cracked.

"Not unless you want me to."

"Not particularly."

They were met by one of the President's aides, a woman who looked no older than thirty. Jonas had been to the White House before but never the West Wing, and he was struck by how much smaller everything seemed than what he had expected. It was like walking onto a television studio set and finally sensing the actual proportions of something he had only ever seen on TV, and it left him feeling underwhelmed. He knew that would change as soon as he met the President.

"He's running late," the aide said. "Shouldn't be too long a wait."

"Where are we meeting?" Sidams asked.

"Roosevelt Room."

She led them down a short corridor and escorted them into a conference room. A long table with more than a dozen chairs sat in the center of the room. The walls were a creamy yellow, the color of aged paper. A large painting of FDR occupied a spot next to a grandfather clock that softly clicked away the time.

"Maybe fifteen, twenty minutes," she said. Her teeth were perfect, Jonas noted, something she must have been well aware of since she used every opportunity she could to smile. "There's water on the table. Can I get you anything else?"

"Do you have espresso?" Jonas asked.

"We're *fine*," the Senator said, his words stomping with authority over Jonas's query.

"Very well, then." Another smile, a delicate turn, and the aide disappeared from the room, closing the door behind her as she left.

Sidams turned. "We're in the White House for chrissakes. Ask for something American, will ya?"

"Like shitty watered-down coffee?"

"Exactly like that."

"Noted."

Jonas sat at the table and spread papers before him like a dealer at a blackjack table. He studied his notes for a few minutes before realizing he was at the point where if he studied more, he'd forget it all. He needed to divert his attention.

"I think I'm in love," he said.

The Senator buried his face in his hands. "Oh, sweet Jesus."

"Yeah, I think so."

"How many times have you slept with her?" Sidams asked.

"Once. About nine hours ago."

"That's not love, son. That's just the endorphins talking."

"You don't think it's possible?"

Sidams shook his head, an Army General disappointed in his troops. "Shit, Jonas, I didn't even love my wife until the fifth year of our marriage."

"That's just sad."

"But true nonetheless. Anything before that is just lust mixed with curiosity. Only when those two things have worn off do you find out what's really left."

"That's really depressing," Jonas said.

The Senator dismissed the comment with a wave of his hand. "Not at all. It's heaven. But only if you get to travel a lot with your job."

Jonas reminded himself yet another time never to get married. They spoke on the subject of love and marriage for several more minutes until the banter threatened to give way to Jonas having to reveal true emotion, so he let the conversation die a quiet and noble death.

A comfortable and lengthy silence settled in between them, the kind that can only exist between two people who are more than mere colleagues. They were friends, Jonas knew, and because of that he felt a growing need to tell the Senator more about what he had been doing with his free time. It had become almost a conspiracy, he thought. With Anne, Jonas was tracking down a serial killer, something he had no right or skill set to do. But it was personal to him, which, in his mind, somehow afforded him latitude.

Of course, they had no way of actually knowing Sonman was the killer so sought after, and their inability to afford evidence permitted them to keep all the information to themselves. Jonas's involvement had surpassed the point where he should have told the Senator about it, and each passing day the prospect of doing just that became all the more pressing and simultaneously less appealing.

"I need to tell you something," Jonas said.

The Senator was distracted by his BlackBerry. "Mmmmm-hmmmmm?"

"Michael Calloway."

Sidams kept his gaze on the glowing little screen.

"What about him?"

Jonas squeezed his eyes shut for just a second, releasing his words along with his breath. "I think I know ..."

Sidams's head turned toward him.

"Know what?"

Then the door opened and the President of the United States walked in the room.

CHAPTER TWENTY-NINE

JONATHON ROSWELL CALDER was a tall man, the kind of tall that imposed rather than towered. Broad. Solid. His physical traits helped with the election – during the debates, the moment he shook hands with his opponent it was clear to all viewing who could kick ass and who could do nothing but take a beating. Despite all the issues that divided the two candidates, some polling experts posited that Calder's menacing stature *assured* Americans.

They called it the Schwarzenegger Effect. It didn't hurt that the Calder served with distinction in Vietnam, earning two Purple Hearts.

The President walked into the room and immediately owned it. Following him was William Stages, the U.S. Ambassador to the U.N. and a smaller but powerful player in the Accords. Jonas knew Stages by reputation but had never met him.

"Robert, how are you?" Calder extended his hand and Sidams took it with obvious pleasure, not because the Senator needed to kiss the President's ass but because he truly admired the man. Calder had been in office less than a year, shattering the hopes and dreams of millions of Republicans who had enjoyed White House and Senate majority occupation for sixteen years. In ten months, Calder had enacted enough programs to make the conservative right scream socialism and the moderate left feel proud about the path the country was taking for the first time in almost two decades.

"Mr. President," Sidams said, gripping Calder's hand. "Good job on *Meet the Press* last weekend."

"I hate those things."

"Presidents don't normally do them."

Calder allowed himself a stolen grin. "But I'm not a normal President."

"Yessir." The Senator turned to Stages. "Bill, good to see you."

"I'm pleased to be helping you with the Accords," Stages said. His enormous belly threatened to breech his shirt. "I think this could be the right team to get something done finally."

"Amen to that." Sidams turned to Jonas, who only just realized he was standing at military attention. "At ease, soldier," Sidams cracked.

"Old habit," Jonas said. He quickly slid his sweaty palm against his pant leg before extending his hand to the President. "Jonas Osbourne, sir. I'm the Senator's Chief of Staff."

Calder took his hand and shook it. Jonas felt the raw strength in the grip; it wasn't the iron grip power players sometimes give just to overcompensate, but rather the reserved grip of someone who could really do some damage. Jonas fleetingly thought of George Washington, who was rumored to have been able to break open a walnut shell with one hand.

Calder released first. "Of course, Jonas. How's your father doing?"

Jonas was stunned. The President must have been briefed.

"He's fine, sir." The statement felt empty, and Jonas felt a disservice to his father for saying it, even to the President. "Actually," he added, "he's not well at all, but I appreciate you asking about him."

"Nasty disease," Calder said. "Very hard for the family to watch."

"Yes, sir."

"We served at the same time in Vietnam," Calder said. "I didn't know him. I was on the ground. He was in the air."

"I'll give him your regards when I visit him."

"Please do," Calder said. The President took a step past Jonas and surveyed the room, while Jonas introduced himself to Stages. There was a knock on the door and a different aide entered before permission was granted.

"Mr. President, we're running about twenty minutes –"

"Adrian, I know the schedule," Calder said, looking at the grandfather clock. "We're late. We're always late. They can wait."

"Yes, sir." The aide disappeared.

Calder turned and looked at Jonas.

"You were a Ranger."

"Yes, sir."

"Mogadishu. Ninety-three."

"That's correct, sir."

Calder nodded, his approval clear.

"You were wounded by one of your own men," he said.

Where is this going? Jonas wondered.

"A private in my command reacted adversely to a tense situation."

"I read up on you," Calder said. His voice had a hint of New England inflection. "I know Robert here is the name attached to the Peace Accords, but I also know how much he likes to delegate. The Accords are critical for my presidency, so I make sure to know about all the players involved." The President paused as he looked at Jonas. The grandfather clock ticked quietly away behind him. "He threw a grenade at you," Calder said. "That's what the report on the incident says."

"Yes, sir. He killed a Somali family."

"Jesus Christ." The room fell silent as Jonas wondered whether he said too much. "Somalia was a mess as it was," Calder continued. "Doesn't help when your own men go rogue."

"Yes, sir." Jonas had a sudden and burning urge to tell the President everything. Everything he wanted to tell Sidams. Everything about Rudy Sonman.

"Tell me about Denver," Calder said, changing the subject. "I don't want the details, not yet. Give me the overview."

Everyone in the room remained standing as Jonas did as commanded. He gave his briefing, mentally slicing through his rehearsals and lopping off details he could sense the President didn't want. He spoke for less than five minutes, and the whole time President Calder remained silent and motionless. Unreadable.

Jonas finished and no one stepped in to fill the void. Finally, Calder nodded his head. "Good," he said. "Good." Then he took a step toward Jonas. "Jonas, I don't want this to be a bullshit summit. Every President has a bullshit peace summit. The leaders meet for a photo op of a handshake, then they go home and keep pushing bulldozers through houses. I don't want that. If we can't get something done in Denver, I don't even want to have it. Trying is not enough."

Sidams spoke. "We understand, Mr. President, and we're completely committed to this effort."

Calder turned toward the Senator. "I know you are, Robert. Your political capital is on the line here. Bill's, too. We all have our careers at some kind of risk here, don't we?" The President took a step back to better address all three men in the room.

"Gentlemen, let me tell you what I want. I want a Palestinian state by the end of my first term, just like I promised. We're not likely to have another summit, so this is our best shot while everyone's sitting at the same table. I want to be tough and I don't want bullshit promises. Israel and the PLO are as close politically as they've ever been so the time is now or never. But we're going to have to ask Israel to give up more than they have ever been willing to do. Asking will be the easy part. Getting them to do it will take both brains and balls. Understood?"

"Understood," Sidams said.

Calder turned back to Jonas. "You look like a tough son of a bitch. You up for the task?"

"I am, sir."

Sidams quipped, "He just got hit by a car and lived to tell about it."

"Yeah," the President said, shaking hands and preparing to leave. "I read about that. But let me tell you something. If I had to choose between a speeding car or a pissed off Israeli coming head on towards me, I'd choose the car."

CHAPTER THIRTY

CALL ME

Anne's text message glared at Jonas. He wondered what she wanted.

"Good job," Sidams said. Jonas kept a half-step behind Sidams as the men walked away from the White House. "There'll be more briefings as we get closer, but that was good. You didn't seem nervous."

"I was scared as hell," Jonas said.

"I doubt that."

"Okay, maybe a little anxious."

"You did fine." The Senator sucked in a heavy breath. "Goddamn we have a lot of work to do before this thing."

"That we do." Jonas slowed his pace. "I'm going to make a call – mind if I meet you back in the office?"

"No problem." Then the Senator stopped. "Hey, what were you talking about earlier? About Michael Calloway?"

Jonas thought through the several different ways he could go with this before deciding on the easy out. "It's something I need to talk to you about, but I think it can wait a bit."

"Are you in over your head with something? Are you losing time at work over it?"

Yes, Jonas thought. And *yes*.

"No."

Sidams nodded. "Good enough for me, then. I trust you. Fill me in later, but it better not be something that bites us in the ass."

"Yes, sir."

The Senator continued his walk alone towards his office as Jonas dialed Anne.

"There you are," she said. "How was your meeting with the President?"

"It was good," he said. "I outlined my health care plan for him and he seemed to like it?"

"Oh, yeah? What plan is that?"

"Survival of the fittest. No doctors. No medicine. Just Darwinism."

"Oh, that sounds just like something a Democrat would *love*."

"Hey, it would save a ton of money."

"Seriously, Jonas, how was it?"

"It was great, actually."

"Tell me all about it later?"

Jonas smiled into his phone. "I'd love to. So your message sounded urgent. Or are you usually an all-caps texter? Because that could get annoying."

Anne's tone changed instantly. "A woman was beaten to death a couple of weeks ago in Cleveland."

"Sonman?"

"She was killed in her home. But there was security video inside a grocery store where she had just been shopping. Shows her interacting briefly with a man who followed her out of the store. He's unidentified, but police entered his physical description into the NCIC database."

"Let me guess. He had a nasty scar on his ear."

"I've had a standing order to flag any ear injuries that come across the database. This is the first hit."

"It's not his M.O. Why would he beat a woman to death?"

"Hold on. You think I would call you with this kind of flimsy story? It gets more interesting."

"Tell me."

"The video image was shown on the local news. It was picked up by other affiliates in the region. There had been a few tips, but nothing that's been fruitful. One of the tips came from a woman in Pittsburgh. Name's Rose Fitzgerald."

"So?"

"So, she says she thinks she knows the guy. Said he looks like her long lost brother, who ran away from home when he was seventeen. Said he had a horrible wound to his ear."

"What else did she say?"

Anne paused. "She said his name was Rudiger."

CHAPTER THIRTY-ONE

JONAS LOOKED AT the clock on his computer. Just after ten. Even with the longer days the sun had disappeared hours before he'd last gotten up to get more coffee, and now he found himself alone in the office, the halogens above him humming like a distant swarm of insects. Even the workhorse Senator had gone home. Jonas had work to do, in fact he had so much it didn't matter how much coffee he drank because he'd never get to it.

But that wasn't why he was still at work.

His phone chirped the arrival of a text message. Anne.

She's here.

Okay, Jonas thought. Here we go. He punched the tiny keys on his BlackBerry.

Same address you gave me earlier?

Yes.

Be there in 15.

The drive was easy, especially at this time of night. Jonas felt a gnawing anxiousness as he gripped the steering wheel.

Tonight, Jonas thought. *Tonight we're going to have to tell the FBI everything.*

They met at a safe house. Jonas had never been to one before.

The safe house was in fact a dilapidated townhouse, one of several in a grouping that extended a city block. Ugly, homogenous, forgettable. Perfectly sensible for the purpose it served.

Jonas checked the address as he walked along a cracked sidewalk toward the unit. He noticed a grey sedan across the street with two silhouettes in the front seat. Jonas tucked the image not far beneath the surface of his most conscious thoughts.

Anne opened the door before he knocked. She kissed him on the cheek as she let him in.

"Why are we meeting here?" he asked.

She nodded to the gray sedan across the street. "They're doing us a favor because I was the one who saw the significance of her tip. If we went straight with her to the Hoover Building, there's no way we'd get to talk to her first. I have a friend who's letting us talk to her here first. We get an hour."

"That's a good friend."

"I told him we'd get more out of her than they will. They still don't know what they have here."

Jonas walked in the townhouse and peered into the living room, seeing no one. "Where is she?"

Anne nodded and shut the door. "In the kitchen."

Jonas turned the corner past the living room and found the woman sitting at a dusty glass kitchen table, a can of Diet Coke nestled inside the loose grip of her right hand.

She was hunched over the table. Skinny. Pale skin and a faded long-sleeve t-shirt. Dirty blond hair sprung from darker roots in uncombed ropes, hanging down, hiding her face. Jonas noticed the tattoo on her left arm, some kind of serpent, the ink faded, the outline washed. Tribute to a decades-old decision.

"Hello," he said, hoping not to startle her. "I'm Jonas."

She looked up, her bright blue eyes flashing at him. They were the only features of her face that still held beauty. She wasn't old, but she had aged hard, as if she crammed a life's worth of living in a few short years. But he could see that once she was probably the type of woman men fought over. Now, she was a few years and a handful of bad decisions short of beautiful.

"I'm Rose," she said. "Rose Fitzgerald."

Anne entered the kitchen and took command. "Rose," she said, "Jonas is helping me with this investigation. As I explained in the car, we'll be talking to you for a little bit here and then you'll be interviewed more thoroughly by the FBI. Between all of us we are desperately trying to find your brother."

Rose looked at Jonas. "You with the FBI?"

"No, ma'am. I have a personal interest in this case that goes back to my time in the Army. I served with your brother."

Jonas asked, "When was the last time you saw your brother?"

"When he was seventeen. I was fifteen."

"Where was that?"

She nodded out the window. "Close to here. Virginia, where we grew up."

Jonas noticed her accent.

Anne took a seat at the table across from Rose. Jonas remained standing.

"Where are your parents now?" Anne asked.

"Mom is dead. Car accident. Dad's still in Virginia, though a different town. Don't talk to him much." Rose took a sip from her soda. Jonas watched her effort to swallow.

"When did you move to Pittsburgh?" Anne asked.

"'bout ten years ago."

Anne's questioning was slow and casual. Friendly, but cautious. "What do you do for a living, Rose?"

"Worked at Home Depot until about three months ago. Got laid off. Bad economy and all."

"That must have been hard for you."

"Not lookin' for pity."

Anne let the silence settle in the kitchen for a few moments. Jonas watched her study Rose, just the way she had studied him the first time they met at Calloway's funeral. She was scanning for a connection.

"What we're here to do is understand more about your brother's background. Anything that might help us find him. Now, we don't have much time, so do you mind if I go ahead and ask you some questions about him?"

She shook her head. "That's what I came here for, right?"

"Right." Anne leaned forward in her chair. "Rose, did you ever marry? I ask because you and your brother don't share the same last name."

"No. He was always Fitzgerald. Must have changed it." Her words were heavy and dull, dropping out of her mouth like lead. "I jes know it was him, though. I mean, the image on the video wasn't that clear. But ... it was *him*. At first I didn't see it, because he looked so different. But the way he stood. The way he *leaned*. And his ear."

"Tell us about his ear."

Jonas spoke up. "It was a childhood injury," he said. "I remember it from the Army. I don't remember what he said happened, but there's a scar that ran down the side of his left ear and onto his cheek."

"Knife," Rose said. "Happened to him when he was twelve ..." Her voice trailed.

"He never made contact after you last saw him?" Anne said. "Not with your parents either?"

"No. Nothing."

Anne took a moment to study Rose. Then, she said in a low voice, "Did you think your brother was dead?"

"Why would I think that?"

"It's ..." Anne shifted her gaze briefly to Jonas and then back to her subject. "It's a sense I get from you. You ... you connect death with your brother somehow."

Rose looked uncomfortable. "What do you mean 'sense?'"

"Anne is very intuitive," Jonas said. "It's what makes her a good investigator and why the FBI uses her services."

Rose looked from Jonas to Anne and finally to the table. "No, I didn't think he was dead. I guess I never thought about it much. We were never close."

"Rose, why did Rudy leave home? What happened to his ear?"

Dampened shouts from a domestic argument bled through the walls of the townhome, the man's voice deep, full of bass and vitriol. Jonas couldn't make out the words, but he didn't have to. Rose shifted in her seat and tapped a long, painted nail on the side of the sweating soda can.

Anne didn't repeat her questions. She sat and patiently waited for Rose to speak first.

Jonas focused on the argument in the neighboring townhouse. He made out a garbled *bitch* and a *fucking*. The woman yelled something and then enough silence settled in to make Jonas wait for the sound of a gun firing a single shell. It didn't come.

Rose began to tell her story.

CHAPTER THIRTY-TWO

"I WAS JES ten," she said, "when Rudy came back home ..." Rose's voice was slow and controlled; her words soft. Appalachian drawl laced with melancholy. Her gaze remained fixed on the table. "I remember when he opened up the front door. It was night, jes after dinner. The search for him had died down. It'd been two months and all, and, though no one ever said it out loud, I think we all thought Rudy was gone forever."

Rose tapped on her can again. A short but powerful burst of a yell came from next door, but she didn't seem to even notice.

"He'd been abducted?" Anne asked.

"Yes. That's right. Abducted at twelve years old."

Anne placed a recorder on the table. In her softest voice, she said, "Do you mind if I tape this?"

Rose shrugged.

Anne pressed the record button and nodded at Rose to continue.

"Rudy opened up the front door and looked like little-boy death. Skinny. Dirty. Dried blood all over his face. Eyes wide like a doll's. Unblinking. No one moved for a moment. We all jes thought he was a ghost, you know? Least that's what I thought.

I was scared to death of the boy at the door. He sure wasn't my brother – least not the one I remembered. Then finally my mom screamed and ran over to him, falling all over the skin and bones standing in the entryway. She scooped him up and she jes cried. My dad called the police, and I sat there and watched it all, unbelieving. Rudy was back."

Jonas leaned forward. "What happened to him?"

Rose didn't look up. She shook her head and kept staring at her soda can. "Rudy didn't talk for the first three months he was home. Not a word. Took him to all sorts of psychologists and counselors, but he just sat there, dumb. They knew he'd been abused. Had a long nasty cut along his ear." Rose drew her finger along the left side of her head. "Bruises on his face and body. Damn nearly starved to death. And doctor said he'd been raped. Repeatedly."

Jonas tried to see the face of a twelve-year-old Sonman in his mind and couldn't. "Jesus Christ."

"Police found a dead man a few miles away in an old abandoned house. Throat cut and mouth split wide open. Ear missing. Found a basement with locks on the doors and found Rudy's blood down there on an old mattress. No one knew if Rudy killed the man or someone else did, but his death allowed Rudy to escape."

"Did they find out who he was?"

"Rudy called him the Preacherman."

"So Rudy started talking?"

"Never about what happened to anyone but me. And that was jes one time."

"What did he say happened?"

The world seemed heavy on Rose. "It was five years later, jes before he left home for good. Rudy was different by then, and

I was too self-absorbed to really give a shit. My parents had split up and my mom went to go live in Phoenix with some guy she met at a conference. But Rudy was the stain on the family. He was so smart, but he was horrible in school. Failed every class."

"How do you know he was smart?" Anne asked. Jonas noticed she wasn't pressing Rose to tell them what Rudy said happened to him.

"Because ... because he could do, like, insane math problems in his head. And he was always doing word jumbles."

"Word jumbles?"

"Yeah. You know, like in the paper. Rearranging letters to form a word. Like 'rose' can also be 'sore.' But you could jes tell him a word and he could tell you what other words you could make from it. Did it all the time. It was ... well, to be honest it was creepy. But impressive, too." Rose stood and walked to the refrigerator, helping herself to another soda. "Some of the kids called him Rain Man."

"Was he ever diagnosed with any kind of condition?"

"Condition?"

"Yes, like ... well, like autism. Or one of the spectrum conditions of autism, like Asperger's Syndrome."

Rose looked confused. "No, not that I know of. Don't suppose my parents ever gave it much thought. Though my dad always said he was special."

"Was your family religious?"

She managed a weak laugh. "Hardly. But Rudy ... after he came back. He got all religious." Rose turned to Jonas, her eyes dull with fatigue. "He would quote Christian scripture to you about anything, but mostly about the Rapture. It was really annoying. I never knew what the hell he was talking about. We were all hoping it was a phase but he was that way until he left."

"Did he ever go to church?"

"Never."

Finally, Anne reached out across the kitchen table with her hand, not touching Rose but letting her know she was nearby. "Rose, what did Rudy tell you happened to him?"

Rose flicked her gaze upwards and studied the ceiling fan for a few seconds. "He joined the Army when he was seventeen and my dad did nothing to stop him. Fact, thought it might be good for him. Bring him out of his shell. Maybe make him normal again. About a week before Rudy left, I went into his room. I asked him if he was taking his CD player with him to the Army, because I wanted it. He just stared at me for a long time, like *I* was the crazy one or something. Then out of the blue I asked him. I asked what happened to him in those two months."

Jonas felt his breathing quicken. "What did he say?"

Rose took her time before answering. "Said a man named the Preacherman took him. Older man. Elephant skin and rotten breath, Rudy told me. Said the man locked him up. Made him eat dog food. Hit him. Raped him. Would strangle him until he was nearly dead then let him breathe again."

"Jesus," Jonas muttered.

Rose put her head down and let the words spill out. "Said this Preacherman had a woman who followed right along in it all. Even laughed when the Preacherman cut him with a knife, nearly taking his ear off. Rudy thought he was gonna die and wanted nothing more than death, until he started reading the Bible. Bible that the monster gave him. Rudy said it gave him hope, because one day there would be judgment, and Rudy knew he'd be all right then. So he waited it out. One day, Preacherman wasn't careful enough, and Rudy got his knife and sliced the old man up. Kilt him. Came home that day." She paused, then looked up. "Said he never saw the woman again."

Rose stopped talking.

"What else did he say?"

"That was it. He didn't say nothing else about it. One week later he was gone, and I never saw him again until that video played on the news. He ... he killed that woman in Cleveland, didn't he? I know it's been such a long time, but the man on the tape was him. I jes know it."

"We don't know, Rose. We just need to find him."

Jonas glanced to his right and looked out the kitchen window. It was dark, but a streetlight glowed in the distance, casting dying embers onto the house. For a moment he thought he saw something move in the window, a head quickly pulling out of view. He looked at Anne and she to him, and he searched her eyes for a flicker of intuition to confirm his paranoia. He saw nothing, then dismissed his concern.

"Why would he want to kill her?" Rose asked.

"It's nearly impossible to say," Anne responded. "For someone like him, with his history of abuse, a number of things could trigger violence."

Jonas looked at the window again. Nothing was there.

A knock at the door.

Rose jumped in her seat.

"It's okay," Anne said.

The door opened and a portly man in a rumpled grey suit stepped inside. He seemed winded from the walk up the stoop. "Time's up, Ms. Deneuve," he said.

"Okay," Anne said. To Rose: "These men are with the FBI. They're going to ask you a few more questions and then you can get to your hotel."

"I'm going with them or we're doing it here?"

"You're going with them," Anne said.

Jonas saw a flash of fear in Rose's eyes.

"It's okay," Anne said. "I work with them. You'll be perfectly safe."

"Okay," she said.

Jonas stood and walked over to the agent, introducing himself. He received a nod and mumbled hello.

"You were across the street the whole time?" Jonas asked.

"Yeah. Why?"

"You see anyone outside. Lurking around?"

"Lurking?"

"Yeah, you know. Hanging around suspiciously."

"I know what lurking is."

"Then why did you ask?"

"Because I wasn't sure if you were being serious. You think me and my partner missed seeing a lurker when you civvies are interrogating someone in conjunction with a serial killer?"

Rose's voice called from the next room. "Serial killer?"

"Nice work," Jonas said.

The man squeezed his forehead, as if he could push out the negative thoughts as easily as popping a zit. He looked up defeated.

"Jesus Christ. No," he said. "No lurker. Or peeping Tom. Or interloper of any sort. Okay?"

"Yeah," Jonas said. "Take it easy. I was just asking."

"We need to go now," the agent said. He put a hand on the back of Rose's elbow and guided her toward the front door.

When she reached the door, she turned back to Jonas. She looked at him like a beaten dog still searching for approval in her master's eyes. Jonas knew all she wanted was someone to tell her everything would be okay.

He nodded at her. "It's okay, Rose. You'll be okay."

She nodded back and walked out the door. Jonas couldn't help but feel he just lied to her.

CHAPTER THIRTY-THREE

A RINGTONE WOKE him up before the alarm did. Jonas reached over and checked his phone. The first thing he noticed was the caller: Anne. The second thing was the time: 4:32am.

Jonas shook the sleep from his head as he answered.

"Anne, what is it?"

Silence for a few seconds.

"She's dead, Jonas. Rose is dead."

Jonas pushed himself up. *"What?"*

He heard a sniffle. She'd been crying.

"I just got called by the office. A ... a grey sedan was found parked next to a city ball field, about two miles from the safe house. Inside were three bodies. He fucking killed Rose, and he killed the two agents who were taking her to debrief."

"Oh my God."

"Jonas, I just –"

"Dead? All of them? For sure?"

"Yes."

"Oh my God, he was out there. Last night. He was outside your place."

"I know. I –"

"And you didn't feel anything? Sense him at all?"

"No, Jonas. It doesn't always work that way. Sometimes it does, but not always."

"You say that a lot. Goddamnit. Why didn't you feel him out there?"

"It's not my fault they are dead, Jonas."

He squeezed his eyes shut and let out a slow breath. "I know. I know. I'm ... I'm sorry. I just ... fuck. I can't believe this." A thought occurred to him. "Are you home now?

"Yes."

"You should get out of there."

"Jonas, he doesn't want me. He's not still around here."

"He might be. You need to be safe."

She ignored his request. "Jonas, he used a knife on them. On *all* of them. He overpowered two federal agents, both of whom were armed, and he killed them all with a *knife*."

"God, I ... I told her ..."

"I know, Jonas. You told her the same thing I did. We told her everything would be okay. And now she's dead."

Jonas stared at his curtained window and tried to understand what it all meant, but he couldn't focus. The only thing he saw was Rose's face as she stood by the door, looking for approval.

Jonas had sent her to her slaughter. No matter how everything else turned out, he didn't think that was something he would ever get past.

Another memory that would haunt him forever.

PART II

CHAPTER THIRTY-FOUR

JULY 21
DENVER, COLORADO

SWEAT RUNS OFF Rudiger's chin and drips onto the stained concrete floor of the abandoned airplane hangar, slickening the surface. Close to a hundred degrees outside. Little cooler inside, but not much. He wants to prop the doors open and get some of the Denver breeze, but can't chance it. Doors closed and locked. No windows.

He's pleased with his work. His muscles are developed perfectly for the task. For the cutting, the lifting. The drilling.

The crucifixes will take another day to complete – longer than normal. But this isn't a normal job. This time there'll be three instead of one. He uses a small blade to carve ornate designs into the wood of the heavy beams in the main cross. It'll be his final work. Final crossing, the good Lord had said.

Three months since the last killings.

He thinks of the last time he watched a person die.

The woman. His sister. Rose.

He'd tracked her down after attaching a GPS tracking device to Jonas's car. When he'd seen Rose through the window of the safe house back in D.C., he knew it was her. She'd looked right at him, and though she had only seen darkness, Rudiger saw his sister. She was older, weathered. She had none of the vitality he'd remembered from their youth. But her eyes, their family eyes, were exactly the same as they once had been, and though it had been over two decades, Rudiger could not have been more positive who she was. But he could neither believe nor understand it. There she was, sitting at a table with Jonas Osbourne. The last time he remembered seeing her was on his front porch as he left for the Army. She barely even said goodbye, barely looked up as he left. Bitch didn't care, even though he'd told her about the Preacherman. He hadn't told *anyone* about that except her, and she didn't give two shits about it. She had just wanted his CD player.

Seeing her back in D.C. had been a sign, one that he hadn't even needed his abilities to unscramble. Whatever Rose had meant to him in the past, her sudden presence was a threat. She was trying to stop Rudiger from doing what it was he needed to do. And he couldn't let her do that.

Rose needed to die.

Used a knife on her and the two Feds. Next day, it was all the news people could talk about.

Rudiger takes a moment to rest from his work, straightens his body, and wipes the sweat away with a dirty forearm. The hangar is dark – he doubts electricity has flowed through the overhead lights in years – and only his head-mounted light allows him to see what he's doing.

He'll need to get a generator and proper lighting.

It's a small hanger, probably never housing more than a Cessna or two. It decays in the open farmland ten miles east of downtown Denver. A hundred feet away an empty house rots.

Rudiger is lucky to have this place. A fortunate discovery. Nobody'll bother him here, and by the time they do it'll be too late.

He twists his neck and the beam of light atop his forehead sweeps along the rusted steel walls of the hangar. Pieces of chewed gum hold hand-torn strips of newspaper to the metal. Articles written about Rudiger. A lot of them. Rudiger's become quite famous in the last few months. He's collected them and made a shrine to a life he's still only beginning to discover.

Ever since his sister died, the story of the serial killer has been all over the press. Rudiger read about his life.

The killer's name is Rudiger Fitzgerald, the stories said. Grew up in western Virginia with two normal parents and a younger sister. When he was twelve years old, Rudiger disappeared coming home from his paper route. His bike was found on a dirt road on a wooded area of his town, but Rudiger had vanished. Two months later Rudiger returned home on his own, bloody and abused, but never spoke of what happened to him. The body of Thomas Wilcott, a 62-year-old drifter and self-anointed preacher originally from Kansas, was discovered two miles away in an abandoned house, with severe stab wounds to his mouth, neck, and side of his head (his ear had been removed). The murder weapon was never found, and it was never confirmed Rudiger was the killer, but Rudiger's blood in the home's basement did confirm this was where the boy had been kept – and abused – for two months. After returning home, Rudiger rarely spoke, except to shout passages from the Bible, an influence from his time in captivity. His trauma seemed to amplify a talent his parents noted since he was a young boy – the ability to hear or see words and almost instantly find anagrams of them. Rudiger excelled at complex problem solving but failed miserably at school. Had been an asocial teenager. Other kids referred to him as Rain Man. A Bible freak.

Dr. Sanjay Gupta on CNN said Rudiger might have Asperger's Syndrome.

When he was seventeen, Rudiger changed his last name to Sonman and joined the Army. Shipped off to Somalia.

There was an incident in Mogadishu, the press reported, though details seem hard to come by. A whole family had been killed. Rudiger Sonman swiftly disappeared.

Yeah, Rudiger thinks. I did disappear.

He scans the articles again, reading but knowing he won't find a single one that says how he was able to get out of Somalia and back into the U.S. Not one reporter figured it out, but that's only because they'd have to talk to two Somali men who gave him medical treatment for bullet and shrapnel wounds, then agreed to smuggle Rudiger onto a cargo ship in exchange for five thousand dollars. Rudiger hadn't killed them. But they didn't get their money.

He peers closer at an article in the *New York Times*, written just a week ago. The reporter is smart, having been the first person to pick up Rudiger's trail after his time in the Army. Woman by the name of Gloria (*"Liar go,"* his mind reads) connected Rudy Sonman with a man named Rudiger Mortisin who worked as an independent building contractor in Salt Lake City as recently as two years ago. Interviews with co-workers said little except that Rudiger worked hard, kept to himself, and had an ugly scar on his left ear that he never spoke about. One day he was gone, not unusual in that field. His ex-boss remembered him once saying something about going on a trip.

Two years later people started getting nailed to crosses.

He steps closer to the tattered newspaper and breaths slowly through his nose. He soaks in the words in front of him. Rose connected the Rudiger of the past with the serial killer of the present. She knew about the scar on his ear. She recognized him on the security tape.

The Jesus Killer.

That's what they're calling him. He doesn't understand. He doesn't want to kill Jesus, after all. He wants to *bring Him back.*

Rudiger leaves his wall of fame and goes to the door on the south end of the small structure, throwing it open and letting the daylight pierce the innards of the hangar. He feels like an insect whose rock shelter was just removed by a curious little boy. Exposed. Naked.

A breeze rustles through the high dry grass and licks his sweaty torso, cooling him. He thinks about the task before him.

He has all the supplies he needs. He has shelter and privacy. Tools. Food and water. Six wooden beams.

Peace, the priest in that D.C. church had said. *You need to find peace.*

The Peace Accords start in three days. Rudiger was certain this time he had chosen correctly.

In a few days it'll all be over. He'll be done. People will remember him until the final days of existence.

He turns back inside to resume his work, letting the door blow closed behind him. The daylight disappears from inside the tomb once again, leaving Rudiger in a darkness he is growing more and more accustomed to.

CHAPTER THIRTY-FIVE

WASHINGTON D.C. SUBURBS
JULY 21

"That one? Really?"

Jonas looked at the couch on the floor of the showroom, considering it as he would someone else's dog that wouldn't stop licking itself.

Anne heaved out a sigh. "What's wrong with it?"

Jonas ran his hand along the curved leather arm, letting his fingertips graze the large copper buttons attached to the seam.

"Kinda busy for my tastes."

"White bread is busy for your tastes. Live a little, Jonas. Put some style in your life."

"I thought that's what you were for."

She rolled her eyes. "Fine, put some style in *my* life. Buy this beautiful couch so I have something nice to sit on when I come over."

"I thought that's what *I* was for."

"Christ, you're exasperating."

"I know."

"Good thing I love you."

"Don't I know it."

Jonas scanned the piece of furniture with his gaze, which then ended up resting on Anne's legs. He raised his eyes and took her in fully into his mind, letting this woman swirl through his senses all at once. She did love him, and he loved her.

How the hell did *that* happen?

"Maybe this is how it starts," he said. "First you convince me to buy a couch because you tell me I need style. Then it's a new kitchen table, new bed, maybe new car. Next thing I know you're moving in."

She swung her head around and a piece of her long black hair whipped like a horse's tail.

"Is that what happened with the others?"

Jonas shook his head. "No one else ever wanted to bring more than an overnight bag to my place."

She laughed quietly, closing her eyes as she did. Her next question came with her eyes still closed as if she didn't want to read his reaction.

"Is it such a bad idea?" she asked.

"It's a horrendous couch."

"No, stupid." Her eyes squeezed tighter shut. "Us moving in together."

He looked over at her.

"No, Anne, it's not such a bad idea. Not at all."

She opened her eyes.

"Well, then."

"Well, then."

She smiled and leaned in to flip over a tag hanging from the left arm of the couch.

"It's nearly four thousand dollars," she said.

"I can't afford that."

"Let me buy it. I want to give it to you."

"That makes it sound like a venereal disease," Jonas said. "Which I think would be more attractive than this couch."

"Fine," she said, spinning delicately on her toes. She began walking toward the door and he followed her. "Just don't think my offer will stand once we walk out the door."

He reached her and ran his fingertips down the back of her thin silk shirt. "We shouldn't be inside on a day like this anyway."

She turned around and kissed him. "Don't worry," she said. "We don't have to talk about this now. We have enough going on at the moment."

It was an abnormal July day in Virginia. The sun had scurried away any trace of haze and humidity, and the air felt crisp, almost cool. Jonas breathed it in, knowing with certainty in another day or so the atmosphere would be back to its normal wet blanket of insufferable nastiness.

"I can't believe you convinced me to go shopping when we leave for Denver in two days," he said.

"I can't believe I convinced you to go shopping at all."

He rubbed the back of his neck. "God, I have so much to do before I leave." He liked to think he was playing an instrumental role in developing a potential lasting peace between two parties whose hatred ran long and deep. But he was still mired waist-deep in dinner-party seat assignments and speaking order.

The details are what kill you, he thought.

"It's not punishment, you know."

He grabbed her hand as they walked. "What isn't?"

"All the shit work you've been doing in preparation for the Accords. It has to be done. The Senator isn't punishing you."

"I know." Jonas wasn't sure he believed it, though.

With Rose Fitzgerald's death had come a deluge of media attention, and within two days Jonas's involvement in the case and connection to the suspect was widely circulated. The Senator wasn't pleased with the distraction to his peace accord efforts, and Jonas had been told in blunt terms he was no longer to be involved in the investigation unless subpoenaed. So much for being a hero.

Jonas was happy to comply, but, even though three months had passed, the Senator remained chilly towards him. It didn't help that the press loved Jonas. Jonas Osbourne had become a minor celebrity despite having really done nothing but narrowly escaping death from the hands of a serial killer. Twice.

"After next week it'll be the Senator's name on everyone's lips and not yours."

"It's not fame he wants," Jonas replied. "He just doesn't want the focus shifted away from what's important, which is making actual progress in Denver." He squeezed her hand as they passed store after uninteresting store in the outdoor mall in the D.C. suburbs. "Besides, you're a bigger name than I am."

As if on cue, Jonas noticed something out of the corner of his eye. Something pointed at them. Instinctively, he stepped in front of Anne in the direction of the movement, shielding her.

A man with a camera tracked them for a few seconds before getting back in his car and slowly driving away. More media, Jonas thought.

"They like me because I have a wacky job," she said.

"And you're hot as hell," he added.

"Yeah, that doesn't hurt."

They were a *known couple*, Jonas and Anne. The ex-Ranger Chief of Staff and the exotic psychic criminologist. It was too much not to attract attention during a slow news cycle, particularly when the commonality between the characters in the story was a serial killer.

He slowed and pretended to look interested in a cargo-shorts display at an Eddie Bauer storefront.

"So, any leads?" he asked.

"Leads? Leads on what?"

He shoved his right hand into his pocket and looked at her sideways. "You know ... the case."

"Jonas, you know you can't be asking me that."

"It's not like you can't discuss it with me."

"First, it's *exactly* like that. Second, you are under strict orders from your boss – a U.S. Senator – not to involve yourself to any degree with the Rudiger case. You might want to be a hero, but you don't get to be one this time."

He turned and felt his face warm with frustration.

"Look, it's been three months. *Three months* since we spoke to Rose together. Three months since he's killed." The guilt still gnawed at him daily, as he knew it did to Anne. If Rose had gone straight to the FBI offices, she would still be alive. As would the two agents. "Three months since my hand was slapped and I've been forced away from the case. And since that time, I have not once asked you about it, even though we've seen each other nearly every day."

"And night," she added.

"Exactly."

"Yes," she said. "I have to admit you've surprised me. You've had to rely on the tabloids to get your information."

He took a step closer to her. "Look, I know I can't help. I realize that. I know there's a whole taskforce set up to find him, and you're working with them."

Her words came playfully. "I can neither confirm nor deny that."

He pressed on. "I know you think something might happen in Denver. That's why you're going with me."

"It's not because I can't stand to be without you?"

"Maybe there's some kind of connection. Something to do with the Middle East and his time in Jerusalem? What are you guys looking for in Denver?"

"Jonas ..."

"Anne, c'mon."

"And what would you do with the information I told you?"

"Nothing. I swear. Look, we leave in two days. My mind is exploding with all the shit I need to remember to do before we leave. But I'll be honest with you, I can't stop thinking about ..."

"Him?"

"Yes, him."

"What do you think about?"

Jonas started walking again, slowly, with no real destination. Anne walked along his side.

"I know him. I *know* him. I'm the only person he's tried to kill twice and lived through it. I ... I don't know. It's almost like –"

"Like you have a bond?"

He looked at her. "Yeah. Something like that."

"You do have a bond, Jonas. You have a deep and intimate bond. And a horrifying one. Rudiger places some degree of importance on you, perhaps because you were there when he first ..."

"First what?"

She looked around and saw only the typical complement of milling shoppers. She pulled him into a Starbucks.

"Get me a coffee," she said.

"And then what?"

"And then we'll talk."

CHAPTER THIRTY-SIX

HE ORDERED TWO espressos and they walked to a small outdoor courtyard where a collection of empty park benches stood in formation. They chose the one farthest from the shops and sat.

"Let's be clear – we're only doing this once. Right?"

He nodded.

She took a sip of her coffee and considered her words. "Rudy Fitzgerald, aka Rudy Sonman, aka Rudiger Mortisin definitely seems to have some form of developmental impairment."

"Wow," he said. "Breaking news."

"Look, if you're going to be an ass –"

He held up his hands. "You're right, I'm sorry. Please. Continue."

She studied him for a moment, as if waiting to see if any more quips were forthcoming. Then she continued.

"Best guess is Asperger's Syndrome."

"That's what CNN said."

"Someone in the task force leaked that to CNN – that's the only reason they mentioned it. Be that as it may, it makes sense given what we know about his mental capabilities, his intense focus on certain subjects. Like religion. And his asocial behavior. Asperger's is basically a high-functioning form of autism."

"But he held jobs. He was in the Army."

"Like I said. High functioning. There's been strong anecdotal evidence that Jeffrey Dahmer had Asperger's. Maybe Ted Kaczynski. Most people with Asperger's have similar characteristics – lack of eye contact, socially inept, emotionally disconnected. Usually brilliant in one form or another."

"Like an idiot savant?"

"In a way. Or just able to process things much faster. Apply greater focus. Rudiger has been able to find private cell phone numbers, put something on your desk at work undetected, not to mention his ability to rearrange words in his own head. He is incredibly resourceful. He can't be underestimated. The man's not just psychopathic – he's likely a genius."

"And he's a physical threat. Guy is built like an Olympic athlete."

"One trait he doesn't seem to share with most who have Asperger's is the ability to handle change. He handles it quite well, which isn't common. But aside from all of this, which alone might have been enough to allow him the homicidal tendencies we know he has, there's the matter of his abduction."

"When he was twelve."

"He was sexually abused, starved, and beaten for two months. His ear nearly cut off and crudely stitched back on. All of that comes from the doctors who examined him, because he never spoke about it to anyone, except that one time to his sister."

"Who told us about the Preacherman."

Anne nodded. "The Preacherman. Thomas Wilcott. He's the one who raped the boy while probably spewing quotes of hellfire and damnation at him at the same time. You add an experience like that to a boy who is already showing autistic characteristics, and it's a recipe for a serial killer. It's likely Rudiger was the one who killed him, and even cut off his ear as an acknowledgement of what Wilcott did to him. Imagine killing someone so brutally when you're just twelve. Think about what kind of impact that would have had on Rudiger."

"Rudiger? You on a first-name basis?"

"The task force refers to it as the Rudiger Case. He has so many last names it keeps things easier." She brushed a strand of hair behind her ear. "Rose mentioned Rudiger liked to talk about the Rapture. The Second Coming. In his mind, maybe he thinks that by crucifying people he is helping the Rapture to come about. He has also shown that he likes rituals, which is another trait of Asperger's."

"Rituals?"

"His crucifixions are meticulous, all the way down to the burials. The patterns he's shown in his past killings reveal an increasing level of detail."

Jonas thought about that. "As if the first couple were just practice rounds?"

She nodded. "We think he's getting ready for his grand finale."

"In Denver?"

A shrug. "Perhaps."

"What's he looking for? I mean ... why is he killing at all? He's just a Jesus freak who wants to bring about the Second Coming?"

"There is no official theory. Just a bunch of speculation from a lot of smart people."

"What piece of speculation do you ascribe to?"

She remained quiet for a few moments as Jonas sipped his espresso, which had already cooled.

"I have a friend on the task force. David Preiss. Smart as hell. He was brought on because of his background in world religion. Does a lot of work on religious hate crimes."

"And he has a theory?"

Anne nodded. "Look, we know Rudiger is obsessed with the teachings of Christianity, ever since his abduction. Probably developed an obsession with it as a defense mechanism against what had happened to him. He escaped inside himself. He probably clung to this obsession through the years that followed in order to quiet down some of the other thoughts that were probably starting to formulate in his young mind."

"Dark thoughts," Jonas added.

"Very dark. Religion was an outlet for him. Could have been anything. Could have been baseball cards, for all that any of it matters. The important thing is the dark thoughts got stronger, and eventually won out."

Jonas watched as a mother and her child strolled hand in hand along the sidewalk. The little boy pulled at her fingers and laughed as they walked.

"So he joined the Army," she continued. "Maybe he hoped that sanctioned violent conflict would fulfill his needs. He was likely hoping to find any kind of distraction to keep his thoughts away from homicide, because back then he still probably knew the difference between right and wrong. And he was successful for a while."

"And then there was Somalia," Jonas said. "Why do you think he did what he did?"

Anne shook her head. "Hard to say. Your first-person account is the only one we have of that day. We've been able to track down other members of his unit, and most describe him as a loner, but pleasant enough. He always obeyed orders, and if he wasn't the most social solider out there, he certainly didn't cause any trouble."

"Until he killed an entire family," Jonas added.

"Could have been the stress of being under attack by the sniper. Maybe when he saw the other soldiers being killed Rudiger was overcome with bloodlust. The best guess from FBI psychologists is that he just snapped."

"Snapped? That's the diagnosis?"

"Most likely he had a psychotic break, where he finally and totally disconnected from reality. He found himself suddenly free to act on the impulses that had been brewing beneath the surface for years." She dipped her fingertip in the remnants of sugar and espresso and touched it to her lips.

Jonas thought about that for a moment. "So he killed that family out of bloodlust?"

Anne shrugged. "There are a lot of reasons why serial killers do what they do, but most of them are convinced what they're doing is *right*. That's important to remember. Rudiger seems to fit the category of a visionary killer, someone who feels compelled to kill by entities like God or the devil. Rudiger seems to be a God-mandated visionary killer."

"I remember him saying he read some sign. Must have been in Somalia. He said it was a message." Jonas struggled to reconcile any of this with the image of the baby's headless body on the floor of the Mogadishu apartment.

"That goes along with what Rose told us about his ability."

"How the hell could he believe God wanted him to brutally kill an innocent family?"

"I didn't say it made sense, Jonas. That's the whole point of psychotic breaks – it's a complete detachment from reality."

"I still don't understand."

"It could have been a test," she said. "Some on the task force think he believes God commanded him to kill the family as a test to see if he could do what he was later called upon to do."

"You mean the crucifixions?"

"Exactly."

"But ... he lived for years, with yet another new name, without killing anyone after that."

"Not that we know of. Most likely, that's not the case. He probably remained quiet for a long time. He somehow walked away from both the bullet wound you gave him and the grenade explosion undetected. Probably received help from some Somalis. He then got himself home from Somalia without detection by the military. Best we can tell he worked a series of manual-labor jobs and saved up his money, staying out of trouble the whole time. As he became more comfortable with his freedom, his darker side would have come out. Maybe he killed sometime during this period, but it might have not been an organized, ritualistic killing. It might not have had focus, which is why there's nothing tying him to any unsolved murders."

Jonas stood and stretched his legs. "And then came Jerusalem."

Anne also stood. "If Somalia was his mental awakening as a killer, then Jerusalem was his spiritual one. Jerusalem gave him the focus he needed to make his bloodlust justifiable, if only to himself. We found records of his travel. He had an episode there."

"Episode?"

Anne explained what the medical report on Rudiger detailed about his outburst at the Church of the Holy Sepulcher.

"Holy shit."

"That's about right."

"So he comes back home and starts crucifying people because that's what God told him to do?"

"Basically."

"What does God want from it all?"

"That's a little out of my league."

They started walking back to the car. A small breeze wafted down the narrow pedestrian walkway. Jonas turned his head in small degrees, searching for any paparazzi, seeing none.

"Rudiger is recreating Jesus's crucifixion," Anne said. "Down to the burial in a tomb. None of the victims are related. Except for one thing."

"What's that?"

"Remember what Rose said about Rudiger's ability?"

"The rearranging of letters in his head?"

"Yeah. Well, there are geeks at the FBI who live for that kind of thing."

"What kind of thing?"

"Figuring out what kind of anagrams may have set Rudiger off. Like Michael Calloway's personal ad on the website? It was an anagram for *"Holy blood enter."*

"And you think that was a clue to Rudiger? He was supposed to crucify whoever wrote that ad? And it just happened to be Michael Calloway?"

Anne shrugged. "That's a theory. We think he's looking for someone specific to kill and he hasn't found him – or her – yet. We think he's getting clues from ads, billboards, bumper stickers … anything that can be rearranged to form clues. And that college kid?"

"Yeah?"

"He had written an article in the campus newspaper. The title was an almost-perfect anagram for *"bring me reveal Christ."*

"Damn, that's creepy. How'd the FBI figure that out?"

"Just running anything they could find about the vic through their computers."

"What about the ears?"

"Trophies. Common among serial killers. Reflects his own mortality. His own wounds. What the Preacherman did to him. And it's very Old Testament. Eye for an eye, and all that."

"What about me?"

"What about you?" Anne stopped and kissed him.

Jonas looked at her. "Why did he attack me?"

Her face tightened – only a little, but enough for Jonas to notice.

"A man was killed on the side of a Virginia highway," she said, pulling back. "Shot to death – road rage incident, most likely. No witnesses to the crime itself, but someone driving by reported to the police a man fitting Rudiger's description standing next to the vic's pickup – no sign of the vic. When police found the pickup, the vic was in the bed of the truck, covered by a tarp. In the cab of the truck was a *Soldier of Fortune* magazine. The cover story was about the Rangers."

"You think Rudiger killed him?"

"Might have been a wrong place-wrong time kind of thing. But maybe after Rudiger killed the driver, he saw the cover of the magazine and took it as a clue to go find you. He attacked you just a couple of days later, so the timeline fits."

"You think he was trying to crucify me?"

Anne tilted her head as she continued walking. Her face wore traces of a smirk. "You ever think in your life you'd be asking that question?"

"No. At least not literally."

She sighed. "I don't know. I doubt it, but maybe. You're connected to him and that connection means something. You might be a target. You might just be a clue to him."

He could sense her starting to pull back from the conversation, and he knew he wouldn't get much more from her. "So then you do think I'm still a potential target." It wasn't a question.

She stopped and stared ahead for a few moments, as if trying to figure out what kind of face to wear when she turned to look at him.

It was a vulnerable face.

"Yes. That's possible."

The answer didn't upset Jonas as much surprise him.

"So what's taking him so long?"

"The significance of the Peace Accords is huge," she said. "It's about the Holy Land. Rudiger might use the Accords for his next killing to make a statement. Plus he knows you'll be there."

"So I'm bait."

"No, Jonas. It's just a theory. And trust me, you might think you're vulnerable, but you'll have extra eyes watching you the whole time in Denver."

"There'll be a protective detail on me?"

"If we get any kind of alert, yes."

He wasn't sure how much he liked that. "Wow, I'm special."

She reached out and touched his forearm. "You were with him at his awakening. Yes, Jonas, you *are* special to him. Maybe you're the one he's been searching for all along." She let out a small laugh, as if she realized she just made her boyfriend and a serial killer sound like lovers.

Jonas squeezed her fingers and pulled her along as they walked back to his car.

"If you want to tie me up and make me scream out God's name, that's one thing," he said. "But I don't think I want him doing it."

CHAPTER THIRTY-SEVEN

LESS THAN TWELVE hours remained until Jonas had to get on a flight to Denver, and he now realized there was no way in hell he was going to finish everything he had to do. His office was awash in clutter; despite the Senator's best green initiatives, paper was stacked in enough bricks around Jonas's desk to make any single page within them virtually meaningless.

V walked into his office.

"What are you still doing here?" she asked.

"Staring at things and doing nothing."

She looked around. "Good job."

"Thanks."

"You should get some sleep."

"I know. So should you."

She rolled her eyes. "I plan on sleeping in the office every day you all are away. It's like an extra paid vacation."

"Way to be a team player."

She arched her eyebrow. "Way to invite me to Denver."

He groaned. "It wasn't my decision."

She let out a sing-song voice. "You all have to understand that a pretty girl like me can get a lot more accomplished at any negotiation involving men than crusty old politicians can." She raised her skirt and flashed some thigh at him.

"Please tell me you're only pretending to be this stupid."

She dropped her skirt. "Wow, boss, when did you stop being fun?"

He considered her question seriously. "I'm not sure," he said. "But it was definitely sometime before I turned thirty."

She leaned over across his desk, resting her palms on two stacks of paper. "Go home. Now."

Jonas rubbed his eyes and stood. "You're right. Thanks, V."

She turned and left the office. "Good luck in Denver, boss."

He grabbed his briefcase and plane tickets and turned the light off in his office on the way out.

Luck, he thought. If only it were that easy.

* * *

It was close to midnight when he pulled into the parking lot of the Jefferson Memory Care Residence. The parking lot was silent, and only his own scuffled footsteps along the cracked asphalt indicated life. Dead of night.

He hadn't been able to sleep. Too much on his mind. Normally he would have convinced himself that staying in bed without sleeping was at least some kind of rest, but not tonight. Tonight was different, because out of the millions of nighttime thoughts and images racing through his mind, one seized him and wouldn't let go.

He wondered what his father was doing at that exact moment, and the image haunted him.

He pictured him in his bed (or maybe someone else's, since the residents all wandered). He pictured a dark room and a scratchy blanket covering dry and withered skin. He pictured the Captain sleeping fitfully, his mind unable to dream when asleep and unable to see reality when awake. His father was trapped in a dark and haunting loneliness, and Jonas decided he wanted nothing more than to spend some time with his dad before leaving for Denver.

Fuck sleep, Jonas thought. I can sleep next month.

He walked through the double doors and signed in at the unattended reception desk. The daily visitation log showed the last visitor to the facility signed in over four hours earlier. No one came to visit in the middle of the night.

He suddenly wished for Anne. That she would sit with him, next to his father. But Jonas had only briefly mentioned his father's condition to her, because as close as he and Anne had become, some things he held close to the vest. Someday, maybe.

He walked down the corridor and keyed in the code to open the first set of doors. The fluorescent lights buzzed above him as he passed through the wing on the way to the Captain's unit. The nurse's station at the end of the corridor was unattended and all of the resident doors were closed. His shoes squeaked on the faded linoleum floors.

Antiseptic fumes wafted past him.

At the far end of the corridor a resident's door creaked open, and Jonas reflexively slowed. No one came out, and Jonas kept walking. He expected to see a nurse come out after checking on someone, but the door had merely opened a few inches and then remained that way.

The overhead lights seemed to buzz louder, like a swarm of insects slowly getting closer. The nurse's station remained empty, but a crackling radio somewhere nearby was the first sign of life he'd heard.

As he passed the open door, Jonas shifted his eyes and looked inside the room. He saw only darkness, but a voice whispered to him from within.

"Come here."

Jonas couldn't tell if the voice was male or female, only that it was old and tired.

He stopped and looked into the darkness.

The door opened a few more inches and the light from the hallway illuminated the face of an old black man peering from around the edge.

"You got business here?"

Jonas thought the man must be at least ninety but knew dementia could age someone a decade or more. Dark, leathery jowls hung like sacks off the side of his face, as if years of obesity had rapidly succumbed to the disease's appetite for flesh. Patches of wispy, curled hair seemed glued to his scalp; his sunken eyes belied both mischief and fear.

"I'm visiting my father," Jonas replied in a whisper.

"Your daddy in here?" The man's voice was sandpaper.

"He's in the north unit."

"Ooh." The man's eyes widened and he looked like he was either going to laugh or scream. "That's the *bad* place."

Jonas turned more fully toward the man.

"Why do you say that?"

The old man smiled, his yellow teeth large and obscene. "Because everywhere in here the *bad place*." He let himself laugh though the act of it seemed to pain him. "It's all bad, boy. All bad." Then the smile disappeared from his face and his eyes widened. A naked, bony arm reached out from behind the door.

"I don't know where I am," the man said.

It wasn't a question, just a statement of fact.

"I'm sorry," Jonas said. He reached out and let the man grab his fingertips, something he never would have seen himself doing before the Captain took up residence at Jefferson. But he learned a lot about Alzheimer's, and one thing was clear: despite how much of a person's mind had been eaten away by the disease, they still responded to human touch. It was something they needed, sure as they needed food and water. Maybe needed it more.

The man gripped Jonas as if he was the singular rope thrown to a dozen drowning people. "You hear me, boy?" he said, his voice a hiss. "I *don't know* where I am."

"I can't help you."

"I didn't *ask* for your help."

Jonas patted the top of the man's hand.

"No, I guess you didn't. I have to go now."

"Go *where?*"

"To see my father."

"He in here too?"

"North unit."

"Ooh. That's the –"

"Bad place. Yeah, I know."

The man's lips drew in a circle of surprise. "You know, do you?"

"Yes."

The man suddenly yanked on Jonas's hand, pulling him toward the door. Jonas couldn't believe the strength the man still had despite the toll age and disease had taken on him. Jonas could have pulled back, but he let the man do what he wanted, because he knew that, even if just for a fleeting moment, the act gave some degree of satisfaction to him.

The smell of the man's dinner came from his mouth in a tangy wind.

"*You ... don't ... know ... anything.*"

That was when Jonas forced his hand free and walked away, leaving the old man in his room, where he repeated those same words, over and over, until Jonas was finally out of earshot.

Jonas was thankful when he finally reached the north unit.

He let the wedge of light from the open door guide him inside his father's room. The Captain was sleeping in his bed, a twin Jonas had bought when his father first moved into Jefferson. Jonas hadn't wanted his dad sleeping in some old mattress that God-knows-who had excreted God-knows-what onto. The Captain was sleeping soundly, as was his roommate, a seventy-something Wisconsin native named Paul who shouted birdcalls whenever the mood struck him, which was just about always.

His father's breathing was slow and steady, and he slept flat on his back, his nostrils flaring with every exhalation. Jonas immediately felt a sense of relief. Whatever his father was dreaming, at least he was asleep. To Jonas, that made things easier.

He leaned over and kissed the Captain on his forehead.

"Hi, Dad," he whispered, hoping for a second to see his father's bright eyes but then happy not to have woken him. Paul stirred a moment in the bed on the other side of the room and then fell back into silence.

Tonight Jonas didn't want to talk. He just wanted to be close, and that would be enough. He pulled over a plastic chair and sat next to the bed. Jonas removed his laptop from his leather messenger bag, then powered it up to check the latest AP wire stories before his morning flight. He positioned himself so he was able to browse the Internet with his left hand while using his right to hold his father's hand. The Captain's fingers were cold. Jonas stroked the back of his dad's bony hand with his thumb.

The glow of the laptop ghosted the small room as Jonas read a dozen articles about the upcoming Peace Accords. Security would be huge. Lots of protests expected. The President continued to press his message of cautious optimism, while the Israeli and Palestinian leaders seemed content to let the American President speak for everyone. For now.

It's either going to be a success or a failure, Jonas thought. He believed it because that's how the President and the Senator wanted it. There would be no middling compromise, no empty handshakes. There would be no status quo after the Accords, despite history's overwhelming forces that push everything from all sides at the same time, making peace progress an almost immovable object. There would be shouting, threats, delegations walking out of meetings, walking back in, and then walking back out again. But, with luck, nerves will be just raw enough to actually allow for progress. The idea of a Palestinian state had been debated for decades, but they were closer now than ever to it becoming a reality. If the Accords succeeded, there could be a recognized state in a year, with its official capital in East Jerusalem. If the Accords failed, the Jewish settlers would continue to build in the territories while the Palestinians continued to do everything they could to stop them.

Jonas squeezed his eyes shut and wondered if there was any real possibility for sleep that night. He didn't think so, but the morning was still far enough away to make the prospect of staying awake for the rest of the night a daunting task.

Then he got an idea.

Thinking of his recent conversation with Anne, he Googled the word *anagram*. The first entry was for an anagram server, allowing him to type in any words he wanted to see what anagrams could be made from them.

He started with his name. Jonas Osbourne.

There were almost two-thousand responses. The first one almost made him laugh out loud.

Onerous banjos.

Jesus, Jonas thought. Does Rudiger's brain really work like this? It didn't seem possible any human mind could calculate the hundreds or thousands of word combinations one could make from rearranging the letters of other words.

He scanned the first hundred entries on his own name and found nothing biblically significant about any of them, though his knowledge of the Bible left a lot of room for error. Then he typed in Anne's name. Only fifty-nine results, the most interesting one being *a need uneven.*

The Captain wheezed, coughed, and gave Jonas's hand a squeeze. The grip tightened, making Jonas think of his earlier interaction.

that's the bad place

Jonas held on tight and typed another name into the anagram server.

Robert Sidams.

Nearly 20,000 results. Jonas scanned the most relevant. *Broader Mists* was an interesting result, but not biblical. Still, if Rudiger was going to the Peace Accords for his next victim, there had to be a significance to it. The biggest name associated with the Accords was President Calder, but Jonas highly doubted Calder would be a target – that just seemed too unlikely given the impossibility of the task. Sidams was another big name, as was Jonas himself. But no anagram made sense, if in fact that was what was necessary to Rudiger for him to select a victim. Maybe the target was someone with one of the foreign delegations?

He tried a few more names and phrases until the words on the screen did nothing but sting his eyes. The FBI had a lot of people working on the case – Jonas knew his futile late-night efforts would do nothing to help. He put the laptop to sleep and wished he could do the same for himself.

The door opened and a nurse walked in. Monique. The hallway light silhouetted the Haitian's kinked hair, which sprung from the top of her head in tight coils. She startled when she saw Jonas.

"Oh, Mr. Osbourne," she whispered in a thick French accent. "You scared me."

Jonas stood and walked toward her. "Sorry, Monique. Just came here to see Dad."

"At midnight?"

Jonas shrugged. "I was missing him."

She nodded and smiled. "You are a good son."

Jonas remained silent.

She leaned into him. "He ate very much today. All his dinner."

"Good," Jonas said. The Captain finishing an entire meal was a rare event. "Maybe he'll sleep all night."

"Oh, yes. Definitely." Monique slid past him and briefly checked on Paul. She went to the Captain's bed and looked down at him before straightening the pillow beneath his head. The Captain didn't stir.

"You look like him," she whispered. "Same *pretty* eyes."

"Osbourne eyes," Jonas replied. "My grandfather had the same color."

Monique turned to him and gazed into his eyes, as if searching for an answer. Her proximity startled Jonas, but he didn't step away.

"Maybe," she wondered. "Maybe you have same soul, too."

"Soul?"

"Yes," she said. "Same spirit."

Jonas didn't understand what that was supposed to mean. "Maybe," he replied.

"You are a fighter. From war, no?"

Jonas shook his head. "I was in the Army. I wasn't really in a war. And that was a long time ago."

She dismissed his answer with a shake of her head. "You are a fighter. Your father. He is a fighter, too. Very, very strong."

"Yes. He is."

"Same soul," she said. She seemed suddenly certain in the assessment. "Same soul."

"Then I'm a lucky man."

She leaned in one last time, this time so close he thought she was going to kiss him.

"Yes," she said. "You *are*."

What the hell is going on here tonight? Jonas wondered. First the resident telling him the north unit was a gateway to hell or something, and now Monique proclaiming that Jonas and his father have some kind of mind meld. Jonas wondered if the horsemen of the apocalypse were going to ride in any second.

Monique pulled away from Jonas. "You stay long tonight?"

"I don't know," Jonas said. "I think maybe so."

"Can I get you something?"

He thought for a moment. "If I fall asleep, don't let me sleep past six in the morning. I've got a flight to catch."

"OK, Mr. Osbourne. Six o'clock. Good night."

"'night, Monique."

She shuffled past him and left the room, the door softly clicking in place behind her. The room was lost in darkness, and Jonas returned to his chair. The courtyard lights from outside the bedroom window were enough for him to see traces of his father, the outline of his nose, the sweep of his forehead. The darkness suddenly overwhelmed Jonas. Maybe darkness was all he needed. Maybe that was enough for him to shut off his mind for awhile, to drift off, to be at peace in the middle of an Alzheimer's facility.

What a crazy fucking world, he thought.

Cradling that as his last memory of the night, Jonas leaned forward in his chair, closed his eyes, and rested his head on his father's chest, wishing he could be a little boy all over again.

CHAPTER THIRTY-EIGHT

DENVER, COLORADO
JULY 25

THE SUN BAKED the streets and Jonas wondered why he assumed it was always snowing in Denver. He could see the mountains in the far distance, but downtown the scorching dry heat reminded him of Fresno. The delegations from the Middle East must find the weather very accommodating, he thought.

He walked into the lobby of the downtown Hyatt and the air conditioning washed over him. Day One of the Accords was almost over, and, so far, nothing disastrous had occurred.

There was still plenty of time for that.

He passed the lobby bar. Even though it was only four in the afternoon, the bar was bustling. The bar would be the place most, if any, progress would be made by unofficial spokes people speaking on the condition of anonymity. Whatever was said publicly would be stretched and pulled and dissected by faceless staffers with American beers clutched in their fists. Even some of the Muslims would be drinking.

"Jonas."

Jonas peered into the lounge and saw William Stages, the U.N. Ambassador. Stages waved him over.

"Bill, how's it going?"

"Fine, Jonas." Stages gestured to a hawkish man in his mid-forties standing next to him. "Jonas, this is Eli Chazon. Eli's a Knesset member on the Foreign Affairs and Defense Committee."

Jonas reached out his hand. "Of course. I know you by reputation, Mr. Chazon. Welcome to the United States."

"It's Eli, and thank you." Chazon offered his hand. "I know of you as well. You've been instrumental in setting up this conference. I hope it turns out to be fruitful."

"As we all do," Jonas said.

Stages squinted his eyes at Jonas. "Eli and I have been discussing Sidams's plan." He paused for a moment, giving Jonas the second he needed to process the magnitude of what Stages just revealed. Sidams's plan wasn't supposed to be unveiled until tomorrow.

"Have you?"

Chazon leaned toward Jonas. "It's about what we expected, but not what we hoped for."

Jonas met his gaze and could tell the comment was official. A necessary salvo.

"Unfortunately the process will not be an easy one for any side," Jonas said.

"This is true." Chazon raised a beer to his lips. Fat Tire, Jonas noted. Local Colorado brew. "But one of my jobs is to ensure that whatever is decided will be in Israel's best interest."

"I would think peace would be in your best interest."

Chazon smiled. "Jonas, I truly hope you are not that naïve. Peace is something that does not exist in the world. What you call peace is merely moments of tense silence in-between wars."

"I suppose it doesn't really matter what you call it," Jonas replied. "As long as it's anything *but* war."

"L'Chayim." Chazon raised his glass.

Jonas looked at his empty hands. "Looks like I need to be drinking with you gentlemen."

Stages revealed a tightly controlled smile. "You read my mind."

* * *

Four hours, five drinks and one very expensive dinner later, Jonas called it quits, knowing he'd had too much to drink considering the work he still needed to do before he even got the idea about sleeping, which probably wasn't going to happen anyway.

Eli Chazon was his new best friend, and Stages had been brilliant by leaking the Senator's peace plan to the Israeli a day early. It was an important gesture – it allowed the Israeli delegation time to formulate a calculated response. And since Israel was really being asked to concede more than the Palestinians – at least in terms of real estate – the gesture could prove an important one in reaching an agreement.

On the way to his room on the seventeenth floor, Jonas checked in with the Senator. Sidams was on the thirty-forth floor, and Jonas found it easier to phone. He briefed the Senator on the meeting with Chazon, and Jonas knew Sidams was happy about the situation.

All in all, not a bad day, Jonas thought.

He got off the elevator and walked past his room. He knocked on the door three down from his own.

Anne opened it.

"Hey, baby," Jonas said. "I wasn't sure if you would be here or not. Do you have to work tonight?"

They had seen little of each other since landing in Denver.

She leaned in and kissed him, though it was a hurried kiss. She's distracted, Jonas thought.

"Of course," she said. "I feel like I haven't stopped working since we got here."

"I know the feeling."

He walked in and took off his jacket. "I still have a lot to do tonight." He looked around her room and saw one bed still unmade, the other piled with notebooks and binders. "Making any progress?"

"Hard to say," she replied. "Nothing going on. No sign of him anywhere. No indication he's even in the area."

He noted the doubt in her voice. "But ..."

She looked at him. "He's here, Jonas. I know it. He's here and he's close."

"You're sensing it?" He didn't add that she didn't have the same feeling the night Rudiger killed Rose.

She hesitated for only a moment. "No, I don't so much sense it as I know it *makes* sense."

"What do you think he's going to do?"

She looked at him and started to answer, but held back. There was a glisten in her eyes.

"What?"

"Just ..." She grabbed his hand. "Be careful."

"You think he's here for me?"

"I ... like I said. I'm only going off what seems to make sense."

"I haven't seen anything unusual."

"That's good. And, we have people watching you."

"How closely?"

"You had chicken piccata for dinner."

"That's close." He wondered who'd been watching him that closely in the lobby bar. "Are they monitoring conversations? There's some sensitive issues being discussed and the Senator wouldn't want to find out the FBI is listening in on his chief of staff."

"Don't worry," she said.

"That doesn't answer my question."

"Don't worry."

"Are they watching anyone else?"

"Jonas, I can't really discuss this much more."

Jonas stepped closer to her until her breasts touched his chest.

"Are they watching right now?"

She smiled and shook her head. "No. But they might be listening."

"Good," he said. "Let's give them something to listen to."

CHAPTER THIRTY-NINE

AT FOUR IN the morning, Jonas finally put his head on the pillow in his own room. The curtains were still open and he could see the three-quarters moon beginning its descent over the Rocky Mountains in the distance. Sunlight was only a couple hours away, and the day would be hot and chaotic.

He reached over and rang the front desk, asking for a six o'clock wake-up call. It would be a long day, but he was capable of complete functionality on two hours of sleep. As long as he didn't sustain that for too long.

Jonas picked up his BlackBerry and set its alarm as well, just to be safe. Then he texted Anne.

You sleeping?

He waited a minute. No answer. Then he texted again.

Night, sexy. See you tomorrow.

He pictured her sound asleep, her hair spilled out over her pillow. He could hear her small, shallow breaths, her occasional murmur. He could see the side of her face, the moonlight on her mocha skin, the outline of her aquiline nose.

Jesus, he thought. *What is this woman doing to me?*

The answer came just as he drifted off to sleep.

Does it matter?

* * *

Protesters swarmed as close as they could to the entrance of the
hotel. Jonas walked outside and slipped on his sunglasses. It was
only nine in the morning but the sun was already intense, and
the noise from the crowds just made everything feel hotter. He
scanned the area and saw more pro-Israel than pro-Palestine signs,
and an equally divided amount expressing hate against both sides.
Then there were the groups who didn't care at all about peace –
they just knew a lot of cameras would be there so free publicity was
available for the taking. Tea Party demonstrators rallied against
the oppressive U.S. tax code. The pro-lifers and the pro-choicers
squared off across the street, and anti-war protestors were shouting
something that was lost in the din. Jonas spied a little girl dressed
in pink with her long hair split into pigtails. She wore a summer
dress and a blank expression, and in her little hands she hoisted a
sign that read *God Hates Fags*. She was probably eight years old.

"Wonderful," Jonas said to himself. "Great publicity for
America."

The security was tight and men and women wearing dark sunglasses and darker suits dotted the perimeter. The initial meetings
this morning would be inside the hotel, and Jonas was part of a
small group of dignitaries assigned to escort the delegation members into the conference. Most of the Israelis were staying at the
newly built Four Seasons and would be taking limos to the Hyatt.
The Palestinians were at the Brown Palace. President Calder
hadn't arrived in Denver yet, but when he did, he'd be staying at
the Ritz.

Jonas scanned the crowds and wondered if Rudiger was really in
Denver. If so, was he watching Jonas right now? He swept his gaze
a hundred and eighty degrees and saw nothing but anonymous

faces and news cameras. How could the FBI and Secret Service figure out which face in a sea of faces meant trouble? It seemed impossible.

To his left, a woman in a dark-grey suit with her hands clasped in front of her watched Jonas from fifty feet away. Her dirty-blond hair was pulled back tightly behind her head, and her corded earpiece was white, highly visible. Jonas made eye contact with her and she gave him the slightest of nods.

She's here to watch me, he thought.

The thought of having his own security detail was intriguing, though he knew Rudiger wasn't stupid. If Rudiger really wanted Jonas, nobody was likely to stop him.

"Sleep much?"

William Stages appeared on Jonas's immediate left.

"Not much. Enough. You?"

Stages shook his head. "I'll sleep next week. You here to do the meet and greet?"

"I am. I've got Israeli detail. You?"

"Palestinians." Stages grabbed at the knot in his tie. "Goddamn it's already hot as hell out here. Nothing worse than sweating inside a suit." His corpulence looked suffocating.

As they waited the crowds seemed to swell, though the barricades remained exactly where they had been all along. To Jonas, it felt like a tide of anger and frustration was coming closer to crashing on the shore. The protesters seemed louder, the streets hotter. He looked over at Stages, who looked more annoyed than worried.

Maybe it's just me, Jonas thought. Too little sleep, too much to do, and not enough time.

He wanted to wipe off the gathering sweat on his forehead but his only options were his fingers or the sleeve of his suit coat. He let the perspiration build until a few drops rolled down the side of his face.

"Here." Stages handed him a handkerchief. "You don't want them to see you sweating."

Jonas grabbed it and dabbed his face. "What, they don't sweat?"

"Not until it's over a hundred and twenty outside."

Jonas took a deep breath and mentally worked to control his core temperature. He didn't think about the long day ahead. The frustrations. The pressure. The miscommunications and the media spin. The pressure from the Senator. The demands of a President. He would let it all happen as it happened, and he would do the best he could, which he knew was usually enough. It would all be fine, and tonight he would sleep. Maybe he would even be able to share his bed with Anne, if she didn't have to work all night.

But as much as he calmed himself, Jonas could not escape the immediacy of the crowds surrounding the Hyatt. Then it occurred to him. He wasn't tired. He wasn't unfocused, or even worried about the Accords. It was something else, wasn't it? The same sense Anne possessed. The sixth sense that makes the air still around you. The same sense Jonas remembered outside his apartment in D.C., right before Rudiger attacked him.

He's here.

Rudiger is here. Right now. Somewhere out here.

Watching me.

Jonas swept his gaze over the crowd again, this time focusing on as many faces as he could, looking for the man with almost translucent skin and a jagged scar down the side of his head. But there were too many people, and they were too far away. Jonas could barely tell man from woman, let alone find the madman among them.

"What's wrong?" Stages asked.

Jonas was pulled from his focus. "Nothing. Nothing's wrong."

"You look like you want to kill someone."

Jonas tried to relax his stance. "I do?"

"Yeah. Not the posture you want to assume at a peace conference. Just relax, will ya?"

Just then a limousine arrived and Jonas knew it was the first car of the Israeli delegation. The protestors increased in volume, and Jonas couldn't tell if it was in support or opposition, though no one in the crowd could really be sure who was inside the gleaming black sedan. There was only chaos, and that was never good.

"This is you," Stages said, nearly shouting in Jonas's ear.

Jonas walked up to the limo and waited for security to open the door. He looked to his left and saw the woman with the security detail sweeping the crowd.

Jonas dabbed his forehead one last time. News cameras pointed down at him from the top of three separate news vans. A man who could have been a middle linebacker for the Middle East's first football team walked around the limo and opened the car's door. The first person to get out was not a staffer, as Jonas expected, but the Israeli Prime Minister, a small, balding man who wore the wrinkles of time and worry on his face like a badge of honor. He gave Jonas a firm handshake and a smile of true affection.

"Mr. Osbourne, how are you?" he shouted.

"Very well, Mr. Prime Minister. And you?"

"I am very happy with your city here," he said. "The views are beautiful."

Jonas didn't correct him that it wasn't *his* city, and he had in fact never been to Denver before. But such was the mentality of those from a country like Israel, whose entire land mass was a third of the size of Colorado.

"Excellent. Right this way, please." Jonas escorted the Prime Minister toward the porte cochere of the hotel as three Israeli staffers exited the vehicle and hurried to surround their boss.

There were shouts from the crowd, and Jonas heard at least one *"Go home!"* The Prime Minister blocked it all out with the professionalism of someone who was used to hearing insults hurled at him, and he turned and took a few seconds to wave to the crowd. An Israeli flag bobbed for a few seconds in the sea of people before being swallowed.

Jonas turned and touched the man's elbow, a gesture meant to tell him it was time to go. Though the delegation was enveloped by security, Jonas couldn't help but feel he was directly responsible for the Prime Minister's well-being.

Jonas felt the heat pour over him. Stages was right – sweating in a suit was miserable. The shouts seemed to grow angrier, as if the entire tone of a thousand people suddenly shifted.

"We need to go, Mr. Prime Minister."

An Israeli security agent gave Jonas a look. The man wore the eyes of a soldier, and Jonas could read the expression on his face.

Let's get him inside.

Then, for some reason Jonas would never fully understand, he looked up at the face of the towering Hyatt. He did so because, at that moment, something told him it was what he needed to do.

Instinct.

Rudiger Sonman stared down from a third-floor guest room window.

Jonas saw him for maybe three seconds, but, even from the distance, there was no mistaking him. Rudiger wore a dark grey suit with a bright red tie, painted like blood against a white shirt. He stood with his hands loosely clasped in front of him.

Jonas froze, his hand still on the elbow of the Prime Minister. The Israeli security agent leaned into Jonas.

"What is it?"

"It's a threat," Jonas said, his voice controlled but his mind racing.

The security agent reacted immediately. "In, in!" The Israeli towered over the Prime Minister and hurried him back to the car, his body expertly blocking that of his boss's from the front of the hotel. The three other members of the Israeli delegation panicked and scattered in different directions, but none in the direction of the Prime Minister. Within seconds the limousine tore away from the hotel and down the street, nearly running over a Denver police officer who was trying to restrain the crowd.

There were shouts from the crowd, none of whom knew what the situation was but all of whom knew there was indeed a situation. People looked up and all around, and everyone seemed to tense and wait for the inevitable sound of gunfire.

Then people started to run.

It started with a few people on the fringes of the crowd. Had they just walked away, there wouldn't have been a problem. But they ran, which told the others *something* was going to happen. In the purest form of group panic, the others began to run as well, and it took only seconds before those who were most confined by the crowd struck out the hardest, running over those whose feet failed them.

News producers screamed at camera operators to *get everything*, even though it wasn't clear what there was to get. So the cameras whirled in frantic circles, looking for the best snippets of chaos for their live feeds.

Police told people not to run. People ignored the police.

Jonas had one last flash of Rudiger, who smiled down at the scene he created with no effort other than appearing in a window. He then looked at Jonas, raised his right hand, and made a sign of the Cross on his chest. Then he stepped away from the window, disappearing in the shadows of the hotel room.

"What is it?"

Jonas looked to his left and saw the woman who he'd assumed was part of his own security detail. She didn't wait for an answer. Instead, she grabbed his arm and raced him into the hotel lobby, away from the pandemonium in the street outside.

Radios chirped from every direction in the lobby. Curiosity seekers ran outside, while others from outside ran in. Nobody knew where to go or what to do, but standing still seemed the one thing everyone agreed not to do.

Inside the lobby the woman flashed a badge. "Special Agent Difranco, FBI." Her words were fast but clear, and she gave him a full two seconds to scrutinize her badge. "I'm part of a team assigned to you."

"That's what I figured," Jonas said. He was still looking around the lobby until she used her hand to point his face in her direction.

"Focus on me, Jonas. What did you see?"

"He's here," Jonas said. "I saw him."

"Rudiger?"

Jonas nodded. "Upstairs. Third floor. Maybe fourth. He was standing in the window of a guest room."

Her hand squeezed her radio. "You sure it's him?"

"No doubt. Grey suit. Red tie. Looks bald. Maybe short blonde hair. Big scar –"

"Yeah, I know about the scar." She raised the radio to her mouth and repeated Jonas's sighting and description to whomever was on the other end of that frequency. Jonas wondered if Anne was one of them.

"I don't think he was targeting the Prime Minister," Jonas said.

Difranco holstered her radio inside her jacket, which she opened long enough for Jonas to see the butt of her handgun. "No, I doubt it. What did you say to the bodyguard?"

"He asked me what I saw and I told him a threat. Then he took off with the Prime Minister."

"Starting a fucking panic. Jesus, what a mess outside."

Jonas felt guilty. "I didn't know what else to say."

"It's okay. Just stay the fuck away from any reporters."

"You have a hell of a mouth on you," Jonas said.

"No shit." A pair of hotel security guards ran to the revolving doors and stood in front of them. "We're starting to block all exits. You could be helpful if you're up for it."

"What do you need me to do?"

"Canvas with me. Rudiger isn't stupid. He's already changed clothes and is probably wearing a hat. Stay in the lobby with me." She led Jonas by the arm toward the front desk, where they had a better view of the lobby. "He's sending a sign. He wants something."

"Yeah," Jonas said. "I think he wants me."

"Maybe." Difranco's eyes darted back and forth.

Jonas thumbed his BlackBerry and dialed Anne. She didn't answer so he left a message.

"It's me," he said. "Rudiger's here. I saw him in the hotel. Call me as soon as you can."

Difranco snapped her attention to him. "Who did you call?"

"Anne Deneuve. She's working with you guys."

Difranco nodded. "She's offsite. She'll be coming here quick."

They watched as more security guards covered all areas of the lobby. Anyone leaving the hotel was asked to show I.D. No one was being let in.

"You think you can find him in here?" Jonas asked.

She scanned the crowd as she spoke. "Eleven hundred rooms in this place. He could have registered under an infinite number of names. He had enough time to get to the parking garage before we knew you'd seen him, or he could be hiding in a different guest room and it'll take hours to canvas the building." She responded to a radio call with an affirmation that Jonas was with her and was assisting in canvas detail at his own request. When she finished, she hooked the radio back on her hip and turned to him.

"There's no way in hell we're finding him in here."

CHAPTER FORTY

IT DIDN'T TAKE long for the first news station to catch wind of what was happening. News cameras weren't the only form of technology present at the scene. A local Fox affiliate crew also had a parabolic microphone in use, a device used to pick up sounds from hundreds of feet away. A boom operator reacted quickly during the confusion, training the microphone on the epicenter of the commotion, which was Jonas.

It wasn't long before the name Rudiger was mentioned.

* * *

Jonas looked down at his BlackBerry, the third time in a minute. Still no word from Anne, though he had called her twice and texted her once. It wasn't unusual – her personal phone was probably off and she was likely hurling herself headfirst into the recent Rudiger development. He wasn't exactly sure how the Feds would use her, but knowing Rudiger was in the vicinity would play well into her abilities.

She had sensed it, Jonas thought. She knew he was close, and she thinks he's here for me. She was right about the first thing. I wonder if she'll be right about the second.

It had taken only an hour and a half for the hotel to receive an all-clear, significantly less time than Agent Difranco had guessed. There was no sign of Rudiger anywhere, and although every news channel carried sensationalist lead-ins (*Terror in Denver?* CNN wondered), no one at the actual Accords seemed to notice or care about the recent developments. The delegations came back to the Hyatt shortly after receiving assurances there was no threat from the suspect. Neither the Israelis nor the Palestinians cared about one crazy man on the loose. They were used to playing their odds with safety all the time, and this Rudiger Sonman seemed like a small threat.

"Would you stop looking at that thing?"

The Senator peered over Jonas's shoulder at the BlackBerry. They were seated next to one another at a round lunch table in the grand ballroom at the Hyatt, picking their way through light Mediterranean fare. The conversation around them was cordial but otherwise hushed.

"Sorry. Just trying to get hold of Anne," Jonas said.

"You hoping she's going to tell you what's going on?"

Jonas thought about it. He actually didn't know why he felt he had to speak to her. He just wanted to. "Maybe," was the best he could offer the Senator.

Eli Chazon sat to Jonas's immediate left. He wiped his mouth with his napkin and leaned over toward Jonas.

"It is my understanding that you are the one who spotted this ... this person."

Jonas felt his guard go up. Everyone looked at him.

"I was," Jonas said after a moment. "Maybe I was wrong. Maybe it was someone else."

Chazon chuckled. "I drank heavily with you last night, Jonas, and that makes us friends." His accent was thick and his English perfect. "I feel I know you now, and one thing you are not is over-reactive. You are not the type. If you say you saw this man, you saw him."

This prompted the Israeli Ambassador to the United States to speak up. "What does this man want? Or, should I say, *who* does he want?"

The Senator barged in. "Let me assure you this man poses no threat to anyone here, and I'm sorry for the annoyance this incident caused."

"Oh, Senator Sidams, I quite understand that, and I believe no one here feels in danger." The eight other people around the table all offered nods of agreement. "I am merely curious about Mr. Osbourne's opinion. I understand he has a connection to the criminal."

A woman next to the Ambassador – his aide, Jonas remembered – opened her eyes a fraction wider at the statement.

"What kind of connection?"

Jonas heard the Senator softly groan.

"I don't really have a connection," Jonas said.

The Senator gave him a look that was unmistakable. *Shut the fuck up.*

The Israeli Ambassador cleared his throat. "I understand you served together in the Army, and he almost killed you."

Shit, Jonas thought. *How does he know that?* He looked over again at his boss, who had barely restrained anger on his face.

"Jonas can't comment on that," the Senator said. Jonas read his boss's body language, and it was clear. It was time to change topic.

But the Israeli Ambassador was too fast. "I have to tell you," he told the table. "I have been following this case in the news. It is fascinating. American serial killers far outnumber those of any other nation. Did you know that?"

No one seemed surprised.

"This man. This *Rudiger.*" The name snaked from his mouth. "He was in my country. He reportedly had an incident at the Church of the Holy Sepulcher. He was admitted for psychiatric treatment in Jerusalem."

Jonas looked down at the table. He could feel the Senator wishing for the whole conversation to drop. Jonas wished for nothing more than to be anywhere but where he was.

"And soon after he returned to the United States," the Ambassador continued. "The killings started. The *crucifixions.*"

All of this had been reported in the news, so no one seemed surprised.

"How did he almost kill you?" Chazon asked Jonas.

"I ... I really don't want to speak about that," Jonas said. "That was a long time ago."

"It is no coincidence, I think." The Ambassador sat up in his chair and scratched at his beard. "Let me go back to my original questions. What does this man want? *Who* does he want? This man recreates the death of Jesus Christ, even down to the cave burial. And now here he is, at these Accords, which concern the holiest lands on the earth."

The Senator could take no more. "Mr. Ambassador, with all due respect, I don't think this man deserves averting our attention from the monumental task we have here at hand."

"Respectfully, I disagree. Often distractions prove just the thing to be able to forge ahead." The Israeli Ambassador spoke with the patronizing arrogance of a department store Santa Claus. "Fascinating," he repeated. "It is all very fascinating. Do you realize the amount of physical strength and stamina it would require to crucify a person all by yourself?"

His aide put down her fork. "I think perhaps the Senator's right. Perhaps this is not proper conversation during a meal."

The Ambassador huffed and leaned back into his plate. "As you wish," he said.

Jonas looked over at his boss, whose face showed a modicum of relief.

Chazon leaned in close to Jonas, lowering his voice enough to keep the others from hearing. "It is true," he said. "It seems more than coincidence this man is here now. At this time."

"Don't worry, Eli. You don't have anything to worry about."

Eli shook his head. "My friend, it is not *me* I am worried about."

* * *

Jonas walked down the long corridor to his hotel room, loosening his tie as he thought how good it would feel to collapse on his bed. The sun was low in the sky, and diffused light filtered in through the window at the end of the hallway. The meetings were over for the day, but the negotiations went on, and Jonas had about thirty minutes before the late-afternoon and evening social events commenced. Just enough time to change clothes. Not enough time for anything else.

Still no word from Anne.

He opened the door to his room and the first thing he noticed was the piece of paper on the floor near his door. A note card, folded in half. Jonas poked his head back in the hallway and looked up and down the corridor.

No one.

He stepped inside his room and closed the door. He knew before picking it up who had left the note for him: Rudiger. No question.

Had he managed to leave the note before fleeing the hotel, or was he still close?

Jonas picked up the card and opened it. The writing was tight and careful. Controlled.

There was only one sentence.

Leave your cell phone on.

CHAPTER FORTY-ONE

DENVER, COLORADO
JULY 26

His BlackBerry screamed at him, waking him from the little sleep he'd been able to achieve. Jonas rolled over and lunged for the phone, hoping it was Anne. He wasn't sure if he had ever fallen asleep – if he had, he'd had less than an hour's worth, at most. Not talking to Anne, especially after seeing Rudiger, filled him with anxiety.

He could see the beginning of the day starting to seep around the edges of the hotel room curtains, but since his alarm hadn't gone off Jonas knew it was earlier than six.

He stared at the small screen.

Unknown Number

It was either Anne calling from a secure line or it was Rudiger, Jonas thought. Two extreme ends of the spectrum.

He sat up in bed and braced himself.

"Hello?"

"Mr. Osbourne?"

Male voice.

"Yes?"

"This is David Preiss. I'm with the FBI task force assigned to the Accords."

You mean assigned to finding Rudiger, Jonas thought. He remembered Anne mentioning Preiss. Said he was an expert in world religion.

Jonas felt his muscles relax a little. It wasn't Rudiger, but *goddamnit* where was Anne?

"Yes, David."

"Sorry to wake you. I know it's early, but ..."

"But what, David?"

The slightest of pauses. "Is Anne with you?"

Jonas felt his muscles stiffen again. "No. Why?"

"There ... there are some people looking for her."

"Who?"

Another pause. "Everyone."

Jonas stood. "Are you telling me she's MIA?"

"It appears so. She was last seen yesterday afternoon. She was working offsite but drove back to the Hyatt after the suspect was spotted. No one's heard from her since. We were hoping she was with you."

Jonas felt panic rising in his chest. "No. I haven't been able to get a hold of her either."

He has her. Holy Jesus. *He has her.*

Preiss's voice didn't register surprise. "Did she mention anything to you? Anything that could have made you think she was going to leave Denver?"

"No," Jonas said, trying to recall their last conversation. She had warned him to be careful. "Can you GPS her cell phone?"

"We tried. Her phone must be off."

Shit.

Jonas walked to the window and parted the curtain. "David, listen to me. Trust me when I tell you I'm not prone to panic or overreaction."

"Okay, Mr. Osbourne."

"Rudiger has her."

Jonas heard the man let out a weak sigh.

"It's not inconceivable," Preiss said.

"You already thought that, didn't you?"

"We checked all hospitals and accident reports in the last twelve hours. When nothing came up, well, yes, it occurred to us she could have been the victim of foul play."

"So what are you doing about it?"

"We're looking for her, Mr. Osbourne. Trust me when I tell you that. But it's important we try to understand what he would want with her."

Jonas felt anger rising through his body. "David, the man fucking *crucifies* people. He's not looking for a bridge partner."

"He's not going to crucify her, Mr. Osbourne."

"No?"

"No. She doesn't fit his profile."

"So what does he want?" Jonas looked down to the streets below. Wooden police barricades littered the blocks surrounding the hotel.

Jonas felt sick to his stomach.

"We think he wants *you*, Mr. Osbourne. If he has Anne, he can use her to get to you."

Jonas crumpled up a wad of the thick curtain in his fist. Then, as he released it, he concentrated on breathing slowly.

"Mr. Osbourne?"

"I'm here."

"It's just a theory."

"He asked me to leave my cell phone on," Jonas said, exhaling.

"What?"

"There was a note under my door. That's all it said on it."

"Did you tell anyone?"

"I left another message for Anne. But no, no one else."

"We need to meet."

"Where?"

"We have a suite in the hotel. Room 407. Can you be there in an hour?"

"Of course. I ... I need to tell Senator Sidams."

"That's another thing I wanted to talk to you about."

"What?"

"Sidams."

"What about him?"

"He could be a potential target."

"The *Senator?*"

"Yes. And Ambassador William Stages."

"Are you *shitting* me?"

"That's not the kind of personality I have, Mr. Osbourne."

"What makes you think that?"

"It's not my theory, but it makes sense. Based on Rudiger's patterns, we think he's got something more elaborate in mind this time. He's not a thrill seeker – he's purpose-driven."

That's pretty much what Anne had told him, Jonas thought.

"And he hasn't found what he's looking for yet," Preiss continued. "We know he's trying to recreate the crucifixion of Christ for some purpose, but what he hasn't done is recreate the entirety of the scene."

"Meaning?"

"Meaning Christ wasn't the only person crucified that day. There were two others. Common criminals."

Jonas paced. "So let me get this straight," he said. "You think Rudiger is going to crucify three people, and the Ambassador and the Senator are supposed to represent the criminals."

"Yes."

"Why them?"

"Mr. Osbourne, one of the things we've been doing is searching anagrams, because that's how Rudiger's mind operates. It's one of the ways he gets his clues."

Exactly as Anne had explained.

"And?"

"And the two criminals, though never mentioned in the Bible, are generally attributed the names Dismas and Gestas. There are various spellings one can find for those names, but in the most common form, they are perfect anagrams for Sidams and Stages."

Jonas let it sink in, but it seemed impossible.

"Do you know the probability of something like that?" Preiss asked. "It's almost incalculable. That's why we think they could be targets."

"And I'm supposed to be the main event in all this?"

"Again, it's a possibility."

"Why? My name isn't an anagram for Jesus."

There was a lengthy pause on the other end. Jonas thought he heard a siren in the background.

"I know. We're not sure. Similar names, though. Jonas and Jesus. Five letters, two syllables, two vowels, same beginning and ending letters. I know. It's not perfect. But there's more to your history with Rudiger to suggest you could be the ... however you called it ... *main event.*"

"What's he going to do to Anne?"

"He's going to use her to get you to cooperate. Listen, Mr. Osbourne, it's probably best we talk in person. We need to meet with you, the Senator, and the Ambassador. I'll leave it to you to get them to come in for a briefing. But we need to keep everyone's safety the priority here. We'd like to do this without affecting the schedule of the Accords, but that will be up to all of you."

"You can't interrupt the Accords," Jonas said.

"Then we need everyone's cooperation. One hour, suite 407. The three of you, and anyone else you think needs to come. We won't take long."

"The Senator needs to be at the meetings starting at eight thirty."

"Shouldn't be a problem."

"You need to guarantee it."

"I guarantee it."

"Fine." Jonas looked at the clock radio on the bedside table. Five thirty-five.

"And keep your phone on, Mr. Osbourne. We'll start monitoring it in case Rudiger calls."

Preiss hung up and Jonas stood in the hazy morning light, wondering where he would be standing at the end of the day.

If he would be standing at all.

CHAPTER FORTY-TWO

HIS SHOWER LASTED less than five minutes, but the powerful jet of near scalding water was exactly what Jonas needed for his mind to focus. Or refocus.

Shave. Dress. Call the Senator. Senator calls Stages. We all go to the suite, then the FBI tells us what to do next.

What happens if Rudiger calls in the next hour with different plans? Then what do I do? I don't even have Preiss's number if I need to change the plan.

But Preiss said they're monitoring my phone, so they'll know if he calls.

Is Anne hurt? Would Rudiger hurt her before he gets what he needs? Will he hurt her after?

Jonas jumped out of the shower, dried, and threw on his suit. It took him less than a minute to shave and he was ready to go. He still had nearly forty-five minutes before the meet time. He grabbed his BlackBerry to call the Senator.

The screen glared at him.

One missed call.

Jonas cursed. It must have been when he was in the shower.

No messages. He checked the call log.

Anne Deneuve

Jonas stared at the phone in his hand like it was an alien arti-fact. Is this real, he thought. Did Anne really call?

He immediately called back. He could feel bile creep up his throat when her voicemail greeted him.

"Anne, it's me. Jesus, you just called. *Where are you?* I'm ... I'm going out of my mind here. Listen, I'm meeting with –"

A thought stuck him. Was Anne with Rudiger? If she was, he was going to hear this message. He didn't want to tell Rudiger too much.

"– well, never mind," he said into the phone. "Just call me back immediately and let me know you're okay."

As soon as he hung up the phone rang again. In his haste to answer, Jonas almost hit the button to ignore the call.

Unknown number.

Fuck!

"Hello."

"Jonas, it's David. We heard that call."

"So you saw that Anne called?"

"We did. Her phone is off again. But we were able to track it within a city block."

"Where is she?"

Jonas heard papers rattling in the background, but no other voices.

"Jonas," Preiss said, his voice low and steady. "We think she's in the hotel."

Jonas felt the need to sit down. "So ... so she's okay? He doesn't have her?"

"We don't know, Jonas."

"Has her room been searched?"

"Yes, she's not there. Jonas, you need to come sooner. This hotel is going to be swarming soon, and it's going to affect the Accords. There needs to be a change of venue."

"Impossible," Jonas breathed.

"Jonas, call the Senator and get everyone here immediately. It has to happen now. We don't have any time to lose here, do you understand me?"

The reply was a reflex. "Yes, sir."

"Good." The call disconnected.

Jonas dialed the Senator.

He got voicemail. Jonas cursed, hung up, and dialed again.

Sidams answered on the fourth ring.

"What is it, son?" The Senator's voice was gravelly with sleep but his tone was serious. Both men knew Jonas wouldn't wake his boss for an unimportant matter.

Jonas gave him the highlights in less than a minute, as professionally as any solider ordered to provide a concise *sit rep*.

Sidams was silent for a long period.

"Give me fifteen, then come up to my room." He hung up.

Jonas spent the next fifteen minutes sitting on the corner of his bed, feeling as useless as a dead man on a battlefield.

CHAPTER FORTY-THREE

When Robert Sidams opened his door, he was as polished looking as if he'd had two hours to get ready. The lights were still dark in the room and Jonas knew the Senator's wife, Patricia, was probably still sleeping.

Sidams stepped into the corridor and closed the door behind him.

"What did you tell her?" Jonas asked.

"She didn't even hear me get up. If she wakes up before I get back, she'll call me."

Good, Jonas thought. No need to worry her prematurely.

Sidams walked toward the elevator and Jonas followed.

"Morning, Brian." Sidams nodded to the security agent in the blue blazer standing next to the elevator.

"Good morning, Senator. Early for you, isn't it?"

Sidams nodded and smiled. "That's an understatement."

"Need a detail?" Brian raised his radio.

Sidams put a hand up. "I'm meeting with a bunch of Feds in the hotel. I don't think I need a security detail."

"Hope everything goes well today," Brian said.

"Me too, son. Me too."

Jonas and Sidams stepped into the elevator, and Jonas marveled at his boss's coolness.

"Did you get a hold of the Ambassador?" Jonas asked.

"No need," Sidams said.

Jonas looked at him. "What do you mean?"

"I mean let's see what our friends want to tell us before we start getting everyone in the world involved with this." Sidams checked the cuffs on his shirt, pulling them down a fraction more.

"Preiss was pretty insistent."

"Well, Jonas, I can't say I know who David Preiss is, but he sure as hell knows who I am. That makes me the one calling the shots here. So until he earns my trust and confidence, I'm not in the mood to start taking orders." He looked at his watch. "Christ on a Ferris wheel, it barely past six o'clock."

"You don't seemed concerned."

Sidams shrugged.

"You don't think this is a real threat?" Jonas asked.

"Might be. Might not be. Don't have enough information to tell. Until I do, no real use fretting about it, is there?"

The elevator slowed as it reached the fourth floor. "I agree," Jonas said. "But I'd be lying if I told you I wasn't worried sick about Anne."

Sidams looked over at him and his face softened for the first time during the conversation. "I know you are, son. Let's just talk to these boys and see what they want us to do."

He didn't say *Anne will be fine*. The Senator didn't like making promises he couldn't keep.

The elevator doors opened and the men took a left toward room 407. Thick corridor carpet muffled their footsteps, and the faint smell of room-service leftovers wafted from a collection of trays left outside of guest room doors. Copies of *USA Today* papers lay like doormats in front of nearly every door.

The two men walked nearly the length of the entire corridor before reaching their destination.

There was no paper in front of 407.

Jonas could hear the sound of the television bleeding through the door. A news program. What he didn't hear was a team of FBI agents discussing an action plan.

The Senator cleared his throat and knocked on the door.

"Hope this is fast," he muttered. "I've got enough horse-shit to do today."

Jonas took a step back from the door and looked at the rooms to the left and the right. They were spaced evenly apart, as were the ones directly behind him on the other side of the corridor. If 407 was a suite, it certainly didn't seem any wider than any of the other rooms. Unless all the rooms on this floor were suites.

Something wasn't right.

The Senator checked his watch again.

Jonas heard footsteps inside.

"Senator ..." Jonas started, not knowing what his next words should be.

The pinpoint of light in the security eye disappeared as the person inside looked through it.

It was wrong, Jonas thought. All wrong. There was no team of FBI agents in there.

The lock on the door slid open.

The Senator turned to Jonas, a tired look on his face. "Hmm?"

There was no time to react. The door opened wide and on the other side stood Rudiger, holding a 9MM handgun in his right hand and a Taser in his left.

Both were pointed at Senator Sidams.

CHAPTER FORTY-FOUR

"YOU HAVE THREE seconds to move into the room." Rudiger took a step back and held the door open with his foot. "You first, Senator."

Jonas felt his stance reflexively shift to a defensive one as the Senator remained motionless.

"Don't, Lieutenant," Rudiger said, training the gun on him. To Sidams: "Now, Senator."

Sidams walked into the room, his steps small. Jonas followed, and Rudiger's gun remained pointed at Jonas's head. Rudiger stepped away as Jonas entered the room, giving more space between the men.

In the room Rudiger ordered them to sit next to each other on the bed with their hands on their knees.

"Where's the Ambassador?" Rudiger said.

Jonas listened to the voice. It was lower than the one on the phone, but he could sense the familiarity. Same drawl.

"It was you," Jonas said. "There is no David Preiss."

"There is a David Preiss. You jes weren't talking to him. I asked a question. Where's the Ambassador?"

"I didn't call him." It was the first time Sidams spoke. "And I'm goddamn glad I didn't. What the hell do you think you're doing, anyway?"

Rudiger's face was a blank canvas as he stood silently, pointing the weapons with both hands. Jonas studied the man and tried to reconcile him with the person he remembered. He was older than the young soldier in Somalia, but that was a given. He was more than just older. His face showed the lines of a lifetime – not wrinkles, but deep creases of someone who spent his life never looking in the mirror. His hair was shaved to a blonde fuzz that sloped in a V down the top of his forehead. Except for the shark-grey scar running down the left side of his head, the man's skin was the color of milk. Rudiger wore a tight grey t-shirt over dark grey suit pants, and his physique was even more impressive than what Jonas remembered. The muscles in his arms could have been sculpted by an artist.

Rudiger was completely motionless, the weapons raised at eye level.

"We need to get him," Rudiger finally said. "I specifically told you to bring him."

Jonas noticed Rudiger struggled with eye contact.

"Where's Anne?" Jonas asked, keeping his voice as calm as possible.

Rudiger pulled a cell phone from his front pocket and handed it to Jonas. There was a picture on the screen.

Anne.

All he could see was her face, lit up in green, like a nighttime video shot with an infrared camera. The camera was close to her face, and her eyes dated back and forth, but her head barely moved. Her pupils were dilated, so Jonas knew she must be in the dark. She looked desperate. Panicked.

Rudiger pulled the phone away.

"You see, Lieutenant. She's running out of air."

"I swear to God I'll kill you."

"Maybe you jes will, sir. Maybe you jes will." He turned to the Senator. "Call Stages."

The Senator asked blandly, "And if I won't?"

"Then she dies. Don't believe me?"

Sidams nodded. "I believe you."

Jonas looked at his boss. He wanted to tell him not to make the call, but he couldn't.

Sidams picked up his phone. Before he could dial, Rudiger spoke.

"If you call anyone else, I'll shoot both of you. Then she dies."

No you won't, Jonas thought, soaking Rudiger's image into his mind. *You need us, and you need Stages. You can't just kill us in this hotel room – that would be meaningless to you. You need us for your special event.*

Sidams dialed and spoke in a normal voice into the phone.

"Bill, yeah, it's Robert. Listen, I know it's early, but I need you to come to room 407 in the next ten minutes. It's important." He listened as Stages asked something. "I'll explain when you get here. And ... sorry." Rudiger raised the gun a fraction of an inch. "Sorry ... um ... for waking you."

He disconnected the call.

"He's on his way."

"If he brings anyone else, the other person will have to be killed." Rudiger made the pronouncement as more of statement of fact rather than threat. "I just need the three of you. Anyone else will be left in this room."

Sidams looked down at his hands. "What do you want?"

Jonas marveled at how calm the Senator's words were.

"Want you to listen to me and stop asking questions."

"But now we have ten extra minutes you hadn't planned on. Seems like a good time for you to tell us what you intend to do."

"Unnecessary. You'll either do what I ask or people will die."

"Not much for conversation, are you?"

Jonas thought of something. He turned to the Senator. "Some people think Rudiger here has Asperger's Syndrome. It's a form of autism. People who have it are usually ... socially awkward."

Rudiger lowered his weapons and checked his watch. "Doesn't matter what you think my psychological condition is, neither."

Jonas continued. "Some people think Dahmer had Asperger's. That guy thought he was doing some kind of important work, but at the end of the day all he did was cook up some skulls for dinner."

Sidams gave Jonas a look Jonas knew well. *What are you doing?*

Jonas gave his boss the slightest of nods, telling him to go with it.

He looked up at Rudiger. "You think you're doing God's work, Rudy? Is that it?"

"You have no idea what God's work is."

"When you killed that family in the Mog, that was God's work, too?" Jonas stiffened his spine and leaned forward on the bed. "When you cut that baby's head off, God told you to do that?"

"That," Rudiger said in a hollow voice, "was a test."

"A test? Is that what that was? Biting that little girl's ear off – that was a test, too? Because it sure as shit just makes me think you're crazy."

"Don't matter what you think." Rudiger checked his watch again.

Sidams leaned forward and joined the conversation. "What I want to know is why this guy has such a hard-on for you, Jonas.

First he tries to kill you in the Army, then he tries again outside your house."

"And again now," Jonas said.

"True. Guess he's hoping the third time's a charm."

"Maybe he just likes a challenge. He hasn't been able to kill me yet."

Rudiger raised his gun. "Maybe I'll just kill you now."

"No," Jonas said. He felt the heat rise through him. God, how he wanted to just slam that bastard against the wall and smash his fists into his face. But he couldn't. He couldn't because of Anne. Rudiger wasn't bluffing. Jonas knew *she would die* if they didn't do exactly what Rudiger wanted. "You need me," Jonas continued. "You need me up on that cross, don't you? Somewhere you have three crosses waiting for us, and if you shoot me now you won't get what you want."

Rudiger's face twitched. "You have no idea what I want."

"Then tell us," the Senator said. "Listen, son, I'm not a psychologist, but I can pretty well guess that serial killers need psychological help. You can get that. We can help you. Just tell us what you want."

Rudiger suddenly rushed up to the Senator and shoved the gun into the neck, pressing Sidams down against the bed. Jonas jumped up and towered over Rudiger, poised to strike.

"I'll tell you what I want," Rudiger said. "I want you to play your role, because you're *supposed* to play your role. You don't have a choice. It's how it's supposed to be. You are not the One, but you are still important." His eyes closed and his hand shook as the barrel of the gun pressed harder into the Senator's neck. "The sun will be darkened, and the moon will not give its light; the stars will fall from the sky, and the heavenly bodies will be shaken ..." Rudiger seemed to have disappeared, replaced by something Jonas remembered from Somalia. He was the devil. The devil quoting scripture. "They will see the Son of Man coming on the clouds of the sky, with power and great glory ... I tell you the truth, this generation *will certainly not pass away* until all these things have happened."

Jonas had seconds to make his move. Rudiger's back was to him. He could punch the gun away and square off for a fight. The Senator could grab the weapon and that would be it. It could be over in seconds.

Do it, Jonas. Now.

Now.

The adrenaline surged through his body. He readied himself. Rudiger was still on top of Sidams, and the Senator was now wheezing. We'll take him alive, Jonas thought. He'll tell us where Anne is. He will. We'll make him, no matter what we have to do to him.

Do it now. Only seconds left. *Don't wait any longer.*

A knock at the door.

Jonas felt himself lose balance. The knock pulled him back just as he was ready to attack.

Rudiger pushed himself off Sidams and back into the middle of the room – it happened so fast Jonas barely had time to register what was happening. Rudiger was undeniably a powerful man, regardless of his mental state. He was both strong and fast, Jonas knew, and not to be underestimated.

Rudiger trained the gun on Jonas. "Would be a mistake," Rudiger said. "I know you. You want to be the one in charge, but you can't be. Not here. Not now. I don't care about dying. But I promise you your girlfriend does."

Jonas didn't move.

"Back on the bed."

Jonas sat.

Another knock at the door.

"Stay still."

Rudiger turned and went to door, looking through the security hole.

Jonas tensed.

Please, God. Let Stages be alone.

Rudiger took a step back into the room.

"Come here," he said in a loud whisper to Sidams. "Open the door."

"Why?"

"Because I'm telling you to. Move now."

The Senator stood and walked slowly over to Rudiger. Jonas noticed a small round welt on the Senator's neck where Rudiger had pressed the gun.

"What do you want me to say?"

"Nothing. Just open the door and gesture for them to come inside."

"Them?"

"*Do it.* Now."

"Don't," the Senator said. "*Don't.*"

Rudiger raised his gun. "Last chance. Open the door."

"Don't do this. I'm begging you."

A third knock.

Rudiger steadied himself and drew a deep breath. Then he shoved the Senator with massive force back into the room, catching Sidams off-balance. He sprawled to the floor and missed slamming his head into the corner of the bedside desk by inches.

Jonas watched everything in slow motion.

Rudiger slipped both of his weapons in his belt and opened the door. His body blocked Jonas's view, but only for a second. Rudiger grabbed Stages arm and yanked him inside the room. Like the Senator, Stages lost all control and his large body tumbled with a heavy thud onto the carpet. He had barely let out a *What the fuck?* before Jonas saw the second person standing there. It was a young man, maybe thirty, wearing a dark grey suit and a bright yellow tie. Jonas had met him before. Greg? Craig? He worked for the Ambassador, that's all Jonas knew.

The man's brown eyes widened in fear at what had just happened, but then grew even wider when Rudiger pulled out the gun.

"Inside," Rudiger said.

Jonas shook his head at the man. Run, Jonas wanted to yell. *Run.*

The man took three tentative steps inside the room. His face lost all color.

Rudiger shut the door.

Then locked it.

The Ambassador yelled. "What the hell is all this?"

The Senator watched everything from the floor. Jonas studied Rudiger's eyes.

It was too late.

The Ambassador's aide spoke one word to his boss. "Bill?"

Rudiger reached down and pulled a knife from a sheath strapped to his ankle. Hunting knife. Black blade, about six inches.

No one had time to react.

Rudiger attacked from behind, grabbing a fistful of the aide's hair, yanking back his head. The knife sliced his throat wide open. Blood sprayed against the cream-colored walls. Against the armoire.

The man barely made a sound as he collapsed and died on the well-worn carpet of the hotel room.

CHAPTER FORTY-FIVE

RUDIGER WATCHES THE man fall to the carpeted floor, his body making a thud. Sounds like a suitcase falling off a bed. Then, nothing. Gone.

Wipes the blade on his pant leg and sheaths the weapon.

Good, Preacherman says in his ear. *Nice and clean. You sure know your way around a knife, boy.*

He feels it. Feels the rush. Just like every other time. He doesn't want to admit it, but he only has himself to be honest with. Death warms him. Excites him. He feels power, even only for a fleeting moment. Makes him want to kill more.

Maybe it's true, he thinks. *Maybe I'm jes crazy.*

A man is howling. Rudiger looks over. The Ambassador.

"Shut up," Rudiger says.

The man is hysterical. The fat hanging off his chin shakes and wobbles with his cries.

Rudiger takes out his gun. Doesn't want to use it – too much noise anyhow. But it should get the point across. He aims it at the man's head.

"Shut up now. Understand me?"

The fat man nods his head. Screams fade into foolish whimpers. Snot creeps from his left nostril.

Disgusting.

Am I crazy?

He holsters his weapon and thinks about what Jonas has said. About Asperger's Syndrome. About autism. He knows Jonas was attempting to rile him, but still …

Could it be true?

He's crazy, they all say. He's a *serial killer*. And aren't they all bat-shit crazy? Course they are. Must be. Dahmer ate his victims – what normal person would do that?

He kills in the name of God, they say. Uses it as an excuse. The killing just excites him, but he's convinced himself it's done for a cause. A just cause. But it's all a lie, they say. He just wants to kill.

He looks at the body on the floor. The scarlet blood spirals on the hotel walls.

He can't deny the sight of death excites him. But *he knows what he knows*, and he is what he is. He was born thus, and God made him. If he's crazy, it's only because that's how it's supposed to be.

One man's insanity is another man's religion.

Too late now anyway, Rudiger thinks. *I'm so close. Right or wrong, find out soon enough anyhow. Soon it will all be over.*

"Goddamn you," the Senator says. "You didn't have to do that."

Rudiger ignores him, not bothering to tell him that God won't damn him at all. Not one bit.

"Senator, put the bedspread over the body."

Sidams does.

Rudiger tells him to sit on the bed. Tells the Ambassador to do the same.

"Dismas and Gestas," Rudiger says, looking at the older men.

"Sidams and Stages," Jonas replied.

The fat man squeezes his neck. Seems calmer now that the body is hidden under a blanket. "What the hell is he talking about?"

Jonas explains. About the day Christ was crucified. About the two criminals who shared the Glory. Dismas and Gestas.

Rudiger watches the information process behind the Ambassador's eyes. He sees the exact moment when the fat man realizes what it going to happen. What *has* to happen. How the man will die. How they all will.

"No," the man says. "*No.*"

"Calm down, Bill."

The Ambassador is close to hysterics again. Rudiger prays for more strength for the man. Would make things much easier.

"But ... but there are three of us," the fat man pleads to the Senator. "He can't carry us all out of here. And even if he shoots us, it's better than what else he wants to do."

There is a silence and then Jonas explains about the woman. About Anne.

"I'm not dying for some woman I don't even know."

"Ambassador," Jonas says. "Just do as you are told."

"I won't!"

The fat man leaps off the bed.

Rudiger takes two steps forward and backhands him across the face. The man does a half spin and nearly falls before catching himself. The blow feels good against the bones in his hand. Warming.

He worries about the noise. If someone next door heard the yelling, security could be on the way.

"No more time," he says. "We have to leave now."

"I'm not going anywhere."

"Bill," the Senator says, "we're not in a position to dictate terms. Not right now."

The fat man points a meaty finger at Rudiger. "He can shoot me if he wants. I'm not going anywhere with him."

"Bill," Jonas says. "I need you to be strong now. If you don't go, we'll all die. Here. Right now."

"Better to get crucified?"

The Senator lowers his voice, but Rudiger can still hear. "Bill, at least we have a chance if we go with him. We at least buy some time – who knows what might happen? And we don't guarantee an early death for an innocent woman."

Rudiger loses interest in their logic.

"Stand up, all of you."

They do.

Rudiger reaches into a closet and pulls down a backpack, a camera, and a hat. From the backpack he removes a press pass that identifies him as an employee of the Associated Press. He also removes a small wireless transmitter. Slips on the hat and pulls the brim down over his forehead.

Nothing he can do to hide his scar.

He opens the backpack and shows it to Jonas.

"You know what that is?"

Jonas looks. Rudiger watches his face lose a little color.

"Yeah," Jonas says. "I think I know what that is."

Fat man cranes his neck. "What is it?"

"Looks like C4," Jonas says. "Wired and ready to detonate."

"Exactly."

"There's a lot in there."

"Enough to take out the walls around us."

Sidams looks inside the bag just before Rudiger zips it up and puts it on his back.

"What are you planning to do with that?"

"If you do what I say, I'm planning on doing nothing with it."

"We said we'd go with you."

"Never a good idea to take a man's word," Rudiger says. "When we leave here, there'll be a lot of people around us. If you don't cooperate, it won't jes be the four of us blown to all hell. Lot of others will die, too."

Jonas points at the transmitter in Rudiger's hand. It's small, about the size of a cell phone. Small black antennae. Two buttons. "That's the detonator?"

"Like you said. All wired up and ready to go."

Fat Man looks at Jonas. Rudiger knows what he's going to say before the words actually come out.

"How do we know it's real?"

Then Rudiger holds up the transmitter in front of the three men and rests his finger on the left button. The men all seem to stop breathing, and not one of them moves to stop Rudiger. No time. Too late.

Rudiger smiles as he presses the button.

The men all wince, waiting for their bodies to tear apart.

Instead there is nothing but a muffled boom, far in the distance. The building hiccups.

"What the hell was that?" the Senator says.

Rudiger walks to the window and parts the curtain. Within seconds something rains down past their view.

"Top corner of the roof falling down," Rudiger says. He looks down and sees chunks of rubble smashing into the street. A wave of excitement washes over him. Steals his breath for a moment or two. Against all his purpose, he wants more. More destruction. He closes his eyes and steadies himself for a moment.

Then turns toward the men.

"The other button is for the backpack. Clear?"

One by one they all nod. Even Jonas. They will all listen to him now. No other choice.

The fire alarm screeches above them. A light next to the sprinkler system flashes. A deep voice comes over a loudspeaker in the room. No panic in that voice at all, Rudiger thinks. Must be a recording.

"Please evacuate the hotel immediately. Use the stairwells located at either end of your floor. Do not panic. Assist those who need help getting down the stairs."

Rudiger walks around the men and opens the door. People are already in the hallway, scurrying for the stairwells. A bald man in a business suit presses the elevator button and curses at it when it doesn't light up.

Gonna be a panic, Rudiger thinks.

He turns to the three men.

What happens now will happen, Rudiger thinks. There is very little in his direct control, despite what he has told them. He'll kill them if he has to, but he doesn't want to.

Not yet.

It hasn't started yet. So close. What began so long ago is now so near the end. The pain that started with the Preacherman is almost over. The heavens will open up and the good will be saved. Rudiger will be free, for the first time since he was twelve.

Rudiger shifts his weight and squeezes his right hand into a fist.

"Time to go."

CHAPTER FORTY-SIX

JONAS TOOK THE lead, moving past Rudiger and out into the hallway. The fire alarm blared throughout the corridor, and flashing emergency lights stabbed at him from both directions. There were at least two dozen people already headed for the stairs, with more people streaming from their rooms every second.

What the hell happened?

Jonas thought he knew. Rudiger was one step ahead. He'd detonated a charge somewhere on the roof. Probably not enough to do major damage, but enough to scare the living shit out of everyone in the hotel. Force an evacuation. Start a panic. And that makes it a hell of a lot easier to get all of them out of the building undetected.

It also proved the C4 explosive in the backpack was real.

Jonas waited in the corridor for the others, watching as the chaos started to bubble around him.

A family with small children emerged from the room across the corridor. The father was trying to soothe a crying baby while the mother told their little boy everything was going to be okay. The boy covered his ears and stared at the flashing lights. Then he looked over at Jonas, who gave him a nod.

Don't worry, his look said.

Then Rudiger grabbed him by the arm.

"At any time," he said, motioning to the backpack he carried.

"Let's just get out of here," Sidams said to Jonas. "Too many people around. We can't take any chances."

"Agreed."

Jonas turned to Stages, who looked like a fat rabbit cornered by a dog, praying for a heart attack before he's torn apart. "Bill," Jonas said. "Stay close. This is real. Nothing stupid. Understand?"

Stages moved his head, which Jonas took for a nod.

A man shouted at a non-functioning elevator while a woman shouted at him. *We have to use the stairs, idiot!*

A swarthy man with wide shoulders and a long scratchy beard walked briskly with his head down. Jonas recognized him as an adjunct from one of the Palestinian delegations. He made his way for the stairwell among the throngs of people starting to swell in the hotel corridor, but everyone left a wide berth for the Muslim. It was then Jonas realized how smart Rudiger was. The hotel was full of Muslims attending the conference. Now, with pieces of the hotel raining from the sky, everyone would only be able to think of September 11th.

This wasn't going to be a minor panic, Jonas thought. This was going to turn into a riot.

"What's happening to the building?" someone shouted.

"Get to the stairs!"

"I smell smoke."

There was no smoke, only the frenzied imagination of a scared hotel guest. Jonas wanted to tell them all everything would be fine as long as they just went down the stairs in an orderly fashion. He wanted to shepherd them, lead them. It was his natural instinct. But he couldn't take the chance. He had to follow just like the rest of them, because if he did anything out of the ordinary Rudiger might just blow them all into a million chunks of flesh and bone.

Jonas grabbed Stages by the arm as the large man started to fall behind. Sidams led them, and no one around seemed to realize a United States Senator was amongst the throngs of people. Rudiger followed behind Stages.

"No talking," Rudiger said, though none of the men had said anything.

They made it into the concrete stairwell, joining hordes of other people who were descending from the floors above them. It was more controlled than Jonas expected, though a bottleneck immediately formed behind an older woman who, guessing from the size of her, probably hadn't spent much time in her life dealing with any kind of stairs. She apologized for holding everyone up, but it wasn't too long before the wave started to push past her, forcing her to the side of the stairwell and against the wall. She shouted out but didn't fall. Some shouted back at her, some apologized. A waifish young woman in her pajamas grabbed onto her hand and barked at anyone else who tried to push past her.

One floor down, Jonas heard a loud female voice shouting out instructions for everyone.

Move quickly, but don't push. Everything is fine. No need to panic.

Jonas kept one hand on the Senator's back in front of him and the other grabbing onto Stages's arm, coaxing him down the stairs like he was leading a stubborn donkey down a canyon trail. Jonas didn't know what the plan was once they finally left the stairwell and were outside, but it wouldn't be long before they were at that point. Rudiger had chosen a lower floor for his room; their departure had been planned for speed.

Jonas's mind raced through all the different possibilities for escape, and there were several. The most promising was here.

Right now. Among the confusion and the crowds. The natural imbalance on the stairs. He could quickly make a move, shoving Rudiger down and overpowering him.

But Rudiger's hand was on the transmitter, and it was too great a risk. If he hit that button, it would all be over. For everyone. Jonas imagined the power of the blast, which would magnify in the tight concrete stairwell. Devastating.

And once they were outside? When they finally had some distance between themselves and the other hotel guests?

Not going to happen, Jonas thought. There's enough C4 in that bag to kill anyone within a hundred feet, and there's too many people coming out of the hotel to get that kind of separation.

Moreover, there was Anne. Even if Jonas was able to incapacitate Rudiger without the explosive detonating, Jonas fully believed she would die if Jonas and the others didn't do what Rudiger wanted. If Jonas knew one thing about Rudiger Sonman, it was the man didn't bluff.

They reached the second floor and Jonas saw who was shouting out the instructions.

Agent Difranco.

He saw her before she saw him.

Shit.

"Senator!" she shouted, seeing Sidams first.

Sidams nodded and lowered his head, walking past her.

"We're okay," Jonas said, keeping his hand on the Senator's back. He chanced a brief glance back at Stages, whom Jonas had lost his grip on. He was a few feet back, with Rudiger directly behind him, steering him down the stairs.

Difranco then did what a seasoned law enforcement veteran does. Amid the chaos, amid the shouts and screams, amid all the confusion, she picked up on something from Jonas. Maybe it was the way he looked behind him when everyone else was looking forward. Maybe it was the way he dismissed her without even asking her if she knew what had happened. Or that he hadn't asked for extra help with the Senator, arguably the most important guest in the hotel.

Whatever it was, she followed Jonas's gaze as he looked back at Stages. And then she looked at the man behind him, the pasty man with the rigid spine and hollow, sea-blue eyes, who looked like he had no business wearing a baseball hat. The man with the brutal scar running down past his ear.

She drew her weapon and pointed it at Sonman.

"Stay right there!"

Screams erupted. Those on the stairs above Rudiger fought to start going back up, pushing against the tidal force behind them like lemmings changing their mind only feet from the edge of the cliff. Those on the stairs below pushed every harder to make it down, the panic now fully unleashed among them.

Sonman stopped and smiled. Stages managed to push away and reach Jonas's position a few feet away.

"Don't," Jonas said to Difranco.

"It's Sonman. It's him!" Her gun stayed level with his chest. Rudiger stood only feet away.

"I know," Jonas said, as calmly as he could. "Put the gun away."

Someone shouted about a gun above them and more people screamed. Jonas heard the words *terrorist attack*.

"No fucking way," Difranco said.

Rudiger smiled and lifted the transmitter.

Jonas quickly leaned toward Difranco, not wanting anyone else to hear. "He got C4 in his backpack. The explosion on the roof was his. Put the gun down or we're all going to die."

Then Jonas saw the situation wash over her. In all her training, this was something she had likely never been prepared for. Risk the lives of several or let free a known killer?

The panic grew. The force of people from above grew too great. Three people fell onto the concrete landing, spilling at Rudiger's feet. More shouts erupted. A child screamed out something unintelligible.

"What the hell is going on?" shouted someone from above.

Difranco kept her gun trained on Rudiger as she looked at Jonas.

Jonas shook his head. *Don't do it.*

Three more seconds passed, and to Jonas it seemed forever. Everything seemed to be riding on this one moment, this one decision. If this went on any longer the pressure would be too great to overcome, and there would only be death and destruction to follow.

Then, finally, just as quickly as she had produced it, Agent Difranco holstered her gun. "Goddamnit!" she yelled.

Rudiger kept smiling as he walked past her. If anyone pieced together that the thing in his hand was a wireless detonator for a bomb, no one seemed to care. All that mattered was the downward flow commenced once again.

Rudiger walked up to Difranco and said something Jonas could not hear. Whatever it was, the FBI agent did not pursue the group of men as they continued their journey down the stairwell. For all Jonas knew, she wasn't even radioing what had happened, though he doubted it.

Which meant Rudiger had a plan to get them out quickly.

Two floors later his suspicion was confirmed. The stairwell finally gave way to a direct street exit and the barely controlled order from the stairs gave way to total chaos. Once people reached the outside world they bolted, running hard and fast in any direction, as if the building was seconds from toppling over onto all of them. Police shouted, trying to control the direction and the flow of the hotel guests, but it was no use. They were merely pebbles in a stream, futilely trying to control the direction of the current.

Rudiger rounded up his three captives and led them to a nearby surface parking lot. They were never more than twenty feet from other hotel guests, so the threat of a devastating explosion from Rudiger's backpack remained very real.

Rudiger stopped in front of a ten-foot U-Haul cargo van, double parked near the entrance of the garage. Two things jumped out at Jonas: the license plates had been removed, and the cargo trailer door was open.

"Get in," Rudiger said.

"Oh, Jesus, no," Stages said, his breathing labored. "I'm not getting in there."

A woman unlocked the car next to them and scurried inside. Rudiger looked over at her and caressed the button on the transmitter. "Not a question, Ambassador."

Stages tried to climb in the back and fell to the floor. Rudiger pushed him inside with his foot.

"Get in, Senator," Rudiger ordered. "No time to argue." He kept his fingertip on the pager button.

Sidams looked over at Jonas. *I sure hope you have a plan*, his face said. Then he climbed in next to Stages.

Jonas no longer knew what was right. He thought there would be a better opportunity to fight Rudiger and save Anne, but now he wasn't sure. A powerful sense overcame him, a feeling of certainty. *If we get into that van, it's all over. We'll all die, including Anne.*

Rudiger's voice seemed to drop an octave. "Get in."

"You have to promise to let her go. Whatever you do to us, promise to let her go."

"There shall no evil befall thee, neither shall any plague come nigh thy dwelling. For he shall give his angels charge over thee, to keep thee in all thy ways."

Jonas did not understand but knew he had no choice. He climbed in the truck, and Rudiger lowered the cargo door and locked it from the outside. Seconds later the van was moving, pulling tightly to the left, and Jonas knew Rudiger had likely eluded the FBI for enough time to get away without being tracked. They probably wouldn't realize the men were in the back of the U-Haul until the security tapes from the outside the hotel showed what happened. And by then the van would be long gone.

Jonas hoped he was wrong about his intuition. About his feeling of impending doom. For once he wanted to be wrong.

Then a small metal canister dropped through a hole in the van's cab. The cylinder rolled around on the bare floor of the cargo space, stopping when it wedged against the Ambassador, who hadn't moved since getting inside.

When smoke started to pour out of the canister, Jonas knew his intuition hadn't failed him.

It was all over.

CHAPTER FORTY-SEVEN

RUDIGER TOWERS ABOVE them. They're naked, except a small cloth wrapped around their waists. Gotta have a little respect. It's what God wants.

The men are sleeping, and he guesses they'll be out for at least another hour. Maybe the fat one will sleep longer. He'll wake once it all starts though. No way he'll sleep through that. No way.

The two criminals are bound to their crosses. Wrists and ankles eaten by ropes. Crosses still on the floor, but not for long. Got it all rigged to a pulley system. Help to raise the crosses into place when it's time. Still be easier to do the nailing while they're on the floor, though.

The temperature inside the old airplane hangar soars, the heat stifling. *Good*, he thinks. *Should be hot.*

He walks around his work, checking every detail. It all seems, well, just right. Just right this time. Pride flirts with his mind, but he pushes it away. Pride is wrong. No room for it here.

Over to Jonas. He's not on the cross. He's in a metal chair, thick rope around him. Legs bound together at the ankles. Not going anywhere. Rudiger squats in front of him and studies the man, lifting his head by the chin. Jonas sleeps hard. Rudiger runs his fingertips along the man's nose, cheekbone.

"You were there at the beginning, Lieutenant," Rudiger says. Jonas sleeps.

He pushes a bead of sweat along the man's forehead and wonders if he's dreaming. What's in that mind right now? Does he know what's going to happen? Does he know the magnitude of it? Could he possibly understand?

All the scholars in all the world over all the centuries, and no one would have guessed it. Christ is returning, and it's all gonna happen in an abandoned airplane hangar in the Colorado plains. Rudiger smiles. Only he knows. Only He knows.

Rudiger peels off his clothes, leaving on only his underwear. The still air clings to his sweat. He folds his clothes neatly and puts them in the corner of the room.

Rudiger waits.

He's surprised at his own serenity. The quiet calms him.

He keeps his radio off, not wanting to know what's happening outside. Oh, they're looking. Looking all over the place. Looking for a U-Haul van. That FBI lady certainly had them pull up video footage of the hotel exterior, and they probably tracked them all to the parking lot. But it don't matter if they find the van. By then it'll be too late, and the world will just thank him for it anyway.

He shines a flashlight beam along all the old magazine and newspaper clippings, though he's read them a thousand times. The light settles on one article in particular.

From *People Magazine*, the pages wilted by heat and time.

An interview with his daddy.

The face meant nothing to him when he'd first seen it two months ago – he barely even recognized his old man. Cragged lines on weathered Irish skin.

Rudiger shines the light and stares into the face that stares back at him. Steel blue eyes. Flecks of gold.

He remembers him now. Not a lot, but enough. Flashes of a childhood. A time before the badness.

* * *

A trip to the beach, sandcastle eaten by waves. That fleshy Irish face looking down at him. A hand tousling his head. It's okay, the man says. We'll build another one.

But the waves will just keep coming, won't they?

Yes, son, they will. They'll always keep coming. That's jes the nature of things.

Rudiger sees him clearly, thinks he can smell the spice of his aftershave mixed with the scent of the ocean. Waves crash behind them, filling the air with the static of sloshing water.

Let's make this one different, he says.

Different how?

Different special. Because you're special, aren't you, Rudy?

Special how?

He doesn't answer. Instead, he grabs a waterlogged stick washed ashore and writes in the wet sand. The letters clean and neat.

RUDIGER

What do you see? he asks.

I see my name.

What else?

He thinks for a moment. Ride rug, he says.

The man nods. That's right. Ride rug.

A wave comes in and licks away the letters. The man writes again.

OCEAN

Now what do you see?

The boys stares. Ocean, he says. And canoe.

Good, Rudy. Very good. The man leans down and kisses him on the forehead. You're very smart.

Sometimes I don't feel smart.

The father smiles at his son.

You're smarter than me, he says.

Will you take me in the water, Daddy? I don't want to go alone.

Yes, the man says. Of course I will. But you're braver than me. You should be the one taking me into the water.

Don't be silly.

They walk into the water, the salt stinging a recently skinned knee. The boy holds his father's hand as the water comes up to his thighs, then waist. It is forceful and gentle, this water. It guides him and protects him, but it could kill if it wanted to. It chooses not to. The boy doesn't really feel afraid. He doesn't feel much of anything, like usual.

Here, the man says. He reaches and grabs both of the boy's hands. Learn to float.

How?

Hold my hands and let the water do the rest of the work.

The boy does as his father tells him. His feet leave the mushy sand and his legs come to the surface. His eyes are closed for a moment, but once his bare belly breaches the surface, they open. His daddy looks down at him, his smiling face blocking the sun.

That's it, Rudy. That's it.

The man moves a few inches and the full power of the sun bursts down upon the boy's face. It's brilliant. The boy must close his eyes, but does not want to. The light lifts him.

I am very pleased with you, my son.

The boy says nothing. His eyes closed once again, he feels his father's hands let go, and on his own, the boy floats, the water lifting him and the tide pushing him, pulsating with the current, only inches at a time but oceans over a lifetime.

* * *

Rudiger reaches out and touches the glossy magazine page, touching the face of his father. Two months ago the memory came to him, and it is the one memory he needed, the one that solved the puzzle. Since then, there has been no need to search. To find clues. To kill.

There has only been the need to prepare.

"You were right," Rudiger tells the wall. "I am special."

His thoughts are interrupted by a sound from behind him.

It's the Ambassador. The first one to wake.

Rudiger is mildly surprised. Thought the fat one'd be out longer.

The Ambassador begins to scream.

CHAPTER FORTY-EIGHT

JONAS WOKE UP to screaming, but it all still felt like a dream. There was a dream, wasn't there? A snake slithering up his legs, coiling around his body, squeezing the life from him, letting him exhale but not inhale.

He opened his eyes and first saw his knees, but just barely. There was some light, but just a few ghosts of it, not enough for him to understand anything at all.

The heat was stifling.

He was sitting in a chair, that much he understood. He tried to move his arms but couldn't, and then his eyes adjusted enough to the dark to let him see the rope around his upper torso.

The screams continued.

Jonas turned his head and threw up, the vomit dribbling down his shoulder and onto the floor. His head throbbed. *The gas*, he thought. He remembered that much. The van. The canister. The gas. Coughing and holding his sleeve against his nose, knowing it wouldn't help.

But he wasn't dead. Neither were the others. The gas was just to knock them out, make them easier to transport and contain. Nobody was dead. Not yet.

Another scream and then a gurgling sob.

Jonas moved his head again, this time slowly, and looked in the direction of the sound.

They were about thirty feet away. The room was large, whatever it was. Rudiger was standing over Bill Stages. Rudiger wore a headlamp, the light from which poured down over the corpulence of the Ambassador, who was naked save what looked like some kind of loincloth.

Rudiger was hitting him with something.

What is that?

No. He wasn't hitting him, he was hitting a large spike. With a mallet. The spike was going right through the wrists of Bill Stages and into the wooden cross underneath him.

Jonas coughed and another wave of vomit spewed from him.

Rudiger stopped pounding and straightened. He turned in Jonas's direction, the light filling the dark void between them. Jonas looked directly into the light but couldn't see the face underneath it. Rudiger said nothing, and after a few seconds went back to work.

"God, no, please ... no more ..." Stages's voice was weak. A crying child. He would die soon, Jonas knew. From shock if nothing else.

Where was the Senator?

Jonas looked around but couldn't make out enough of the room to see if the Senator was even here.

He felt more awake now, the adrenaline rushing through him. He strained his arms against the rope again, to no effect. Too tight.

Goddamnit. He was the one who made them come here. He was the one who said everything would be okay. *Nothing* was okay. They were all going to die, and it was all his fault.

For all he knew, Anne was already dead.

"Rudiger," he said, soft at first. "Rudiger!"

Rudiger's hammer did not cease. Nor did the screams.

"Rudiger, goddamnit, stop! Just let me talk to you."

The hammering stopped. So did the screams. Stages either died or passed out. Probably didn't matter too much which one. The end would all be the same.

Jonas watched as Rudiger bent down and picked up another spike. He shifted over to Stages's feet, placing one on top of the other.

He's not going to talk until he's all done, Jonas knew.

"Rudiger, please, for Christ's sake just stop. Just for a second."

Jonas thought he heard a muffled laugh before the hammering resumed. The spike pinned Stages's feet to the wood beneath, but the Ambassador didn't make a sound. He was lost in his own black world of silent horror.

Jonas prayed the man was dead. If he wasn't and he regained consciousness, the pain would be unbearable.

Rudiger dropped the hammer on the ground and then picked something else up. Jonas only saw a brief glint. A shimmer of steel.

Knife.

He watched as Rudiger bent over the Ambassador's face and grabbed the side of the man's head. Then Rudiger began to saw, back and forth, and Jonas realized he was removing the left ear of William Stages.

The Ambassador made no sound, which was almost the worst part of it all. Almost.

Jonas closed his eyes.

This isn't happening. Please God, make it all stop.

Eyes opened once again, Jonas saw Rudiger drop the severed ear to the ground, as if giving a scrap of food to a patiently waiting dog.

Rudiger then picked up the base of the crucifix, heaving it a few feet to the left. He lowered it with precision so the base lined up with what looked like a small hole in the ground. Next he pulled on a piece of rope that dangled from the dark ceiling like a vine. He looped it around the top of the cross and cinched it tight. The other end of the rope floated a few feet away. Rudiger donned thick work gloves and pulled on the rope. Jonas could only see what Rudiger's headlamp illuminated, but it was enough. He knew what was happening.

Rudiger grunted as the cross slowly began its ascent. The top of the crucifix angled upwards as the base slipped soundly into the hole in the ground. When the cross was almost fully upright, it slid the rest of the way into its base with a soft *thunk*, shuddered for a few seconds, then was still.

Rudiger yanked the rope, freeing it from the pulley, then walked over to the far corner of the room.

The light on his head went out.

Total darkness inside the room, save the few gaps near the taped doors and windows where sunlight managed to crawl in for a few feet before dying.

Then the brilliance of a spotlight. The light stunned Jonas, almost forcing his gaze away.

But he couldn't look away.

The light shot directly onto Stages, angling down at him from the ceiling, seeming to sear into his fleshy, naked form. The white hot light made his blood brown, and the smears of it across his chest, arms, face and thighs looked like mud.

His weight made him sag, tearing at the holes in his wrists and feet. Still he did not wake, but he was alive. His knees slumped and his chest strained against the force. His lungs screamed to breathe. The man was asphyxiating.

Jonas couldn't look away. This was fucking real. He could see it. *Smell* it. What was happening to Stages would happen to Sidams. And then to Jonas.

"Rudiger!" Jonas screamed. He struggled again in his chair to no use. "Rudiger!"

Out of the darkness Rudiger appeared, just feet away, a ghost materializing. He wore only his underwear, grey-cotton briefs soaked through with sweat. Blood covered his hands and sprinkled his face. He used his right hand to push the sweat up to the top of his scalp, leaving behind a crimson stain, making him look like some kind of albino warrior.

He stared at Jonas for long time, but did not speak.

Jonas knew he could not beg for his life. There was no point.

"Tell me where she is," he said. "At least tell me. Even if she's going to die, tell me where she is."

Rudiger said nothing.

Finally he disappeared back into the darkness.

Moments later, his headlamp burst once again to life. Rudiger walked over to the center of the room and picked up the hammer from the floor.

Then he walked to the far side of the room, which had been ensconced in darkness the whole time. The light from his head arrived at the destination first, and that's when Jonas saw the Senator on the ground, tied to his own cross. The light pointed to the floor and Jonas saw the collection of spikes lined up next to the Senator's leg.

"No!" Jonas yelled.

And then he heard Sidams speak.

"It's all right, Jonas," the Senator called out. Jonas heard the strain in his voice, but the words still seemed calm. Surely the Senator watched what had happened to Stages. But he didn't beg for mercy. Instead, he said simply to his captor, "I can't pretend to understand why you would want to do this, so I won't. You just killed one of my dear friends, and now I suppose it's time for me." He coughed violently before continuing. "I guess if there's anything I could do or say to make you stop, now's the time." He paused, and the room was silent. "All right, then," he continued. "I just hope you keep your promise and let that young girl go. No reason she has to die."

Rudiger spoke, his words grumbled and unintelligible to Jonas.

There was more silence. Then Rudiger kneeled at the Senator's left arm and positioned the spike over his wrist.

"I'll get help!" Jonas shouted. "I swear to God I will get help."

Sidams's voice shook. "You just take care of yourself, Jonas. And make sure you get your girlfriend out of this mess."

"Yes, sir," Jonas said. He didn't want to watch, so he wouldn't. But nothing he could do would keep him from hearing.

The Senator managed a few words.

"The Lord is my shepherd, I shall not want; He makes me lie down in –"

The screaming started.

CHAPTER FORTY-NINE

TWENTY MINUTES LATER the Senator took his place next to Stages. Upright and wrapped in a loincloth. Bleeding and illuminated. Drooling. His hair matted into sweaty clumps, stuck to his forehead. Left ear gone, also discarded to the floor. The Senator was still conscious, remarkably, though only enough to loll his head from side to side. Every millimeter of movement must be excruciating, Jonas thought. Every breath labored. Every hope diminished.

Jonas watched as Rudiger stood back and surveyed his work. Stages, most likely dead. Sidams, struggling against shock and blood loss. He was a tough man, Jonas thought. But he cannot possibly survive long in that state.

"Dismas and Gestas," Rudiger said.

Jonas had tried to free himself while the Senator was being crucified. It had been of little use, though it kept Jonas from focusing all his energy on the pain being inflicted on his friend. Still, his chest had more room for movement than just twenty minutes ago.

"It's just a coincidence," Jonas said. "It's just their names. Nothing more."

"I do not believe in coincidences, Lieutenant," Rudiger said.

"What *do* you believe in?"

Rudiger turned to Jonas, his headlamp shining directly into Jonas's eyes.

"Would think it'd be pretty evident by now."

The Senator coughed, wet, hacking. Blood oozed from his mouth and slid down his chin, hanging off him in a viscous rope, then dropping onto the floor.

Jonas closed his eyes, squeezing them shut for just a moment. Losing himself inside his head. Preparing himself.

"Dismas and Gestas," Jonas said, opening his eyes. "What did they do?"

"They were thieves."

"You think those men are thieves?"

"Don't much matter what I think."

"It does to me."

"Why?"

"Because if I'm going to die, I want to understand it."

Rudiger walked out of the pools of light and again into the dark. Jonas, immobile, had the sense of a night swimmer in the ocean, a shark circling beneath. Seconds later a third spotlight burst into light, holding a tight circle next to Jonas. A third cross lay in the center of the light, its beams nicked and marked in a torrent of symbols and letters. Jonas had no idea what any of it meant.

Rudiger's pale and bloodied form emerged into the light, the shark breaching the surface of the icy waters.

"Who said you're gonna die?" he said.

Jonas exhaled and pushed the rope outward. Inhaling, he guessed the slack. Half an inch, maybe. Not enough. Not enough to do anything. Except whatever he wants me to do.

"I'm not holding out a lot of hope here."

Rudiger bent down and picked up the mallet, its head chipped and scarred from use. "There's always hope, Lieutenant. You should know that."

"Is there?"

Rudiger smiled. "You survived the Mog. That was more hope than you gave yourself credit for." He held the mallet loosely, swinging it back and forth, a pendulum slowly making its rounds. "Almost had you again outside your apartment. Probably didn't have too much hope then neither."

"You didn't want to kill me then."

"No. No, sir, I surely did not. Don't know exactly what I wanted, just knew you had something to do with it. I didn't have the answers then."

Jonas pulled his right arm and felt the rope loosen a fraction.

"You have the answers now?"

"I do. I most certainly do."

"What's the question?"

"Question of salvation."

"You saving yourself?"

Rudiger bent forward and grinned. "Saving *all* of us."

"Where's Anne?"

"She's dying."

"Where is she? Is she close?"

"Close enough to save her. If you can follow instructions."

"I can."

He straightened. "Thought so. Knew I could count on you."

"I can't do much for her nailed to a cross."

Jonas looked over at the Ambassador. In the garish light, he could see the man was already turning blue. His ankles swelled with blood.

The Senator let out a low, hollow moan.

Rudiger walked forward and knelt in front of Jonas. Jonas could smell him, the musk of work. Stench of death. Brutality. Purpose. He reached forward with long fingers, nails bitten to the core. Hand on Jonas's shoulder.

"That cross ain't for you."

CHAPTER FIFTY

HORROR STRUCK JONAS, a twisted fist shoved deep inside, pulling and tearing.

"Don't," he said. "I'm begging you. Don't do this to her."

He had to stop him. He could not watch him do to Anne what he just did to the Senator. Jonas could not watch her die. Not like that. Not in any way.

"*Goddamnit*, you said you'd let her go!"

Rudiger stood and smiled, his lips twisted and tight.

"You're all sorts of panic, sir. All sorts. *Hooah*."

Jonas recalled the voice on the phone. *Hooah*. That felt like centuries ago. He pushed against the rope again. He thought it gave a bit more, but more likely it was his hope outwitting reality. He had to keep trying.

Rudiger disappeared once again into the dark. When he returned, an unlit cigarette dangled off his lower lip. He reached up with cupped hands and lit it, blowing smoke through flared nostrils.

"That is *so* good," he said. "Think maybe I'll even have two."

He smoked silently as Jonas watched him, pushing with his legs and chest against the ropes. The room filled with a haze, the smoke floating in and out of the spotlights, making everything look like a stage production rather than the site of a mass killing. As Rudiger was nearly done with his first smoke he began to speak.

"Preacherman came to me for a reason. God's will. Preacherman stole me from myself, him and the whore. They took and took until there was nothing left, and when he finally had his fill I killed him. My first blood. Wish I got her too, but I didn't. She disappeared like smoke and I never did see her again." He flicked ash to the floor. "That's okay. I found her lookalike back in Cleveland, so that felt pretty all right feeling my fists on her." He looked at Jonas, staring deep into him. "But it was supposed to be that way, don't you see, sir? Preacherman was *supposed* to do what he did, because all God wanted was for me to learn, and learn I did from him. God gave focus to the desires I have. God gave me direction. God gave me a *mission*. Otherwise who knows what sorts of havoc I might have wreaked in my life."

Then he fell silent.

Jonas thought the rope was stretched just enough so he might be able to free one arm, but not without a lot of struggle. With Rudiger in front of him, he couldn't do anything about it.

Then he did as Jonas hoped – walked into the dark. Jonas strained and pulled against the ropes, feeling them dig and burn into his skin, trying to be as quiet as he could. He saw the Senator lift his head and look in his direction, but wasn't sure if there was enough light for Sidams to see him. Jonas was able to move his right arm up a couple of inches, but the ropes were too high on his chest to slip his arm free. He needed more slack.

Seconds later, Rudiger returned to the light. A freshly lit cigarette occupied his mouth. A hunting knife dangled from his right hand. The blade was stained with the blood of ears.

"Then I remembered something else. This time it was my daddy. I was on the beach. He took me out into the water." Long, slow drag. Exhale. Eyes closed. "Don't much matter about the details. But what matters is what he said to me."

Jonas felt the sweat tickle his neck. "What did he say to you?"

"He said, 'I am pleased with you.'" He looked at Jonas. "You don't understand, do you?"

"No. I don't."

"You read the Bible?"

"No."

"Well, that's why, then." Rudiger was silent for many minutes. His voiced seemed to echo when he resumed. "Immediately coming up out of the water, He saw the heavens opening, and the Spirit like a dove descending upon Him; and a voice came out of the heavens: 'You are My beloved Son, in You I am well-pleased.' Immediately the Spirit impelled Him to go out into the wilderness."

Jonas sensed a vague familiarity but nothing more.

"All I needed to do was remember the time before the Preacherman. That one memory of my time in the water with my daddy." Rudiger's gaze burned into him. "Don't you see, Lieutenant? It was jes like Jesus with John. *Jes like that.*"

Fire-eyed and smoke pouring from his nose, Rudiger walked up to Jonas. Down on one knee. Cigarette dropped to the ground. Rudiger lifted his knife and dug deep into Jonas with his gaze.

"Time to go to the wilderness."

Then he cut the ropes off.

CHAPTER FIFTY-ONE

RUDIGER STANDS BACK and looks at him. Ropes cut and twisted on the floor. Jonas doesn't move.

"Get up," Rudiger says. "Slow now. Legs'll be weak from the gas."

Jonas waits a second before standing. He's off-balance when he does.

"Don't try to do anything to me. You'll get that soon enough."

"Where is she?" Jonas asks.

"Not here."

Jonas wobbles.

"You don't get it, do you?," Rudiger says.

"No."

He looks over to Sidams. Man don't have long. Doesn't matter. Those two are just window dressing. Part of the performance. Not the main actor.

"Cross is for me, Lieutenant."

"You?"

"It was me the whole time. The whole time. *I'm* the One."

Jonas takes a step forward. Wobbly.

"Not Anne?"

"No. *Me*." Rudiger loses himself in his memory, clinging to it like the only copy of a rare photograph. "I didn't even need my ability. I jes needed to remember the words from my daddy. He was right all along. I *am* special."

"*Where is she?*"

Rudiger snaps his attention back to Jonas. "Dyin.' Like I said."

"How are you going to get ... on the cross?"

Rudiger squeezes his fists, then opens all fingers. The knife falls to the floor.

"You're going to do it. Just like the others. 'Cept the ear part – that ain't necessary for me. Need to wait a few minutes for you to get your strength. Lot of work."

"You want me to nail you to that?"

"That's the idea."

"You want to die?"

"Not a matter of want. I am the Son of Man."

Silence. Rudiger follows Jonas's gaze, which shifts to the Senator. Back to Rudiger.

"How do I get Anne?"

"You do a good job, I'll tell you where she is. Before I die."

"What if you die too soon?"

"Then she dies, too."

"Is this for real?"

"What else would it be?"

He spits on the floor, dry mouth. Should probably have some water, but doesn't do anything about it. Another cigarette would be nice, but doesn't want to indulge. He walks over and looks at the cross on the floor. Rudiger sits on the floor, then stretches out over the beams. Arms outright. Back stiff against cool wood.

"Take your time. When you're ready, come over."

Rudiger watches as Jonas stumbles over to the Senator. He doesn't tell Jonas not to help the man. *He's smart*, Rudiger thinks. *He'll figure that out.* Sure enough, all Jonas manages is to touch his leg, small gesture. Wipe off some blood. He says something to

Sidams. Rudiger can't hear it. Maybe a promise. Then Jonas goes over to the Ambassador. Stares down at him, but doesn't touch the body.

Then Jonas walks into the dark. Seconds later, the room fills with light. The door he found swings open and Rudiger sees Jonas step out into the daylight. Feeble breeze rustles through the hangar. Death rattle breath. Jonas wants to run, Rudiger thinks. Run into the light. The safety of day. The open plains. But he won't. He'll shut that door and come back to the death around him. Because it's the only thing he can do.

Jonas does just that. Disappears back into the dark. Emerges into the light. Looks down upon Rudiger. Air still and heavy.

"How does this work?"

"Pick up the mallet and a spike."

He nods at the floor next to him, but he doesn't need to. Spikes next to a cross tend to be obvious. Jonas does as he's told, his movements slow and unsure.

"Be easier with you on your knees."

Jonas gets on his knees. Rudiger can feel his breath. He stares at the spotlight above him, burning into his flesh. He thinks he's ready, but he doesn't know. What if I'm wrong?

Preacherman's voice. Preacherman's words.

You ain't wrong, boy. Now do it good and deep.

But I've been wrong before.

Believe in your faith. And don't be a pussy. Pain won't last long.

I don't fear the pain.

Tell him exactly how to do it.

I know.

"Left wrist first," Rudiger says to Jonas. "Between the two bones leading up to the forearm."

"Jesus."

"Don't get sick on me now."

"What if I hit an artery?"

"You won't."

Jonas wipes his forehead then places the sharp end of the spike on Rudiger's forearm.

"Lower."

The metal is cool, despite the heat in the room. The weight against the skin feels satisfying. Solid. Real.

"Here?"

"That'll do it. Get the mallet."

Jonas picks it up. Holds it with a shaking right hand.

"First strike hard, not soft. Drive it through."

"I ... oh, God."

"You can do it."

"I know. Just give me a minute."

"You're important, Lieutenant. Always have been. You're saving the world and don't even believe it."

The Senator gurgles a cough in the distance.

Jonas closes his eyes.

"You praying?"

The man doesn't answer. He's lost somewhere else, another world. Another time. Building a purpose to do what has to be done. Then all is still, like a still that's never been. No more breathing. No more shaking.

He's ready.

Eyes open. Fierce. Resolved. Jonas lifts the mallet. High above the head.

"God bless you," Rudiger says.

The blow is crushing, and Rudiger feels a pain and a glory he hasn't felt since Jerusalem. Excruciating and humbling. He is on the road, no longer lost. Jonas pounds the nail. Two times. Three.

Rudiger says nothing. No scream. No begging. With every crushing blow there is a certainty of right. Of belonging.

He looks down at his arm, the metal protrusion an organic extension of his body. He feels himself smile. Wonders if he is. Blood pours from the wound.

"Where is she?"

Rudiger looks at his right arm. He feels a liquid run from his left eye, not knowing if it's a tear or blood. Then he starts to hum.

"We're jes gettin' started."

CHAPTER FIFTY-TWO

JONAS FORCED HIMSELF to hammer the spike five times before turning away and retching on the floor. Hardly anything came out. His stomach twisted, and his throat burned with fire. When he finally turned back, he could see the pain on Rudiger's face, but the man kept his eyes closed and kept humming.

Jonas didn't recognize the song.

"We don't have to do this," Jonas said.

Rudiger coughed and caught his breath. "Yes, Lieutenant, we do."

"Where is she?"

"Test the nail, Lieutenant. Grab it and pull. Make sure it's hard and fast in the wood. You don't want it giving out."

Jonas didn't move.

Rudiger opened his eyes and glared at Jonas. "Do it."

Jonas reached over and grabbed the spike, which disappeared into Rudiger's wrist. He pulled it weakly toward him. Rudiger grimaced.

"I ... I think it's okay," Jonas said.

"Now the other one," Rudiger said.

"Why are you doing this?"

"The other one, Lieutenant."

Jonas closed his eyes for a moment and tried to escape to a happier place, but there was no happy place to be found. He could smell the coppery blood. The sweat.

He reached out and grabbed the second spike and held it in his hands. It felt heavy as a brick, and the metal became slippery with the sweat of his palm.

Rudiger struggled to find his voice. "That's it now. Do my other wrist the same way."

Jonas slowly placed the tip of the spike on top of the milky wrist and studied it. He held the mallet firmly in his right hand but did not yet raise it up.

Rudiger's voice was raspy and slow. "Be angry, Lieutenant, if that helps. Think of what I've done, if that gets your job accomplished. But I ain't the monster you think I am. When you do what you gotta do, and I do what I gotta do, the heavens will open, the dead will rise, the good will be saved, and the evil will be damned. Judgment day. It all happens now."

Jonas shook his head. "All that's happening here is murder and suicide. You're just going to die."

"Only one way to find out."

"Just tell me where she is, *please.*"

"One more nail, Lieutenant. I ain't gonna make you do my feet. Just one more nail, then that's it."

Jonas looked at the cross and saw the piece of wood extending outward beneath Rudiger's feet. Just a few inches, but enough to stand on once the cross was vertical. Stages and Sidams didn't get that courtesy, Jonas thought. They got a spike hammered through both feet.

"I'll live a little longer that way," Rudiger said. "And once you have me up, I can tell you where your girl is."

"Why?" Jonas asked.

"Why what?"

"Why everything? Why did you kill that family in Somalia?"

"Because I was supposed to. The sign outside the building even said so. It was a test. Make sure I could do what I needed to do later."

Rudiger's face suddenly lost a shade of its already pallor tone and his head lolled briefly to the side before snapping back.

Stop wasting time, Jonas. He's going to lose consciousness and Anne will die.

Jonas steadied the spike.

"Here?"

Rudiger coughed and looked at his arm. "Inch lower."

Jonas moved the spike, and Rudiger gave a feeble nod.

"Those words you see, Rudiger. In your head. Those puzzles. They're just gibberish, you know. They aren't clues to anything. We can stop this all right now."

"She's dying, Lieutenant. Hammer the nail down."

Jonas eyed the rust-brown head of the spike.

Jonas let out a long, slow breath. "Close your eyes," he said. He didn't know why he wanted to give any comfort to the man, but it just seemed inhuman not to.

Rudiger closed his eyes and the humming started again.

Jonas raised the mallet and smashed it down on the head of the spike. The tip punched through the flesh but not to the wood. Jonas struck it again. Three times. Four. Five.

Blood oozed from the wound but did not spurt. The spike seemed as deep as the other, and Jonas reached out and tested its firmness. It moved a little, but Jonas could hammer no more.

Sweat poured from Rudiger's face.

"Good. Good."

Jonas shut off emotionally. He no longer cared what was happening. He had an objective, and that objective was to save Anne. He could only do that by completing the task at hand, and his Ranger training took over. He would follow instructions and do what it took to find out where she was.

"What now?" he asked.

"Use ..." Rudiger coughed harder and his body spasmed. His muscles flexed and contracted, each one pronounced in its definition. "Use the pulley and rope. Lift me. Shouldn't ... shouldn't be too hard. Use the gloves."

One end of a long piece of rope was tied around a hook drilled into the top the cross. The rope ran to the ceiling, over a pulley, and back down to the floor.

Jonas stood. He noticed the base edge of the cross already aligned in a small but deep hole dug into the floor. Once Jonas starting raising the cross, the base should slip into the hole easily.

"Lift me up, Lieutenant. The glory is upon us."

Jonas found the gloves on the floor and put them on, feeling the dampness of Rudiger's sweat inside them. He then picked up the rope on the floor. He knew that once the cross started moving, the pain for the man would be excruciating.

It didn't matter. Jonas had a job.

He steadied his footing and pulled on the rope. Nothing happened. The weight seemed unbearable. But on a second effort the top of Rudiger's cross began to lift from the floor.

Jonas strained and resisted dropping the rope, which his arms were insisting on. He reached up and grabbed more rope and heaved again.

The top steadily rose. Higher.

After the halfway point, just as his arms were sure to give out, the effort eased. The brunt of the weight had been transferred back to the floor, and the cross slid into the depth of the hole beneath it. The cross wobbled, then settled.

Rudiger was raised.

CHAPTER FIFTY-THREE

JONAS RELEASED THE rope and stood back.

Rudiger towered over him, and a bright spotlight perfectly positioned at the ceiling of the hangar shone directly onto the dying man. Sweat covered his body in a sheen. The red of the blood from his wrists looked like rose petals flowering from beneath his pasty skin.

He was conscious. His feet found their pedestal, and, though he seemed weak, he had the strength to support his own weight. For now.

"Now you tell me," Jonas said. "I did what you wanted. Now tell me where she is."

A tendril of drool released from Rudiger's lower lip and stretched toward the floor. He squeezed his eyes, as if willing the pain and the fog away, then opened them and looked down at Jonas.

"Do you understand what I'm doing is good, Lieutenant?"

"Tell me where she is."

"Do you realize this is the end of the suffering? That everything Preacherman and his whore did to me, it all ends here?"

"Yes, I understand," Jonas lied. He understood nothing. "Now please just tell me."

The room grew suddenly quiet. Through the silence, Rudiger sucked in a long, deep breath.

"This is salvation, and you are part of it. God loves you for it." He licked his lips. Tongue like a serpent. "*I* love you for it. Your soul will be saved."

Jonas looked at him, and in the light and through the sweat and the blood, Jonas had never in his life seen a man so in belief of what he was saying. Rudiger was a homicidal sociopath, but Jonas knew he truly believed in what he was saying.

Jonas spoke.

"Let me tell you something, Rudiger. If Anne dies, I'm going to come back and light your body on fire. Hopefully you'll still be alive so you can feel the pain of that. But even if you're not, you won't get what you want, and you'll have died for nothing. You'll be a goddamned chunk of lifeless, smoldering cinder. Now tell me where the fuck she is."

CHAPTER FIFTY-FOUR

RUDIGER WATCHES THE man who watches him. Eye contact is brief, and then Jonas turns and runs from the hanger. When the door opens, bright sunlight floods in like water, and Rudiger wonders what heaven looks like.

He has told Jonas where to find Anne. He no longer has use for him, knowing Jonas would never have come back to complete the ritual of the burial once Rudiger is dead. No matter. There is no need for a cave burial, Rudiger knows, not with him. He may be on the cross for hours or for days, but on the third day the inevitable will happen, no matter where his body is.

The room is silent like a womb. Sidams and Stages are done, ain't no confusion about that. They didn't last long, but shock will do that. Rudiger doesn't feel shock, but he does feel the pain. Pain like never before. Pain like glory.

He shifts his feet and sucks in a breath. Feet struggle to stay balanced on the small ledge. When they buckle, he will fall. When he falls, his arms will tear and his chest will threaten to rip open. He won't be able to breathe, and then that'll be that. He's alive as long as his legs can hold.

He's been near death before. So many times. But never where he had time to contemplate it. Before he had a chance to live. Now he only has the chance to die.

His arms are on fire. The slightest movement sears them further. But the sweat on his face, running down and stinging his eyes, somehow that's worse than anything else. Feels like a thousand flies crawling on his forehead.

Rudiger bows his head, looks at the floor. Sees the blood, spread out like a canyon river on the floor. Sees the hole where the base of the cross disappears.

"I thirst," Rudiger says. This is true, but it's not the reason he says it.

The silence grows louder.

He waits. Waits for something that he should feel. Something he should hear. Something. Anything. Minutes pass, but they could be days. His body shakes, just a quiver. Rudiger is getting cold.

His legs grow weak. Shifts his weight again. He can feel his muscles starting to cramp. Could spasm at any moment.

A small doubt pierces him. It's tiny at first. A single bacteria, barely noticeable. But it starts to multiply. And again. Larger it grows. The doubt starts to take root.

He knows the source. Preacherman is the source, because Preacherman is the root of every dirty thing that has ever touched Rudiger. And now he's back.

Rudiger hears him laugh now.

He sees his yellow, rotting teeth. Smells his breath. Smells like a dead animal, left in the sun.

Can't believe you really did it. Didn't think you were so goddamn stupid.

Rudiger shuts his eyes, but in the dark is where Preacherman shines the brightest. He opens his eyes and Preacherman fades, but only a little.

Rudiger speaks. "Father, into your hands I commit my spirit." They are the final words. The words will save him. He feels his left leg buckling.

Boy, you are a fucking idiot. You let me do it, didn't ya? You killed me, and now you let me kill you. Pretty damn impressive, me being able to kill you from the grave. But here you are. Time to jump, boy. Jump and feel the pain.

More laughter. Rudiger tries to fill his ears with something, anything. But nothing drowns out the laughing. It won't stop.

"You didn't kill me," he says, knowing these are not the words to be said on the cross. But he has to say them. He has to convince Preacherman he is wrong.

The laughing stops. Rudiger feels hot breath in his ear.

Go on, boy. Keep quoting scripture. Keep thinking you're the fucking Messiah. Let yourself go. Let's see if the ground splits open and the earth shakes when you die. Go ahead.

"I'm the One," Rudiger says. His left leg bends and his right arm tears. Pain pulses though him like electricity.

Ain't no One, boy. Never was and never will be. Hell, I'm a preacher and even I don't believe in that shit. You just hopin' for hope, and look what it's done for you. You just minutes from nothingness, boy. Minutes from eternal nothingness. And in that nothingness, I get to fuck you all over again.

"It's not true," Rudiger says. He says it and no one hears.

True and you know it. You're just a monster like me, boy. You don't kill for a reason. You kill because it's just what you do. It's your nature. You are the scorpion on the back of the frog. You just can't help yourself, but you sure try to justify it, don't you?

"No. No. I was told to do what I did. I was commanded."

Commanded by who? Me and Jesus? Boy, if you weren't so fuckin' crazy you might just step back and see how crazy you are.

It's not true, Rudiger thinks. It's not true. I have a purpose. A reason to be here, on this cross. *I am the One. I am the resurrection.*

Sweat drips like rain.

His legs cramp. He can't hold much longer.

You killed me boy. And now you die. I've been waiting years for this. Welcome to hell.

Rudiger disappears inside himself. When he returns, he opens his eyes and stares out at the hanger walls. The light over the fat man's cross illuminates the articles he's put up. He sees the interview with his daddy, the one that triggered his memory. He tries to recall it. That time on the beach. In the water. But now it doesn't feel like the way it did. Did it even happen at all? He looks at the words in the titles, the words in large bold print. He tries to rearrange the letters in his mind, but nothing happens. The words are meaningless. Gibberish.

The doubt explodes in his mind.

Preacherman laughs but says nothing more. The laughing continues and Rudiger suspects it probably will until he is dead.

Rudiger finds strength in his legs and pushes himself upright.

He looks up at his left wrist and to the spike coming from within it. He steels himself and takes a deep breath. He pushes his arm outward, so the bone in his wrist pushes against the spike.

He nearly faints from the pain.

But the spike moves. Just a bit.

CHAPTER FIFTY-FIVE

JONAS DROVE AS fast as the U-Haul van and the laws of physics allowed. The van had been parked outside the hanger, keys still in the ignition. Jonas had no idea where the hell he was, but he could see the mountains in the distance, and that meant west.

The van tore down the dirt road, kicking up a cloud of dust and flying rocks in its wake. Jonas frantically searched for a radio, anything to call to anyone, but there was nothing. It was up to him. He had to get back to the hotel.

Rudiger had said Anne was in the cargo area of an identical U-Haul on the fourth level of the hotel parking garage.

Jonas's hands were covered in Rudiger's blood. He tried to erase the image of what he'd just done to the man from his mind, but he knew that image would be part of him forever, tattooed on his brain.

There. Downtown Denver. The buildings rose in the distance. That was where he had to go.

Jonas finally reached an asphalt road, and when his tires made contact he pressed down on the gas pedal. The van lurched and screamed straight ahead.

CHAPTER FIFTY-SIX

TWO COP CARS – sirens blaring, lights flashing – tailed Jonas as he sped to the hotel. They weren't escorting him. They were chasing him.

Jonas tried to remain calm. Think this through, he told himself. Don't get killed trying to save Anne. You're driving the same van Rudiger had, and you're driving it full speed toward the hotel. For all you know, they think you're him, going to back to blow up the building. The back of the van could be loaded with a fertilizer bomb.

Stop short of the Hyatt. There will be cops waiting at the hotel. If you try to drive down into the parking garage, they will start shooting. Guaranteed.

Jonas wove around two cars on the one-way street in downtown Denver. He had spent at least fifteen minutes getting here from the airplane hangar, but it had felt like years. And as frantic as he'd been, he had to pay attention to where he'd come from. Sidams could still be alive, and he would have to lead a medical team back to the hangar. As soon as Anne was freed.

Please God let her still be alive.

Jonas saw the hotel ahead. There was a swarm of emergency vehicles out front, their lights dancing all together.

Jonas swerved the van to the side, narrowly missing smashing into a Lexus. Horns blared around him. Jonas pulled up onto the sidewalk and pedestrians leapt out of the way.

Jonas stopped the van and got out.

Someone screamed from behind him. Cursing.

The police cars skidded to a stop and the first cop to get out immediately drew his gun. The man was huge.

Jonas raised his hands.

"Get on the ground! Now!"

"There's a woman in the hotel! She's dying!"

"Get on the fucking ground! *Now!*"

Jonas went to his knees and laced his fingers around the back of his head. He saw the cop from the second car get out and flank Jonas, gun aimed at his chest, unwavering, the whole time.

"Please! Listen to me. You have to radio Agent Difranco with the FBI. I'm Jonas Osbourne, and I'm with her. There's a woman in a van just like this one on the fourth –"

The knee hit him on the back and Jonas collapsed face first onto the ground. He felt his arms being yanked down and the cold metal of handcuffs biting against his wrists.

CHAPTER FIFTY-SEVEN

TEN MINUTES.

The longest ten minutes of his life.

Sitting in the back of the squad car, the handcuffs still on. No one to talk to.

Jonas had told any officer who would listen who he was and to call Difranco, but there was so much noise and so much movement he had no idea if anyone bothered to listen. Burly Cop – the one who had cuffed and shoved him into the back of the squad car – stood in a small group of fellow officers and conferred while Jonas waited.

The rock-hard backseat smelled like hot plastic with a faint tinge of vomit. Droplets of sweat ran down Jonas's face, tormenting him, but he could not wipe them away.

He thought of Anne.

Dying.

But was she really? Was she really running out of air?

He thought back to the brief night-vision video he'd seen of her on Rudiger's phone. She was in the dark, and the shot was so close it suggested she was in a tight, confined space. Rudiger said she was in the back of a van, but she must be in some kind of container in the van. A chamber? And how much air did she have?

Rage swelled within Jonas. The minutes he was spending in the back of the squad car may be the exact same minutes Anne had left of air. The cops were doing their job – keeping the suspect away from the hotel and the delegates. But they weren't listening. Goddamnit, *they weren't listening.*

He shouted through the glass. Burly Cop turned his head, just enough to say, *Yeah, bitch, I heard ya. I'm just not going to do anything about it.* Then he turned away.

Jonas stared at the car window. The thought of smashing his head into it suddenly seemed like a brilliant idea. He wouldn't break the window, and even if he did, he'd end up hurting himself. But it would force them to pay attention. They would come over.

More than anything else in the world, Jonas, right now, needed someone to pay attention to him.

Anne was dying, and no one would listen.

Electricity seemed to surge through his body as he leaned away from the door. If he was going to do this, he was going to do it right. He was going to use momentum from his body and then use the side of his head as the primary impact point. He hoped he would only have to do it a couple of times, but he would do it as long as it took for them to come over. He only hoped that he wouldn't knock himself unconscious in the process.

He steadied himself. For a moment, he thought of himself standing in the Beltway, watching the car about to smash into him. Then he thought of his father, who wanted nothing more than to preserve his own mind, and here Jonas was about to self-inflict a concussion.

On three, he told himself.

One ... two ....

Then, from the corner of his right eye, he saw Agent Difranco. She was running toward his car.

CHAPTER FIFTY-EIGHT

"Where? Where did he say? *Exactly.*"

"He said she was on the fourth level. Like I said."

"Where on the fourth level?"

"I don't know."

Jonas and Difranco led an ad hoc team of four other officers on a footrace through the parking garage. Throngs of people had surrounded the evacuated hotel, most of them law enforcement or firemen, and the press were clearly not going anywhere, even if the building collapsed around them. Red lights flashed through the area like tracer fire. Radios spat out bursts of commands. Debris from the small explosion at the hotel littered the street.

The Mog flashed through Jonas's brain. That had been completely different, yet the feeling was the same. The sweat. The urgency. The uncertainty of what the next second would bring.

Difranco opened a path through the emergency personnel, flashed her badge and a spewed a few choice words to the cop in charge of maintaining that section of the security perimeter.

Seconds later they were running down the concrete stairwell of the parking garage. Difranco first, then Jonas, and the four cops in the rear.

Burly Cop was among them, and now he was Jonas's best friend. As they descended the stairwell to the fourth floor, Jonas heard someone radioing for a medical team and a group of rescue workers with any tools possible. Anne could be in a locked gun safe, for all they knew.

They reached level four. Difranco yanked open the metal door with such force it slammed against the wall behind her. The six of them spilled into the parking garage and looked in every direction.

The garage was full. Jonas forced himself to take his time, knowing he could easily overlook the van.

"He said it was the same as the one I just was in. U-Haul. Ten footer."

"Nothing," a cop said.

"Nothing up this way either."

Chatter over the radio. A medical response team was on the way.

Jonas took off running up the parking ramp, scanning the cars as he went. He looked back and saw the others do the same, fanning out. The garage seemed massive, infinitely large. As he ran, and as he saw nothing, he couldn't escape the thought that Rudiger had lied. That Anne was already dead in some location they would never find.

No van. There seemed to be every other type of vehicle ever manufactured, but there was no goddamn ten-foot U-Haul.

"Over here!"

From below. Difranco.

CHAPTER FIFTY-NINE

THE U-HAUL WAS parked between an Xterra and a F-150. A thin coat of grime covered it, making the white paint a dusty gray. Fingerprints were clearly visible in the dirt near the base of the back gate, and Jonas wasn't surprised. Rudiger no longer cared about covering his tracks. Rudiger wanted to be known.

Was this even the right van? Had to be, Jonas thought. Had to be.

He stared at the padlock securing the back gate.

"How do we get this off?" he asked, turning to Difranco.

"A fire crew is on the way," she said. "They'll have something."

"There's no time," Jonas said. "Goddamnit, *there's no time.*" He raced to the passenger and driver's doors, each of which were locked. Didn't matter – there was no access from the cab to the back of the van anyway.

"Shoot the lock. Or something. Just ... can't we shoot it?"

Burly Cop shook his head. "Too risky. Bullet could ricochet. Or go inside and hurt her."

"Damnit, we can't just *wait.*" He slammed his palm into the side of the U-Haul cargo area. "Anne! Anne! Can you hear me?"

Silence.

He hit the side of the van three more times. "Anne! Are you in there?"

Difranco touched his arm. "Jonas, calm down. We'll get her out."

Jonas turned to her and tried to control the panic he felt washing over him. "I saw her picture. She's in some kind of container in there. Tight space. Rudiger ... he said she was running out of air. We have to get her out. *Now.*"

"Jonas, they will be here any –"

"We don't have time. Why won't anyone listen to me? Please, just shoot the fucking lock, will you? Give me your gun. I'll do it." He stepped toward Burly Cop.

Burley Cop put a hand on the butt of his gun. "You need to calm down and step back. You shouldn't even be here."

"I'm begging you."

A hundred feet away, the stairwell door opened. Jonas turned and saw three firemen emerge. One carried an axe.

Goddamn. *Yes.*

"Over here!" he shouted. "Here! Hurry!"

They turned to Jonas and ran the best they could in their gear.

As they approached, Jonas pointed at the padlock. "Please, get that thing off. Please hurry."

The fireman holding the axe said nothing as he studied the lock and steadied his footing.

Everyone else reflexively took a step back.

The fireman lightly tapped the lock three times with the edge of the blade, like an executioner confirming his reach. Then he lifted the axe above him and brought it down with a smash of metal against the lock. A small flurry of sparks lived for half a second before dying. The neck of the lock split open.

Jonas lunged for the back of the truck. He grabbed the handle of the gate and yanked. The gate rattled like a thousand dried-out bones as it lifted.

There was only one thing inside the back of the scratched-metal cargo container.

A silver coffin, wrapped in nylon cords.

CHAPTER SIXTY

JONAS LEAPT IN the cargo area and tried to yank the cords looped around the casket, but they were on so tight he couldn't even get his fingers beneath them. He rapped against the metal cover.

"We're here, Anne. We're getting you out." Silence from within. Sweat fell from his forehead and slid down the smooth casket lid.

He turned to all the faces staring from outside within.

"A knife. Hurry. I need a knife."

Rather than handing him a knife, a fireman jumped into the back of the truck and motioned for Jonas to move out of the way.

Jonas watched as the fireman pulled a folded rescue knife from his utility belt and unlocked the blade. He wasted no time in sawing the serrated teeth of the blade against the nylon cords of rope.

One cord broke and fell from the casket.

The teeth sawed.

Jonas watched, feeling the blood within him pulsing. The tips of his fingers felt on fire.

A second cord fell.

A brief thought went though his mind. Rudiger had already proven he knew how to use explosives. Could the coffin be rigged? Maybe Anne wasn't even in there. Maybe all that was inside was a pressure-mounted wad of C4, set to detonate once the lid was removed.

The fireman kept sawing, the ropy veins in his forearm bulging.

Jonas then decided he didn't care if they all blew up. Whatever was to happen, was to happen. There would be no more wasting time.

Jonas remained silent until the third and final cord fell to the floor of the truck.

Seeing that the coffin opened from the other side, Jonas circled around the fireman.

Jonas opened the lid.

There was no explosion.

There was only Anne.

CHAPTER SIXTY-ONE

HER EYES WERE open. Halfway. Glazed, the look of dreamy death.

Three seconds.

It took three seconds before she blinked, and in those seconds Jonas realized nothing else mattered. Nothing mattered but the woman in the box beneath him.

But she did blink, and when she did, Jonas immediately put his palm to her cheek, as if he could transfer any of his life to hers.

Her hair – matted with sweat and struggle – was spilled over a royal purple satin pillow. Her arms were at her side. She blinked again, and then she looked at him.

Her eyes widened. Just a bit.

Jonas turned. "She's alive. Get her oxygen. *Something.*"

Anne reached up. He could see blood on her fingertips. From trying to claw her way out.

She touched his arm. "I'm okay, Jonas." Her voice was barely more than a raspy wheeze. "I'm okay."

Jonas placed a hand on her forehead. "Thank God. Thank God."

"You came for me."

"Don't talk, Anne."

"Jonas, you came for me."

"Of course I did."

"What ... what happened? Where is he?"

Jonas lifted a strand of hair from her face. Commotion erupted behind him, and he turned and saw a paramedic team rushing toward the U-Haul. He looked back at Anne.

"It's over," he said. "No need to worry about him anymore."

At that moment, a paramedic leapt into the back of the truck and told Jonas and the fireman to get out and give him room.

As Jonas left Anne, he looked up at the coffin lid, held up by its hinge. He noticed two things that he hadn't before. One was the small camera mounted on the inside. The camera that had transmitted the video of Anne to Rudiger's phone.

The second thing he noticed was the hole in the lid. Neatly drilled, the diameter of a pencil.

An air hole, Jonas realized.

Rudiger wasn't going to let her die, after all. He didn't need to. Rudiger only killed when he thought he had to, Jonas realized. He only had to *convince* everyone Anne was dying.

Jonas stepped out of the van. Difranco walked up to him.

"She'll be fine," she said. Jonas knew she had no clue if Anne would be fine or not, but he believed it anyway, so he nodded.

"We need to go back," he said.

"The Senator?"

Jonas nodded. "He might still be alive. I don't think Stages is."

"Where are they?"

"About fifteen, twenty minutes from here. I remember how to get there."

"What happened to Rudiger?"

Jonas was aware of the blood on this hands and clothes. "I'll tell you on the way. But we need to go now."

He turned back toward Anne. The medic had an oxygen mask over her face and was asking her questions. She was nodding.

"I'll be back, Anne," Jonas said. "The Senator needs help, and I'm the only one who knows where he is."

She lifted a hand in acknowledgement.

Difranco led the way back up the stairs and outside the hotel, her pace brisk.

Outside, the sun hit them full force. Jonas squinted as they ran along the crowded downtown streets to her car. Along the way, she radioed in for back up assistance from the police and paramedics, instructing them to follow her.

Jonas and Difranco reached her car and slid in next to each other. He stared straight ahead, through the dirty windshield, and spoke through quickened breath.

"Tell them we're going to need more than one ambulance for what's waiting for us."

CHAPTER SIXTY-TWO

THE MOMENT THEY arrived at the farmhouse, every fiber inside Jonas begged him to stay out in the car. He could do nothing for anyone inside. He knew he should just let the professionals do their job. But he couldn't stay out. What was in there was part of him, just like the small apartment back in the Mog was a part of him. He could not stay out. As Difranco stopped the car and the dirt from the unpaved road willowed around them, Jonas told her very clearly that he was going inside.

Difranco said nothing.

They got out as the four squad cars, two ambulances, and one fire rescue vehicle screamed behind them. One by one they stopped at the farmhouse, sirens blaring at the nothingness of the Colorado plains. One by one they went silent, leaving only their flashing lights on, lighting up the decaying house in pulsing waves of red.

Jonas pointed to the hangar, telling Difranco that was where they had to go. The hangar looked nothing more than an empty shell against a marble-blue sky. But Jonas knew it wasn't empty.

"Let me go in first," Difranco said.

Jonas nodded.

He closed his eyes and said a prayer, which to his secular mind was just a wish. He wished for his friend to still be alive.

Suddenly there was a swarm, and Jonas's mind focused. Narrowed. He heard the emergency crews running from behind. The dirt from the road swirled around him, settling on his lips and face. He heard the shouting of one man to another, and then back again. There was confusion and there was order, and it all coexisted in a perfect slowing of time.

Jonas thought of the Mog.

At least a half-dozen men and Difranco entered the hangar before Jonas did, but in he went, following the rushing masses, sucked in as if his body was helpless to stop itself.

In through the door. Into the darkness.

Jonas thought of the boy he shot in Mogadishu. In the hallway of the rotting building. He thought of the taunting.

Come death, American.

Inside.

The first thing to hit him was the smell, which hadn't seemed nearly so powerful when he'd been inside the hangar earlier. Jonas had never been inside a slaughterhouse, but he imagined this was exactly what it would smell like. A sweet tanginess mixed with the smell of blood and shit. Fresh infection. Disease.

The hangar was a tomb. Dark. Suffocating. Hot like a panting dog's breath.

Jonas's mind focused further as the adrenaline, what he had left of it, spiked his blood like heroin. He could no longer see anything in his peripheral vision, and he only vaguely heard the shouts around him.

Get the ladder! Get the ladder!

No response here. We need to get him down.

Sweet God, I've got an ear on the floor over here.

His mind told him that the emergency crews were doing what they were supposed to. They were trying to save Sidams and Stages, both of whom Jonas knew – he just fucking *knew* – were

already dead. The rescue crews would be grabbing ladders and trying to figure out how to get the bodies down. Some of the police
were probably already headed back outside, securing the scene,
calling in for back up to fend off the reporters that would inevita-
bly digest the scene.

Jonas only knew this in his mind, because the logic of those
actions somehow found a way to enter his thoughts, but only in
the distance. Intangible like a dream.

His actual attention was focused on the middle of the room,
where a powerful overhead light shot down on the figure of a
cross. The beam was perfectly centered on the two pieces of wood,
capturing the ends of the each wooden arm and everything in-between, leaving whatever fell outside the immediacy of the cross in
darkness.

Not a single rescue worker paid attention to this cross. No one
seemed to be concerned with it in the least.

As Jonas stared at the cross, he knew why. But his brain wouldn't
let him believe it.

The cross was empty.

CHAPTER SIXTY-THREE

JONAS KEYED IN the code to the second set of doors and entered Jefferson's north unit, holding the door for Anne as she followed. He checked his father's room but he wasn't there. He turned to leave the room just as Monique was coming in, a blanket folded against her chest.

"Mr. Osbourne, I thought that was you." She reached out and touched his arm. "How are you?"

"I'm fine, Monique. Good to see you."

"I haven't seen you in awhile."

"I've had a rough month."

A slight twinkle in her eyes. "I know," she said, her accent softening her words. "I watch the news."

"Yes, of course. Oh." Jonas turned to Anne. "Monique, this is Anne. My ... girlfriend."

Anne smiled and Monique nodded at her. "You must be someone special if Jonas is sharing his father with you. He's never brought anyone else here before. He's a private man, this one."

Jonas felt himself blush. He willed it to go away, but he knew it was only making it worse.

"How is he?" Jonas asked.

"He is very well," Monique said. "Ate most of his breakfast today. He's in the community room."

"Thanks, Monique."

Monique stood to one side and let Jonas and Anne pass. They made their way down the sterile linoleum hallway, passing door after door of empty rooms. The community room was at the end of the hallway, next to the nurse's station.

Jonas heard the commotion well before turning into the room.

The community room wasn't big-just big enough to hold a few tables with six chairs each, a television, and a closet that held a variety of games and puzzles. It always reminded Jonas of an elementary school classroom, and this was where the residents of the north unit gathered, usually at the request of others, to share in the effects of their commonality and wait for things to finally end. Group therapy.

The television blared an early afternoon baseball game, the only one watching a male nurse. Several residents in wheelchairs moved back and forth with no discernable purpose, looking like battery-powered toys stuck in the corner of a room. Linda, the shrieker, belted out a horrifying series of expletives at Tom, a resident Jonas had never seen move. Three others were getting ice cream from a nurse, while a fourth decided to drop his onto the floor and roll back and forth over it, a wide grin on his face. Jonas scanned the fray for his father, whom he found sitting next to Bennie, both of them silently gazing out the window in the far corner of the room, watching the world go by without them.

Jonas grabbed Anne's hand and pulled her through the room, deftly maneuvering through the chaos. Linda ceased her tirade on poor Tom and focused her attention on Anne long enough to accuse her of stealing her husband.

"She's about to call you a whore," Jonas said, looking back at Anne. "Don't take it personally."

As Jonas pulled Anne past the woman, Linda screeched out with venom.

"*Whore!*"

Jonas found it almost funny enough to smile, until he looked at Anne's face. It was the face of someone not familiar with the demented mind, not yet hardened by the constant exposure to it. It was the face of someone who wondered what these people were like ten, fifteen years ago, when they were full of life and awareness, unable to see the dark and living tomb that awaited each of them.

"It's okay," he said to her. "We can wheel him outside for our visit. More peace and quiet."

"I'm ... I'm fine," she said. "Really, it's okay."

They reached the Captain and Jonas put a hand on the old man's shoulder. The Captain didn't look up. He just stared straight ahead.

Bennie looked up and smiled. "Oh, my," she said. "I know you."

"Hi, Bennie."

Jonas kneeled in front of his dad, and, after a second, the Captain's bright blue eyes shifted, and he looked directly at Jonas. For a moment, his eyes widened and his lips twitched, threatening a smile.

He knows me, Jonas thought.

So much can happen in a month. Jonas was happy his father still knew who he was.

"Hi, Dad."

The Captain's gaze went back to the window, and he started to hum.

"Dad, this is Anne."

Anne stepped closer. She reached for the Captain's hand and picked it up. She didn't shake it but she stroked the back of it for a moment before putting it back down. "It's really a pleasure to meet you."

The Captain didn't look up. Bennie looked Anne up and down approvingly. "Oh, my," she said.

"Sorry I haven't been around, Dad." Jonas straightened the collar on the Captain's polo shirt. "I've been busy."

"Too busy to see your own father?" Bennie tsk-tsked.

"Yes, Bennie. Even too busy for that. It's quite a story."

Bennie smiled. "I like stories. Tell it to us."

Jonas looked at her, studying the wrinkles around her eyes, the wisps of eyebrows, the hair still struggling to be well kept.

"It's not a happy story, Bennie."

"Are they ever?"

"Sometimes."

"It's okay. Any story would be good. Please sit down and tell it to us."

Jonas thought about it for a few seconds.

"Okay, Bennie. I will."

As Jonas and Anne took seats next to the Captain and Bennie, the male nurse who'd been watching baseball came over.

"You're the man," he said to Jonas. "From the news."

Jonas nodded. "Yes."

"This is your father?"

"Yes. He is."

"I had no idea."

"Why would you?"

The man didn't seem to know what to say next, so he stood there and watched Jonas instead of baseball. Jonas wanted to ask him for privacy, then decided against it. What the hell, he thought. He can listen, too.

Then he spoke. Quietly at first, as if sharing a secret. But then louder, drawing more attention to himself.

He gave them the detailed first-hand account so many news stations clamored for but never got. In this place, this world of the forgotten, Jonas never held back. He started from the beginning, from the moment he met Rudiger Sonman, a muscular, scarred youth patrolling the dirt-covered streets of Mogadishu. He decided to tell everything, even more than he thought he'd told Anne. Of all the death. The blood of innocents. The head of a baby and the ear of a girl. Of a woman who died because she recognized her brother. Of people nailed to crosses because a man thought he heard God tell him to do it. And of the horror of that day in Denver.

As he spoke, the walls seemed to dissolve around him, and he realized he wasn't telling a story, but he was convincing himself all those things were *real*. That they had actually happened, and the things he saw would be with him the rest of his life. There would be no suppressing of the images this time. They were a part of him, and that was how it was going to be.

Bennie nodded every few seconds, smiling politely despite the graphic horror Jonas described. The Captain kept his gaze fixed out the window, his humming growing louder occasionally before finally ceasing altogether. The male nurse – his name tag said *Roger* – listened intently, his hands folded in front of him. At one point Monique came over to tell Roger to get back to work, but she too stopped to listen and soon took a chair near Jonas.

Others came, some drifted in and out of the periphery, but many stayed, Jonas realized he was holding court for the north unit, residents and workers alike, and they sat intently and listened as Jonas told of his time in the airplane hangar, and what he had to do to find Anne. He spoke of the horrible deaths of Senator Sidams and Ambassador Stages, whose brutal demises may have, ironically, contributed to the perceived success of the Peace Accords.

Jonas finally finished his story.

The only thing he didn't mention was how Rudiger was not on his cross when they returned to the hangar, nor had any trace of him been found since that day. He didn't know why he didn't include that part. Maybe because he was still trying to believe it himself.

He looked about the room and he realized it was the most silent he had ever heard it. They were gathered around him, school children at a macabre story hour, their eyes pleading for more. All except the Captain, who kept staring out the window, as if something he'd been waiting for his whole life was just over the horizon.

Jonas noticed an old black man staring in his direction. It was the resident from his last visit. The one who told Jonas the North Wing was a *bad place*. The one who told him *I don't know where I am*. Jonas smiled at him, but the man was somewhere distant, a place smiles don't reach.

Then the Captain mumbled, and Jonas went back on one knee in front of him.

"What did you say, Dad?"

And the Captain grinned, the kind of grin that merely replaced thought and function, a reaction of inability. Lips twisted, face twitching, the Captain came alive, aware, present for a moment, if only to speak a handful of words. But they were words, real words, and Jonas heard them even if no one else did. Heard them and understood them, the first words his dad had spoken in clarity in over a year.

"You are my son."

Once spoken, he repeated it, the second time with more strain, as if the words themselves were struggling to find light after traveling from deep within him. Then the Captain's face softened and his gaze resumed its posting at the window. Jonas watched his father drift back into the other world, the one where he now lived, a soft hum slowly building from his chest and coming through trembling lips, the wheezy tune rising and falling, creaking like a ghost ship adrift on a forgotten sea.

ACKNOWLEDGMENTS

THIS BOOK FIRST came to life in 2012 as my debut novel—a major milestone for any writer. My excitement was short-lived, though, as the small publisher folded up shop within months after the book's release. It was a harsh reality but a good lesson. Turns out, this kind of thing happens all the time in the publishing industry. The rights reverted back to me and my agent put the book on Amazon, where it remained on life support for several years. I was very happy when Bob and Pat Gussin at Oceanview Publishing picked it up and brought it back from the nearly dead. Bob and Pat, you guys have been tremendous supporters of my work, for which I'm very thankful. And a huge thanks to the rest of the Oceanview team: Lee, Lisa, Emily—you rock.

What follows below are my acknowledgments from the original publication:

Many read a book by a new author and assume it's the first book that person's ever written. In a few rare cases that's true. Most times, not. So the road to publishing a first novel often has years of struggle and discarded manuscripts behind it.

Write. Rewrite. Collect rejections. Repeat.

Book after book.

All the while, the author depends on a vast support system, so you can understand those lucky enough to see their work in print for the first time have much credit to give. Starting with you, the reader, without whom stories cease to exist. Thank you for letting me tell you a story. I hope I didn't disappoint.

Huge and warm thanks to my agent Pam Ahearn, who has the patience of Job. You guided me into becoming a stronger writer without telling me what to do. You didn't give up on me when you easily could have, and I will never be able to properly express how much that means to me. Thank you to Joe Pittman and the fine people at Vantage Point Books, a scrappy new imprint who took a chance on me. Here's hoping I bring success to you, and you to me. To my friends at Old Possum: Ed, Linda, Dirk, Sean and John. You told me what was good and what sucked, and you were right almost all the time. To Jessica, who not only is my rock and has supported me through this process on so many levels but read everything with a wonderfully delicate eye for detail. To Sole, who makes me happy when she says she's proud of me, and to my beautiful children Ili and Sawyer, who tell their friends their daddy is a writer. To my mom, sister, and the rest of my family, who read every word and supported it all, even the gnarly bits.

Dad, to whom this book is dedicated: you never had a chance to read this, but I think you would have appreciated a good yarn about crucifixion. You were good like that.

Endless thanks to Rioja, Malbec, Sangiovese, and

Margarita. You ladies know how to inspire.
And lastly, to me. Good for you, goddamnit.